Ruins
in the
Mist

Ruins in the Mist

Marion Timmons

WESTBOW
PRESS
A DIVISION OF THOMAS NELSON
& ZONDERVAN

Copyright © 2014 Marion Timmons.

All rights reserved. No part of this book may be used or reproduced by any means, graphic, electronic, or mechanical, including photocopying, recording, taping or by any information storage retrieval system without the written permission of the publisher except in the case of brief quotations embodied in critical articles and reviews.

WestBow Press books may be ordered through booksellers or by contacting:

WestBow Press
A Division of Thomas Nelson & Zondervan
1663 Liberty Drive
Bloomington, IN 47403
www.westbowpress.com
1 (866) 928-1240

Because of the dynamic nature of the Internet, any web addresses or links contained in this book may have changed since publication and may no longer be valid. The views expressed in this work are solely those of the author and do not necessarily reflect the views of the publisher, and the publisher hereby disclaims any responsibility for them.

Any people depicted in stock imagery provided by Thinkstock are models, and such images are being used for illustrative purposes only.
Certain stock imagery © Thinkstock.

ISBN: 978-1-4908-4180-9 (sc)
ISBN: 978-1-4908-4181-6 (hc)
ISBN: 978-1-4908-4182-3 (e)

Library of Congress Control Number: 2014911922

Printed in the United States of America.

WestBow Press rev. date: 7/17/2014

To the memory of the thousands of United Empire Loyalists who were forced to leave their homeland following the American Revolution.

Prologue

Early morning mist hangs over the hills and valleys surrounding the great fortress. Against a backdrop of magnificent snow-capped mountain ranges, the impressive structure sits as it has for centuries high on a jagged cliff rising above the mist, mighty and imposing.

In a land where hundreds of miles of rugged coastline connect with a network of ancient Roman roads, Welsh history runs deep. The imprint of Roman occupation still marks the hundreds of fortresses that have survived throughout the centuries. The struggle against early invaders only served to strengthen the character of this small nation. To the Welsh people, the spirits of the powerful princes will never die. Nor will the music they hear coming over the hills—the sounds of harps and the voices of minstrels—ever fade away. The ghosts of early monks tending their sheep near the abbey haunt the misty moors.

In a child's dream, forces occupying a towering castle silhouetted against the sky prepare for the ensuing battle. He hears the thundering hoofs of the horses as they rush toward the moat. Riders bend forward on their mounts, stirring up dust as they ride. Now the white stallion gallops toward the drawbridge. Soldiers rush out to meet armored knights. The drawbridge lifts. Metal clangs against metal. Bloody swords lash against shields. Screams pierce the air. A crash—

He tries to scream—

Chapter 1

Wales, 1774

"Tomos wake up! Wake up!" Someone is shaking me. I smell smoke.

"What— What's—"

"You were screaming!"

There's another crash. What *is* that racket? My heart is thumping. I throw back the covers and sit up. I rub my eyes. Elen is standing by the bed.

"The smoke. I heard the crash. Is the house—"

"No, silly! It's the wind. You were dreaming," my sister says. Now I'm awake. There it is again.

The wind is rattling the panes. The shutters are clattering. I pull the covers up under my chin. An icy chill slaps my face. Burr. I can't stop shivering. The warmth from below never reaches my bed.

"Come. Breakfast is about ready. It's warmer downstairs," she says. "Look out the window!"

It *would* be warmer downstairs by the fire, but it is too cold to get there.

I should have been sleeping in the alcove. It's always warmer there, but Davydd has taken it.

Oh, well … here goes. I grab a cover and wrap it around

me. I skip over to the window. What does Elen want me to see outside? I can't even see out. Frost covers the pane. I trace the icy pictures with my finger. I scrape away a spot and peek out. Snow! Lots of snow! Drifts of it up around the fence! There *is* smoke. Look at it! It's drifting thick along the lane. Strong peat smoke is coming from every stone chimney. Look, it covers the whole valley. That's where the smoke is coming from. Is that what I smell?

I have Steffan's bed whenever he works away at the quarry. The beds of my other brothers are already empty. Owen and Willym have left early for the mines. How did they get out today? Brynn and Evan must be down by the fire. Why didn't they wake me? Have they all forgotten me?

"Davydd?"

No answer.

Nothing wakes him. Oh, well, let him be. I'll find it myself.

Eight going on nine, and he still doesn't put things away. I'm only seven and I—never mind. I found it. I pull on my trousers and try to tuck in my nightshirt. It won't fit. Oh well. I smell bacon. I slip bare feet into my shoes and run for the stairs.

"Did you see the snow?" I cry as I hurry down the stairs. "Did you see it?"

"I did. There's lots of it!" Elen says.

The heat feels good. I pull my milking stool closer to the hearth. The house is not on fire, but the hearth is blazing. It is the smoke from the peat that I smell. My teeth are chattering. I rub my hands together to try to warm them.

"Not so close!" warns Mama. "Don't be in Gladys's way."

I watch my oldest sister as she lifts tiny curls of bacon from the pan. I *did* smell bacon.

"Time, it is, you were getting up," quips Elen. "Look at you, half dressed!" *She sounds more like Mama every day.*

"No one woke me. Everyone forgot. The noise of the wind—" I try to explain.

"Well, poor little Tomos! Is that why you were screaming?"

"Elen, it was loud. The shutters were banging and—"
Was it really the shutters, or was it the dream?

My sister just laughs as she limps back to the hearth to help pour the batter for the big pancake into the hot fat. She has had that limp for as long as I can remember. Born with it, I guess. This is the second time this morning that they are making breakfast. My brothers would have been up very early. It is miles to the mines.

"Thought the house was on fire," I say timidly.

"Could have been," says Gladys.

"Really?"

"Lots of fires in the winter," says Elen.

"From the peat?"

"Sparks from the peat," she says. "They fly right up the chimney and—"

"Girls! Fifteen and nigh on twelve. You should know better!" snaps Mama. "You'll be frightening him, you will!"

Mama comes over and tries to smooth my tousled hair.

"The house is safe, son. It was just the smell of the peat," she says gently. "Get back to work, girls! The pancake is smoking!"

"How did Willym and Owen get out?" I ask as she tucks in my nightshirt.

"Same as always—walking."

"Walking ... in all of this snow?"

"They'll be ploughing through it today!" Elen says. "They'll be late this morning."

"If they even make it! Expect they will be back. They won't make it in this," Gladys says.

"They should have left after chapel yesterday—that's for certes," Mama says.

"The weather, it has been good. This is the first—"

"But it's too late for traveling the hills. Late November, it is," Mama tells her.

"Why aren't the pits closed?" I ask.

"Should be—that's for certes. Time to put up the picks

and shovels," mutters Mama, "And it's too cold for the boys. Where's Davydd?"

"Asleep still," I say.

"No doubt. You know Davydd—nothing wakes him," Elen says.

"Couldn't wake him, Mama. Maybe he's—"

"You mean he didn't even wake with your screaming?" Gladys interrupts.

"Where's Papa?" I ask, ignoring my sister's teasing.

"He's at the barns, where should he be!" Elen says, knowing it all.

"Brynn is with him," Mama says.

"And where's Evan?"

"He's with Megan. They're hauling water for the animals."

My youngest sister is ten—a year older than Evan. Papa says they're both old enough now to help with the barn chores. Davydd is old enough to help a little. So am I. Our job is to bring in the peat every day. How are we going to get to the peat shed today?

"Gladys, go wake Davydd. Let Elen stir the porridge."

"Yes, Mother."

"Come sit. Ours is ready. The others will soon be here," Mama says, patting my place at the table.

I have been watching as the flames try to lick the bottom of the big iron pot. Gladys returns just in time to remove it and now lugs it to the table. We have it every day. Sometimes we even have bacon and a piece of the big pancake with the porridge on cold winter mornings.

"Get the tea, Elen. It's boiling!"

Mama waits for the others to take their places. I glance across the table at her. I'm hungry, but she has to say grace before we can eat.

"Willym and Owen had to go without their tea at breakfast. Only enough water to make tea for their lunch tins," she says when she finishes praying.

"Why?" I ask.

"The water in the village well was frozen over this morning. Evan had to break the ice before he could dip the bucket."

"We won't be able to travel over the hills for months," Gladys says. "Oh, how I long for spring."

"That will be awhile yet, it will," Mama tells her.

My oldest sister is looking forward to spring. She is excited about taking her first job. She's old enough now to help the family. Mama says it's tough times. She'll be looking after children—something about being a governess at the Morley estate, whatever that is.

"But I'm expected there in March," Gladys says.

"Roads should be cleared by then," Mama tells her. "No need for worry."

"I'll be able to help out. Send a little money."

"You'll be missed at home," Mama says. "But the extra will help."

"Suppose Brynn will be going to work soon," Gladys says as she adds more butter to the pancake.

"In the spring."

"Down in the mines. Just like Owen and Willym. He can hardly wait!" I say.

"Something to wait for—twelve-hour shifts pushing carts in the dark!"

"No, the ponies help with the carts, Elen," I say.

"They're still on hands and knees. It's so low down there. That's got to be scary!"

"Crawling around in the cold water," Gladys says.

"It's the firedamp they really have to worry about. That's what—"

"Enough, girls! That's enough! We don't need all of this talk at breakfast! Besides, Brynn can only go if they work closer to home."

"Do you really think they'll take work closer to home?" Gladys asks.

"Flynt is too far, even when they stay in barracks all week," Mama says. "They are barely rested before they have to be back again Sunday night."

"It's a hard life for young boys. Deep in the pits. Do you think Brynn's ready for that, Mother?"

"Gladys, some go as young as ten. No, they are not ready for that," Mama says. "Not ready at all. But they go anyway."

A sudden gush of wind blows the door open. Papa and Brynn come in from the barn. They each have two more buckets of water. Behind them Evan and Megan are covered in snow. They each have a bucket. Theirs are filled with snow.

"Evan and Megan, hang your buckets over the flame. They'll melt while we eat," Papa says as he goes to the hearth.

"Here, Brynn. Dump that pail of water into the boiler."

"There's room for one more. There … that should do it for now," he says before he turns to remove his coat.

"It's a cold one," Papa says, stomping snow from his boots.

"So it's not warming any?" Mama asks.

"No, she holds!"

They throw off their coats and kick off boots. Wet mitts fall to the floor.

"Come. Sit, you two. Here, Megan, Evan. Get warmed. You'll get your death," Mama says as she lays fresh peat on the fire.

"Well, it's about time!" Mama says when she sees Davydd coming down the stairs. He gives a big yawn as he stretches and then flops into an empty chair.

"We lost one of the sheep yesterday," Papa says as he pulls his chair to the table.

"Will you find her, Papa?"

"No, my boy, it's too late, it is."

"Oh, no!"

"Tom left the gate open!"

"No, Davydd, I latched the—"

"When we put them in the barn last night, we didn't … well … we didn't notice—" Papa tries to explain.

"Did she just wander away, Papa?"

"Aye, she's lost. I've always said, 'A sheep alone is a dead sheep.'"

"But couldn't we find her?"

"But *couldn't* we find her?" Davydd mimics. "Who's job is it to count them?"

I sniff and wipe my nose with the back of my hand.

"What's wrong with you? Only girls cry," Davydd says.

"I'm not crying. Something in my eye—that's all."

"Yeah! Sure!"

Davydd makes a face at me when Mama isn't looking. Mama jumps up from the table. "Enough! Let him be! Take that look off your face!" she says as she cuffs his ear. "Now finish your breakfast before it's time to make supper!" She's trying hard not to laugh.

Davydd thinks that just because he's older he can tell me how little I know. I remember counting. I *did* latch the gate. Now she's gone. We watch as Mama places a thick slice of bread on her plate, slathers it with butter and sugar, and then pours tea over it. It's a habit of hers that's hard to break, I guess. When we ask her why she does it, she just says, "That's how we folks have always done it," so we leave it at that.

As children, we learned very early on that you don't argue with Mama.

Chapter 2

We are used to winter days like this. These storms that blow in over the valleys have a way of keeping families at home in Denbigh. The biggest chore this morning is to feed and water the animals.

"Will you help with the barn chores, Davydd?" Papa asks as he slides his chair back on the slate floor and checks the water buckets.

"I want to help too!"

"Aye, Tomos. That's good."

"Warm clothing. All of you," says Mama. "It's not fit for man nor beast out there. I don't need you all getting sick."

Mama helps me dress properly, and within minutes we are ready to head outside.

"Grab a bucket, Davydd," Papa says as he lifts one of the buckets from the hook.

Water from Davydd's bucket sloshes over the floor before he reaches the door.

He mutters something. I look at him and grin. He gives me a nasty look.

When I step outside, a blast of frigid air hits my face. No one is laughing now. We make our way toward the barn in the deep snow.

I carefully step in the tracks my father has made.

There is always something different about the smell of the barn in winter. Maybe it is the steam from the animals. One of the horses snorts as he waits for the oats. I reach up and stroke him when he lowers his head. "There, Rhun," I say. I rub his nose before I turn back to where Papa is getting ready to do the milking.

I shift from one foot to the other, wishing I had stayed in the kitchen. I let the ewe die in the storm. I listen to the *phish, phish* of the milk as it hits the pail. My father leans against the cow's warm body. She moves away from him.

"She wants Elen," I say.

"Elen will help inside this morning."

I crouch to get a better look. Papa squirts a stream in my direction.

"Papa!"

I jump back and wipe the warm, sticky liquid from my face.

"See that feed bag over there? Scoop some oats for Pany and Rhun in the trough."

Megan comes in with a bucket and waters the two pigs. When Evan comes in, I help him feed the sheep. As I walk behind the horses, Pany lifts her tail.

"Watch it!" Evan calls out.

I jump back just in time. Steam rises from the fresh manure. Davydd and Brynn keep coming in with buckets of water.

"Willym and Owen are back!"

"Knew it!"

"Snow's too deep."

"Eyton waited too late to close the pits for the winter."

"Should have closed weeks ago, Father," Brynn says.

"What about the chickens?" I ask when Papa finishes the milking.

"Aye, the chickens. Do you want to help?"

"That's Megan's job!"

"Not today. She is helping with the water. You can help me gather the eggs. Go back for the basket."

"The big one?"

"Aye. I'll get the feed."

By the time I get back with the basket, Papa has the doorway to the henhouse cleared away. He waits for me to follow him.

"Gently now. Don't startle them," he whispers as he closes the door. He moves quietly and whispers as he checks under each hen. I hold the basket as he gathers the eggs. I keep counting.

He lets me throw the feed, and then we back out. I latch the door.

"Good job. Good job."

"Don't tell Davydd."

"What? That you—"

"That I did girl's work."

"Not to worry. He'll never know!"

By the time we get back inside, Willym and Owen are warming themselves by the fire. I drop my wet mittens and coat on the floor and throw down my cap. I pull up my stool beside them to warm myself.

"Knew you'd not be able to make it out today," Papa says.

"Snow's too deep."

"Eyton needs to close—that's for certain."

"He should have closed a week ago," Willym says. "He's getting every last hour."

"It's too cold now to be walking home after coming out of a wet tunnel."

I knew that this would be a good day for more storytelling if I could persuade my father, but he thought it a better idea that we warm up and shovel the pathways.

"And don't forget the path to the little house," Mama says. "I'll have hot *cawl* and bread ready when you come in."

I go for my little shovel to help the others. I am to help Megan clear the back path. Then I help Davydd and Megan build a snow fort. We have almost as much fun as listening to

Papa tell stories. After an afternoon of being outside we were ready for Mama's hot broth and buttered bread. As we head for the back room to hang our wet clothes, she is already ladling out bowls of hot broth.

"Papa, don't doze off!" I say when I see that he is getting comfortable in his chair. I pull up my stool near the hearth.

"Come," he says as he playfully ruffles my damp hair. "What will it be this time?"

"Tell us another story about the castles, Papa."

Megan sits with her chin resting on her knees, staring into the fire. Davydd flops down beside her on the floor by the hearth. The old sheepdog is stretched out beside them, now dry after she was outside with us. Elen is curled up in Mama's rocker, while Gladys is helping Mama in the back room. Evan and Brynn both look as if they are about to fall asleep in their chairs. That's what Owen and Willym are doing already.

As Papa settles back in his chair, we are ready to hear more of the old stories.

I couldn't get enough of the tales of battles and princes in medieval times. My father made the history of our country come alive. It may have been a time when Wales fought to keep what belonged to our people, but to a young boy like me, it was nothing short of magical.

As he begins the story he asks us to imagine the knights galloping toward the castle, their mounts stirring up dust. I can almost hear the thundering hoofs of the horses as they approach the drawbridge. They are coming to lay siege to yet another castle. I am amazed at how my father makes it all so real.

As he continues to tell the story I can almost hear the sounds of battle.

"Listen to the clash of the swords," he says." "Did you hear the knight hit that shield?"

"I hear it."

"Just listen to those horses thundering up the hill!"

"Are there many?" I ask.

"Do you hear them snorting?"

"I hear them. Are they headed for the drawbridge?"

"They're drawing it up now. Just in time!" And he would keep the story going until it was time to close the imaginary book and prepare for bed. There always seemed to be one more question before I could let it go.

"Are there still battles, Papa?"

"No, son, not like those. Those happened hundreds of years ago when Wales was fighting with England for control. Just like the one between the English and the Welsh at Evesham Abbey."

"I want to hear—"

My mother was standing in front of us.

"Go to bed now."

"Do we have to?"

"It's time we all called it a day. It's been a long one. I'll tell you more tomorrow after the chores are done," Papa says.

Papa starts coughing. He always coughs when it gets cold outside.

"You need some warm milk and onions, you do," Mama says.

"It's just the carath."

"'Tis that darn miner's disease, it is," she mutters. She pulls my ear, and then she steers us toward the stairs. She hugs us and reminds us as she does every night, "Don't forget to say your prayers."

I hesitate at the bottom of the stairs and wait for Davydd to go ahead. He probably thinks I still need Papa to hear mine.

"Papa," I call softly. He gets up and comes over.

"What is it, son?"

"About ... about the counting," I stammered. "I did—"

"Shh. I know you did. That latch needs fixing. Now go to bed."

Chapter 3

But the next night I ask about the abbey again.

"Aye, the abbey."

"What happened there?" I ask.

We gather round and wait for my father to begin. He has a faraway look as if he is remembering something. Then he seems to remember the question.

"A terrible massacre, it was," he begins. "And it's said it happened during a really bad thunderstorm. The English plundered and burned the abbey just like they did to so many of our beautiful castles."

"Couldn't someone stop them?" Davydd asks.

"They were relentless. They went through our land, building their own castles on Welsh soil as they took control. Aye, burning ours and building theirs."

"Papa, how could they burn them? They are so strong—"

"Well you see, some of our castles were built of timber in those days … some fifty and sixty feet tall, so they would burn easily."

"How could they get close enough to burn them? What about the moats and walls? And the guards? Where were they?" Brynn asks.

"They would fill the moat with trees and brush and set fire to it, and then they would move across the drawbridge and throw torches at the walls."

"But the ruins we see now are stone. Were they rebuilt?" Evan asks.

"Aye, at a later time. Many were rebuilt after they were taken over. Remember, I told you how Edward the First started building his own castles after our Prince of Wales was killed."

"Was that the time Llywelyn was fighting to keep control?" Evan asks.

"Aye, almost five hundred years ago."

We listen as Papa explains again the power struggles between the powerful leaders—the struggles that would result in Owain's final defeat in 1416.

"When the war was over, did our people try to build the castles again?"

"No, Megan, there was no need. The fighting was over."

"So is that why the English flag flew on all the castles for so long?" Elen asks.

"Aye, when they took over our castles, they flew their own flag."

"But we will always be proud of our country. We had great leaders. Don't forget that."

"But now we can fly our own flag, the one with the winged dragon," I say proudly.

"Aye, *y Draig Goch* depicts the spirit of the Welsh people in the face of attack. It has been our national symbol now for nigh onto three hundred years."

So the red dragon on the Welsh flag is who we really are. Now I understand.

"Papa, are there still knights?"

"No, not like those knights, Tomos. Those times are gone. There is no need to seize castles and fight for control anymore. If you listen very closely though, it is said you can hear sounds coming from the old ruins—the sounds of harps and music, sounds from the great halls."

"Really? I didn't know that!"

"You have to listen really close to hear it," he says with a smile.

"Papa, is there anything left of the abbey?" I ask.

Ruins in the Mist

"No, the abbey was demolished hundreds of years ago. All that remains is the bell tower."

"Just like the old castle we have at the edge of our village," Megan says as she and Elen get up to leave us.

"Aye, the ruins over Denbigh. But some of those turrets and walls are still standing."

"And the walls go all around the hill," I say.

"Over half a mile of walls, there is."

"Will you take me to see the big, big castle someday?"

"Someday soon."

"Promise?"

"One day I'll take you to see the castle over at Caernarfon. You know, Denbigh Castle once looked very much like it."

"It must be big!" I say.

"Were there many castles, Father?" Evan asks as he gets up from his place by the hearth.

"Many. Hundreds there were, and forts as well."

"Really? Hundreds? I didn't know that."

"Come, Davydd. There's time for one game before bed. Let's go."

And just as if on cue, Mama would announce the time, and the stories would end for another evening.

"It's off to bed, you are," she'd say, guiding me toward the stairs.

"You know you should not be filling this child's head with all that silly nonsense!" she says, turning to my father.

Papa let Mama have the final word. He knew that always worked best.

I stop on the stairs and look back. Papa winks, and a smile lights up his tired face. I wave as we say good night.

"*Nos da*, Papa."

"*Nos da*, son."

Chapter 4

The sound of chapel bells breaks the morning silence. I know that this is not a morning to stay under the covers. Everyone in the family is expected to be ready for chapel Sunday morning even in the dead of winter. Brynn has already let me know that more snow has fallen during the night by rubbing some of it on my face to wake me. I peek out the window and discover that the overnight storm is over, but now everything is covered under a blanket of white. Spirals of smoke rise from the chimneys along the lane. A cloud of mist covers the hills.

My father always says that winter storms have a voice of their own.

"Get dressed! Hurry!" But that is definitely my mother's voice.

Brynn and I are the last to get to use the basins in the back room.

"The water's too cold," I say as I pull back my hands.

"Come on. Don't be a wimp! Willym used the last of the warm water, so this will just have to do!"

"No, Brynn. No!" I cry as he holds my hands in the cool water.

"There now. Was that so bad? Time, it is, you were growing up. You're seven years old now."

"Well, look at that!" Willym was holding up one of his boots. "The sole is coming off!"

"A trip to Jones the cobbler for you!" Evan says.

"Evan, I was wondering—"

"Wondering what, Tomos?"

"Why so many in our village have the same name. There's Jones the cobbler … and Jones the grocer—"

"And Jones the farmer!" Davydd says, laughing.

"It's quite a common name in these parts," Owen says. "One in ten."

"Really?"

"Now you know!"

Everyone else is already at the table, and Megan is helping Elen dish up oatmeal from the big iron pot.

"Quickly, boys, the vicar will be waiting!" Mama says as she tries to tame my tousled hair.

We know that this is not a morning for conversation. Neither time nor Mama will allow it. Getting to chapel on time is important. As we leave our cottage and join others already in the lane, I wonder how they can sing on such a morning. But there they are, clutching woollen shawls as they hurry through the snow-covered lane, singing as if it were summer.

We hear the music of the harps as we get near to the chapel. Even before we reach the door, I can hear what they are singing.

"Mama, they're singing your favorite. Listen!" Often at home we hear her sweet voice singing the familiar words—*Arglwydd, arwain trwy'r anialwch*. Now we all join in the singing of *Guide me, O thou great Jehovah*. The vicar is already at the pulpit but waits until all eleven of us take our place in our pews near the front.

Even as a child I loved to hear the music. And the stories that the old preacher told captured the imagination of even we children. The language was simple—the language of our people. The lessons were explained in plain, farmer language, for the preacher himself had no formal training. One evening as we were talking about the morning lesson, I asked Papa about the preacher's learning. "How does the vicar know so much, Papa?"

"His knowledge is of nature and the old Welsh Bible ... nothing more."

"No other learning?"

"No, Brynn, just that."

"When he speaks of men of old like Abraham and Jacob, we farmers relate to those early shepherds."

"He sure knows how to bring it to life," Steffan agrees.

"Gets a little fired up sometimes," Willym says. "Do we really need to hear all that—"

My father is quick to interrupt and set him straight on a few things.

"He tells it like it is. That's what they need to hear," Owen says when our father has finished.

"I don't understand all that about being sinners and forgiveness. I thought that—"

"A lot of people don't understand it. Let me explain it, Evan."

"I thought that if we live right—"

"It's not about what you do. It's more than that. Remember how we always talk about the Christmas story and what it means to us?"

"I remember it ... the baby Jesus!"

"Aye, Tomos. The Messiah. He's also our Savior."

Willym lets out a big sigh when Papa gets up and takes the Bible from the shelf behind him. We listen as Papa explains the story again. This time I think we all got it.

Each week we look forward to the preacher telling us the stories in our own dialect. Many rely on the parables being brought to life for us because so many cannot read. There are no schools here in the north. The preachers have been setting up chapel schools in the south, but none of my family has ever had any learning. My father taught himself to read, and we look forward to him reading to us every night. I think he even knows a lot of it by heart because he often quotes passages when the Book is still on the shelf.

Ruins in the Mist

More music rings out in the chapel, and this time my mother's sweet voice sings out the words *Blinedig gan ofidiau'r llawr*. I know that "Blest be the Tie that Binds" is another of her favorites because she sings it often at home as she goes about her work.

I'm getting fidgety. There's one more hymn before it's time to go. We are still singing it as we leave the chapel. "Come, thou fount of every blessing. Tune my heart to sing thy grace. Streams of mercy, never ceasing, calls for songs of loudest praise."

It isn't long before we find ourselves back in the lane, picking our steps in the snow. We're still singing, "Here's my heart. O take and seal it. Seal it for thy courts above."

"Don't know why we have to go to chapel when it's this cold," Davydd says as we hurry home.

"Be thankful we only have to go once this time of year," Willym says.

Sundays are the days we look forward to—the days when the whole family is together. Except Gladys—she's away. When she had announced that she was going to the Morley estate, Brynn asked her if maybe that wasn't "above her station." I'm not sure what that means. Even Steffan is home from Penrhyn. My oldest brother has been working in the slate quarry for years now. Owen and Willym are home from the pits at Flynt. Because of the distance, they have been staying in the barracks all week. Just two weeks ago they had gone back to work after the winter shutdown. This late snow is a bit of a surprise. I heard Mama say that Gladys was lucky to get to the estate before it came.

The stories of the morning will be talked about again after our evening meal as we sit around the fire.

"Papa, the story of the shepherd boy tending his father's sheep— Do you think he got lonely by himself?" I ask.

"Oh, I think maybe he did."

"That's why he played his music!" Megan quips.

"That's probably why," Papa answers, smiling.

"I liked that story too," says Brynn. "Sounds like it happened around here."

"Would you like to hear it again?" Papa asks.

He reaches for the Bible and finds the place. We all listen intently as he reads the story again.

"How could he be both a shepherd and a king?" Davydd asks.

"He loved God—that's what the vicar said," I say, proud that I had remembered the preacher's story.

"That's right, Tomos. He was a man after God's own heart. He understood what the Lord wanted for his people."

My mother always says that Papa can quote the Scriptures as easily as he can carry on a conversation. She says we are one of the few families to have the treasured Scriptures because it is very costly to get a copy of the Welsh Bible, if one can be found at all.

Staring into the flickering flames, I would be lost in what my father was reading. Perhaps that is why I didn't hear my mother the first time. But now she stands before us.

"Tomos ... Davydd, it's time you were in bed, it is."

We know she means it, so we lose no time in saying good night to the others. I would barely remember climbing the stairs and falling into bed.

Chapter 5

Spring finally arrives. The warm winds from the Atlantic spread across the land and the isolation of the winter was behind us. Spring brought with it warm days, and it wasn't long before the snow was gone from the fields and the only trace of winter was the lingering snow on the peaks in the distance.

Papa and Pierce, our neighbor, had spent the last few days of March finishing the shearing. Then it was up to Mama and the girls to get the wool washed at the stream and do the carding. Papa has told her for years that she should just take it to the woolen mill, but Mama insists she can do it. The last of the spring lambs have finally arrived. Papa has spent many late nights waiting and checking on the lambs. We boys have been going out every day to see the newborns. Then one morning when my father comes in he is a little more excited than usual about the new arrivals.

"Go see the black one, boys!"

"All black, Papa?" I ask with excitement.

"Aye, all black, it is."

We lose no time racing across the yard to the sheep barn. There it is, black as coal, trying to stand on its long, wobbly legs. We try to help, but the mother nudges us away.

When we return to the kitchen, Evan reminds us that it is almost that time again. "Isn't it about time to take the sheep to the summer pasture?" he asks.

"Aye, the little ones have been in the pens long enough."

"Are they all taking the milk well enough?" Brynn asks.

"Aye, it's time. They're ready."

"Papa, they are so little. Will—"

"They'll be fine. They need feed from the mountain meadows now."

"When do you think—"

"Next week. You can all go and help move the sheep to the higher hills."

"Hurrah!"

And just as promised, the following week we help Papa prepare to take the sheep to higher pastures.

"Ask your mother to pack a lunch for us, and we'll eat on the hills."

"Let's eat in the *hafod*, Papa. That would be fun!" I say.

"We can if you like, Tomos. But better still. Would you like to stay in the *hafod* tonight and come back in the morning?"

"Oh yes! That would be fun!"

This would be our first time of staying overnight. Our father had stayed sometimes, especially if he wanted to make sure everything was all right.

"And we may do the same again in September," he says. Now we are really excited.

"Evan, get the gate! Brynn, don't let them stray in the lane," Papa says as we get ready to leave.

The sheep and lambs follow us up the steep mountain path. Every once in a while we stop to let them rest, taking time to rest ourselves. And all the while Tad keeps them from straying off the path.

"C'mon, sheep. C'mon," Papa calls when we are ready to continue the climb.

"Get that little one, Davydd! It's getting too far from the flock."

My brother starts to chase after the little stray. But there is a shrill whistle from Papa. The old sheepdog bounds after the stray and brings her back.

We arrive at the hut and open the lunch that Mama has prepared, and then we sit outside on the warm grass to eat. A gentle breeze is stirring in the trees above us. Everything in the meadow smells so fresh.

"Listen, boys. Listen to the sounds that the wind makes through the trees. Don't you think it sounds like someone whispering?"

It really *did* sound like someone whispering. I stretch out on the grass and listen to the soft rustling above. We are all quiet for some minutes until I break the silence.

"What do you think it's saying, Papa?"

"Maybe just letting us know that this is a special place."

"Do you mean the *hafod*, Papa?" I ask.

"No, Tomos, not just the hills and the *hafod*. More than that—"

"Do you mean our country, Father?" Davydd asks.

He is thoughtful for a moment. "Aye, our country. The mountains, the sounds of the hills, the harps. It's a very special place."

That faraway look comes to my father's face, but he finally gets up, stretches, and announces that we need to bed down.

It's a warm night. As we lay in the *hafod*, Papa tells us stories from when he was a boy. "My father knew only the life of herding and farming. That's all I want for you boys."

"Is that why you keep us interested in the workings of the farm?" Evan asks.

"Aye, that's why."

"And why you explain about the cows and goats being kept in the paddocks while the sheep spend the summer in the pastures?" Brynn asks.

"That's why. You need to know all of that."

"Brynn doesn't need to know. He's going down into the mines," Davydd says.

Davydd was the first to fall asleep, and before long we were all asleep. No doubt our father soon joined us. That night in the summer hut is one I want to remember for my whole life.

Now that the roads over the hills are open, my father has promised that he and I will soon take a long walk again. None of the others ever have any interest in the walks with Papa. They are our special times—just the two of us. Since late November winter has carpeted the fields, and deep snow has made the mountain paths impassable.

"Papa, is today the day for our walk?" I ask every day from then on. Then one day it is time.

"A good day it is for a walk. Get my walking stick, and we'll be off."

"We won't be missed today."

"Why not?" I ask.

"This is *diwrnod pobi* for your mother and the girls."

Every Friday was baking day—the day when the two large wall ovens would be heated for baking. All morning loaf after loaf of bread would be baked, and then in the afternoon it would be the tarts and cakes. The smells coming from the kitchen were often enough to bring my brothers and me in from the lane, where we had been playing with the neighborhood boys.

"The *bara brith* smells so good, Mama," I would say.

"It will soon be cool enough to have a slice with butter and cheese," she would answer.

Days are always busy in our home. There is always a lot to do, and my father often says how fortunate Mama is to have two girls to help with the chores. And now that the planting is about to begin, Brynn and Evan and even Davydd will help Papa as much as they can. They keep telling me I am just in the way, but Papa always finds something that I can do to help out.

"You'll be able to take Brynn's place when he goes off to work the pits next week," he tells me.

"I can learn the feeding and help with the water."

"That you can!"

The chore of getting water heated for my brothers' washing up after a day in the pits is one that can't be neglected. The conversation is always the same.

"Elen, the water needs to be hauled soon. Take Evan with you," Mama will say.

"Yes, Mother."

"Get the kettles boiling. Out of Eyton's pit they're a sorry sight!"

"Yes, Mother."

"Megan, set out the basins in the back room."

"Yes, Mother."

And as she does every day just before sundown, our mother stands in the open door and watches for them. With her apron folded around her hands, she waits until she sees her boys coming down the lane toward home. Brynn started work just weeks ago.

I sometimes listen to my parents when they think I'm not paying any attention.

"He is too young to be working," I heard Mama tell my papa. I guess they are talking about Brynn.

"He will be all right," Papa tells her.

"The conditions are not good."

"He will be careful," Papa says.

"But you know the youngest are given the jobs of—"

"I know. Opening and closing the ventilator doors."

"That's a big responsibility, Tomos. Too much for young boys." I can hear the concern in my mother's voice.

My father had once worked the mines himself and knew how dangerous the work could be.

"The safety of the mine depends on it, Gwendolyn. It's an important job the young boys have."

"Brynn is so young, Tomos. So young."

"Brynn says it gets monotonous, but it's still better than for some of the young boys working the pumps in the bottom of the pit," Papa tells her.

"Knee-deep in water. It's not fit!"

"At least the boys are home every night now," I hear Papa tell her.

"That's good, it is."

"Aye, I'm pleased they took jobs at Mostym."

My mother has reason to worry. Willym and Owen often talk with Papa about the conditions underground. They all think that more should be done to protect the young boys who have to work loading carts in the cold, damp tunnels. They talk about how dangerous it is and about the accidents that often happen. Sometimes men die. Never come home. Before my father left the mines, he'd been trapped in a heavy earth fall. Owen told me about it. He was one of the lucky ones. Others had died. He never went back to the collieries but instead put his heart into farming.

Now my mother will wait at the open door. I know because I often sat on the step, waiting with her. She will hear the singing. Within minutes she will see them, caps pulled over grimy faces, their tin lunch buckets swinging. She will wave, and the boys will wave back before she disappears inside.

"Hurry, girls. Your brothers are coming. Get the water ready!"

Papa and I arrive back from our walk just in time to join them in the backyard. They are stripped to the waist and trying to wash away the black.

"Look at these arms!" Brynn says as he shows off his muscles.

"Is that from pushing the carts, Brynn?" I ask.

"It's hard work—that's for certain. I'm getting used to it."

"Someday I'll work in the—"

"Not likely, little brother. You've promised Father to—"
"To be a farmer?"
"That you have!"
"Not to worry. That will make you strong," Owen is quick to point out.
"Papa works hard," I say.
"That he does. When you're a bit older, you can work with him." Owen says as he glances at his father.
"I'm working with him now. He's showing me how to farm!" I say proudly. "I do Brynn's chores."

My mother and the girls are preparing the table, and then a long day is rewarded with a hearty meal and the anticipated spicy pudding. Only Steffan is missing tonight, but tomorrow he will make the family almost complete when he comes home from the quarry until Sunday.

Our walk to the hills has been a good one. I want to tell them about the walk and all we have seen, but I will have to wait.

Papa asks the blessing, "Thank you, Lord, for this food, for bringing the boys home safely. Now I pray your blessing upon us. Amen."

"Amen," my mother whispers.

"Time to talk later. Eat before it gets cold."

We never argue with our mother.

Chapter 6

The following week after the barn chores are done, I ask my father if we can take another walk up the mountain path.

"As far as the hills only, we'll check on the sheep today."

Before he can change his mind, I run to fetch his walking stick and hat.

"We'll be off now."

I trot along beside him, and before long we are on the winding footpath leading to the summer pasture.

The trail is dry, and pretty primroses are springing up along the path. Off in the distance traces of snow still dust the high peaks of Eryre. The patches of white that had been on the hills the last time we were here are gone now.

We hear water running somewhere, and as we round a bend on the path, we see water rushing down the side of the rocks.

Coming to a clearing, we walk to the edge of a grassy embankment and peer down over the edge. Below, the patches of green that are bordered by hedges are now pastures for the sheep. The sweetbriar is already in bloom, tangled with the bracken on the hillside, where the sheep are grazing. We sit down to rest, and it is then that we notice that the sun has disappeared.

"Looks like rain," Papa says, looking up at the darkening sky.

"Oh?"

"Aye, listen to the leaves rustling."

Ruins in the Mist

"Sounds like the wind's whispering," I say.

A big smile crosses his face. My father gets to his feet and stands there, leaning on his walking stick. "Look, Tomos! Look at the daffodils on the hill yonder!"

"Oh, Papa, shall we pick some?"

"Your mother likes daffodils .We will have to hurry before the rain comes though."

I hurry ahead toward the yellow flowers that almost cover the hill. When I stop to wait for Papa to catch up, I notice the ruins of the old castle off in distance. I stop to point it out.

"Is it very old?" I ask.

"Aye ... built hundreds of years ago."

"When England was warring with Wales?"

"Aye."

"Why was there so much war?"

"They wanted to take away our independence. They wanted to take away our country."

"So we had to fight?"

"To keep our language and all we held dear, we had to, but in the end we lost."

"I like that our people fought for our country," I say. "But I don't understand it."

"Someday you will understand it all, son. Don't ever forget that our people were very brave."

"I'll never forget," I say.

"The daffodils are ready for picking. Let's go!"

"Remember, this is Saturday!"

"Aye, the boys will be home, and your mother will have a big dinner ready tonight."

Saturday night's dinner is like a celebration. All the family is home, and because this is Easter, even Gladys is home. There is no cooking on Sundays. That is the day for chapel and rest.

By the time I've picked a handful of the bright yellow flowers, the sky has darkened, and the rain has started. Papa decides that we should try to make it to the old castle ruins for shelter before we get drenched. I run up the hill and wait for Papa to catch up.

"Hurry, Papa!"

We make it just as a heavy shower pelts us. We find a spot inside the towering walls where part of the roof is still intact, offering some shelter. Sitting on the damp earth, we listen as the rain forms puddles outside. The smell of the warm rain mixes with the dampness of the old fortress walls, and somewhere inside water is dripping from the stones.

"Look at the vastness of the space," Papa says. "Look at the size of that fireplace!"

"I wish there was a fire in that big fireplace," I tell him. "That would warm us. Just as it warmed the knight's family years ago."

We talked about what it would have been like in times of peace with the families and guests gathered around the huge table, minstrels and poets entertaining them as they ate. So engrossed were we that we hardly noticed when the rain stopped.

"Come, Tomos. Let's be getting home."

I pick up the bunch of yellow flowers now starting to wilt. I know my mother will be pleased with them.

We carefully make our way back down the steep hill and head toward home. Now the path is soft and muddy in places after the heavy rain.

Coming around a bend we meet old Mr. Eyton with a cartload of peat.

"Good day to you, Tomas. Fine day for a walk in the hills."

"Aye, indeed, Mr. Eyton. Now that the rain has stopped."

"We ran to the ruins for shelter!" I quickly point out.

"Ah, you've been picking *Peter's leek*, I see."

"These are for my mother," I say, looking at the pretty flowers.

"And where does the day take you, sir?" my father asks.

"Up to *the Shepherds Inn* with this load by sundown. Been

all day on the moors, I have. Lucky for me the moss was already wet!"

"I must get another load of peat soon. I notice that the peat house is getting low. This past winter has used up our supply too quickly."

"I'll replenish the supply soon," Mr. Eyton assures him.

"Well, you have a good day, sir."

"Good day to you too, Tomos."

We watch as his cart continues up the hilly path, and we turn toward home.

"Papa, why do we not use coal like Dylan's family?"

"The peat does not cost so much. We cannot afford coal again this year. There's good heat in the peat after it has been dried. We are fortunate to have such a ready supply, we are."

"I heard Mama tell Elen the vegetables are running out."

"Oh, we should be all right until the new crop is ready. The crops should be better than last year."

"Was last year a bad crop, Papa?"

"Crops have not been good for a couple of years now, but we'll manage. You don't need to worry."

Before long we pass the stonemason's shop and wave to Mr. Parry, and we walk on by the weaver's shop—quiet on this Saturday afternoon. The women of the village would have finished their shifts on Friday.

A pebble on the path rolls as father's stick hits it, and a startled hare scurries back to his burrow.

"Thought it was a *Tylwyth Teg*," I say, jumping back.

"No, Tomos, the faeries have their own paths in the mountains," he says, laughing.

"Megan told me once they cause bad things to happen. Is that true, Papa?"

"No, son, you do not need to fear the *Tylwyth Teg*. They sometimes cause mischief but will cause no harm."

"Is it true that they sit at the side of the path and watch us as we go by?"

"Aye, during the day that is where they stay hidden."

"Did you ever see one, Papa?" I ask, looking up at him.

"It is said that at night they dance in the dingle with their golden locks flowing in the breeze."

"They do?"

"I'll tell you more about the faeries later," my father says, laughing.

"Tell me more tonight!"

"Tonight I will go with the boys to the pub. But I will tell you more soon."

By the time we reach home, my brothers are already in the backyard, washing away the day's grime.

I hurry ahead and push open the gate, anxious to give my mother the flowers. Before we even open the door, the smells reach our noses. Saturday's meal is always special. It is likely to be potato broth and a big pot of *potch*. I liked the mashed vegetables. Perhaps even lamb or bacon.

"Ah, daffodils for me!" Mama exclaims when I hand her the wilting flowers.

"Mama, there were so many!"

"I shall get them in water right away, I shall. You both need to get out of those wet clothes. You're drenched!"

I start to tell her about the visit to the old castle ruins, but she isn't ready to listen. She doesn't share my enthusiasm for the castle ruins.

I watch as my mother lowers herself heavily into her chair.

"Finally. Thank God for the rest," she says quietly.

"The gravy. You've forgotten the—"

"Megan, let your mother rest. See how tired she is."

As our family pauses to give thanks for the leg of lamb that Papa is about to carve, Mama is quick to remind him of other things we have to be thankful for as well.

"Be sure to thank the good Lord for bringing all the boys home safe tonight."

"And for Gladys and all this good food," Elen adds.

"Why not wait until after we eat to give thanks!" Davydd says.

"Why would you say that?" Papa asks.

"What if we don't like what—"

"God provides it, and we're thankful we have something to eat," my father tells him sternly.

"Enough! Bow your heads," Mama says.

I peek at Mama. She looks tired.

Papa, don't take too long. She'll be asleep.

"Amen."

I join the chorus. "Amen."

Having meat on our table two times this week is something to be thankful for.

"This is better than *quarryman's supper*," Steffan says as he looks in Mama's direction.

"You will have more than potatoes and bacon tonight, you will," she says.

"I'm always glad for your cooking after a week of fending for myself in the barracks."

As they do every Saturday night after supper, my older brothers reach for their caps and head for *the Swan* at the other end of the village. It is their time to find out what the neighbors are doing and what is going on in the village. Mama says Papa goes to look after Willym. She worries after Willym. She says he likes the *cwrw* more than he should. After they have given her their week's earnings, I watch as she gives them each a few pence.

"Here. A few pence," she says. I can tell by the way she looks at Willym that she has given him a little extra. He leans over and kisses her cheek.

"Just one, Mother," Owen says as he kisses her on the cheek and follows Willym out the door.

Papa lays a hand on her shoulder and follows my brothers. She waits to hear the gate close.

"One ... just one!" she mutters to herself. "That cursed devil's brew!" Papa never touches the *cwrw*.

Chapter 7

The day begins as any other. My mother stands by the open door, passing each of my brothers a tin lunch bucket and patting each on the cheek as they hurry out.

"Be safe, Owen."

"Be safe, Willym."

"Be safe, Brynn."

She stands looking after them until they were out of sight. This she does every day without fail. I watch her as she turns and goes back to her duties in the back kitchen. I hear her humming quietly.

Elen is busy at the loom, working on a piece of homespun. She's so intent on the task that she doesn't hear me come up behind her. I watch quietly as she moves her hands, turning the threads of wool into a woven piece.

"What's that you're working on?" I ask, interrupting her as she hums a familiar hymn.

"A piece of homespun for a skirt. Now run outside and play with the others."

Earlier this morning Mama had reminded Megan and Evan that the blackberries were ready for picking. "They're just waiting to be picked. Tonight we will have *bara mwyar* with plenty of double cream."

It's not long before they are back with a bucket of the sweet berries, and Evan hurries to the barn to help Papa finish up the chores.

Suddenly the late morning stillness is broken by the shrill wail of the siren piercing the air.

"The mines!" Davydd yells as he drops what he's been playing with. The other boys all stop what they are doing as well. We stand there, waiting for the siren to stop.

Women are gathering in the lane, looking in the direction of the mines, hoping it might be a false alarm. But the siren keeps blowing. This one is likely to be for real.

"The mines! It's the mines!" they yell as they run into the lane, looking toward the hill.

Everyone knows what the dreaded siren means. By the time we push open the gate, Mama and the girls are already outside and running toward us. Papa and Evan are halfway across the field, running from the barn.

"Help your father, Davydd! Help get the cart ready."

We are all waiting in the lane when Papa hurries the horses through the garden gate. We quickly climb on the cart. The wagon would have given more room for all of us, but Papa knows that the cart will be much faster.

"Shut the gate, Evan!"

"Hurry! We must hurry!" Mama says.

Papa urges the horses on, joining the other carts and wagons as everyone makes their way up the lane. The mine is less than three miles away, but it seems to take forever.

By the time we reach the mine, quite a crowd has gathered. Smoke is billowing from the entrance, making it difficult to see what is taking place. Miners with blackened faces are crowded near the pithead. Families are huddled, waiting. Owen rushes to meet us and helps Mama from the cart.

"What happened?" Papa asks, hurrying to join the others.

"A cave-in no doubt!"

"Where's Brynn? Where's Willym?" Mama asks as she looks around.

"There's still a few to come up. Willym's helping with the rescue."

"Look at the smoke! Owen, go! Find him!" Mama wails.

"Willym is down there now. They'll find them all."

"That cursed firedamp," she murmurs as she wipes at her eyes.

"Who is still missing?" someone calls out.

"Two young boys. Porters they say."

"There's Willym!" Evan shouts when he sees our brother helping a young miner from the pit. His family rushes to meet him. Still no sign of Brynn.

"Someone has to go back for Brynn!" Mama cries.

"Hughes went back for him," Willym says as he throws himself on the ground.

My father holds unto Mama and tries to quiet her, but she's terribly upset. Now we see that something is happening at the entrance. She breaks from my father's hold and runs forward. We all follow her to get a closer look. Still there was no one else emerging from the dust now seeping from the depths. We wait.

Then a miner appears, carrying a young boy, wet and limp. He passes the young boy to a fellow miner and heads back. "Got to find the other one."

Mama rushes to the boy but finds that it is not Brynn.

"Where is he? Where's Brynn?"

"They will find him, they will," my father assures her.

We wait for what seems to be another very long time. Then the word comes that we have all been waiting for.

"They've found him." The news goes through the crowd. "They've found him!"

"See, Gwendolyn, I told you they would." Our family is relieved at the news.

Through the dust we see Hughes staggering from the pit with Brynn in his arms.

The lifeless, blackened, and muddied body of my brother is laid on the ground not far from where the other young boy is laying. My mother drops to her knees beside him. The color drains from her face. I thought she might faint.

"No, no, no! Not my little one!" she screams as she slumps to the ground and gathers my brother toward her. Tears stream down her face as she cradles him in her arms. She is crying loudly now. She rocks back and forth. Finally she falls back against Owen, exhausted.

Papa sits on the ground, his shoulders slumped, his head bowed. I go to him, and he puts his arm around my shoulders. I see now that the tears are running down his cheeks. My own tears are coming, even though I try hard to stop them. I watch as Willym and Owen help Mama from the ground and walk with her to the cart. I see the tears streaming down their blackened faces as well. Everyone is just standing there. For several minutes no one moves, and then slowly one by one they make their way toward home. In the cart Brynn is covered. He doesn't move. We return home in silence, except for the sobbing coming from my mother and sisters.

Later that night a man comes to our home and explains what happened. "Brynn was hit on the head after the cave-in."

"Didn't they know where he was?" my father asks.

"He wasn't able to respond to their calls when they attempted to reach him. Water filled the shaft very quickly. There was nothing more we could do. We tried."

Now the wooden box sits on two chairs by the window. The lid is open.

"Will we keep Brynn here, Davydd?" I ask.

"They'll take him to the hill."

"Papa says Brynn is in heaven. But—"

"Just his soul."

"His soul?"

"Forget it! Don't you remember anything Father teaches us!"

"How does his soul—"

"The angels come, I guess. I don't know."

"Oh, I'll ask Papa. He'll know."

The days that follow are all a blur to me. I just know that

my big brother is dead. Everyone calls it a tragedy. A lot of people are sad, especially my own family. Steffan came home from the quarry, and Gladys came home from Morley Hall. Friends gather to comfort us. Wailing women come to watch. They whisper and sniffle into their handkerchiefs.

"Papa, why do they all come to—"

"It's what people do, son. They've come to 'watch the dead'."

I have Brynn's bed now.

Mama bursts into tears every time she looks at Brynn's body. Evan tells me I shouldn't touch Brynn. It looks as if he is sleeping. Mama lets others attend to the chores that she always insisted were hers.

Dr. Wynne comes to check on her when she refuses to leave her bedchamber. She doesn't even come down to eat with us.

"Let her rest. She needs rest. I've given her something to help her sleep," I hear him tell my father.

The neighbors come with lots of food. The women try to comfort my mother, but she keeps crying.

"This is pain no mother should bear," one neighbor says to another.

"We know her pain," another says.

"More of our sons should work in the quarries. It's safer than in the pits."

The 'soul bell' keeps ringing as the preacher leads the procession to the chapel. The men—our friends—walk in front of the cart, and our family walks behind followed by the women and young people.

The only other sound—besides the wailing of the women—is the wooden box rattling on the rough roadway. The music of the harps can be heard as we near the chapel.

After the singing stops, the old, gray-haired vicar steps forward. "We have lost two young lads this week. God knows the sorrow you feel," he begins. "Today we lay to rest a second son."

"May you be comforted. May you—" He was having a difficult time finding the right words.

"You are troubled now. Troubled by the terrible tragedy that has befallen your homes."

"Look up, dear friends! Remember the words of the Lord. *Let not your heart be troubled. Peace I leave with you, My peace I give unto you—*"

He keeps talking. I am restless. Mama nudges me. Papa reaches over and takes my hand. I listen again to the preacher.

"Comfort each other. God asks us to weep with those who weep."

Finally he finishes. We follow the wooden box to the door. There's a lot of sobbing.

We leave the chapel with the voices of the choir singing, "He bids us build each other up ... and gathered into one. We hand in hand go on."

Now the men carry the wooden box up the hill behind the chapel. Mama's hand clings to the side of the box.

"Brynn! Brynn!" she cries.

Steffan reaches out to take her arm as she collapses against him. Gladys clings to her.

When they put the box on the ground beside the deep hole, I start toward it, but my father pulls me back.

"No, Tomos, it will be all right," he says tenderly.

I watch as the wooden box is lowered into the ground. As shovels of dirt hit the box, the women are crying along with my mother. I guess I am too young to understand what has really happened. All I really know is that Brynn is in that wooden box and they were shovelling dirt in on it. I stand, looking at the fresh mound, and then I reach for my father's hand. When I look up, I can see that he is quiet, very quiet and that a tear runs down each cheek.

So it is all right for a man to cry?

We walk back down the hill, turning only once to look back. We are leaving him there—on the hillside behind the chapel—alone. Shouldn't we go back? Evan says he is dead. Does that mean he won't come back home ever? My own eyes fill with tears. I brush them away with the back of my hand.

We walk home in silence. My father's look tells me everything will be all right. He squeezes my hand and doesn't say a word. Perhaps he can't.

Chapter 8

In the days that follow, Papa spends a lot more time by himself in the fields and barns. My father is a quiet man and keeps his feelings to himself. But then we take a walk to the hills, and his spirits lift. Before long he is telling me stories again, and to a child, that is important. My father is a very smart man.

I often hear Mama weeping. She doesn't even seem to notice when I touch her hands. Gladys explains to us before she leaves that our mother will need extra rest now because she is exhausted.

Is that why she spends so much time in her room alone?

Throughout the summer Evan, Davydd, and I follow Papa in the fields, trying to help wherever we can, but I really don't think we are much help. Our neighbor, Pierce, is the one who helps with the ploughing and crops. They probably think we are just in the way.

"Do you think the rain will hold off till we get the hay gathered?" Pierce asks, looking up toward the sky.

"The sky is darkening, it is. But we should be all right," my father answers, looking toward the threatening clouds as he urges the horse on.

"I'll run and check the little bottle, Papa,"

"Too late for that, Tomos."

The little weather bottle that we kept on the window ledge foretold the weather—or so we thought. My father probably knows more about foretelling the weather than the weather bottle.

Later as we head for the cottage after the last of the hay is safely in the barn, I notice how tired Papa looks. He stops and looks at the darkening skies.

"When are we going to the mill, Father," Evan asks.

"If the weather holds, we'll go tomorrow."

"I can help with the sacks. They are too heavy for you alone."

"I want to go too," Davydd says.

"Me too!" I say.

"Aye, you shall all go with me. We'll leave as soon as the chores are done."

We always look forward to the visit to Piggot's. It is so much fun to see the windmill turning and see the huge stone wheels grinding the wheat into flour.

So the next morning the sacks are loaded on the cart, and we make our way the short distance to the gristmill. There the heavy sacks are hoisted to the sack floor and emptied into the bin. We wait down below for the flour to make its way down the chute to be bagged. When Davydd reaches for the final bag, the miller stops him. He had forgotten about the *miller's toll*. This last bag will be payment for the service that he has provided.

On our way home Papa answers our questions about the mill.

"We want to be farmers," Evan says.

"Just like you," I add.

"I shall hope the fields will call you, that I do."

"It's a good life, isn't it, Father?" Davydd asks.

"It is. I hope that conditions start to improve. That the crops will soon be as they once were."

"Is that why the farmers are worried?"

"There's been a decline in the crops these past two years. But it will get better, it will."

"Are you worried about next year, Father?" Evan wants to know.

Papa shakes his head and smiles. "It will get better, boys. Don't worry. I expect we'll have a good crop of potatoes this year."

As we cross the wooden bridge near the old blacksmith shop, a fox scampers to the nearby woods and disappears.

"Never know what you might see," Davydd says.

"Look, boys. There's Jones the grocer. We're almost home."

"Oh, Papa, could we have a sweet?" I ask.

"No, not today. Your mother will be waiting. My old chair will suit me well, I think."

"Father, why do you work so hard?" Evan asks.

"We have to work hard to make a living."

"But it's so hard on you. Could you not get some help until I'm older?"

"Son, we *gwerin* have always made a living from this harsh, rugged land. It's who we are."

"Why do you stay here, Papa, if it makes you tired?" I ask.

"It's our home. Look at those mountains. I could never leave this. I would miss it all, I would." He raises his hand and points off in the distance where the autumn colors have painted the hills.

"And I would miss the castles, Papa," I say.

"Someday I hope you'll understand why … why I could never leave this land."

"Next week, let's take a walk over the hills to see the castle ruins north of here," he continues.

"Oh, could we?"

"We will leave early. It's a fair hike. Are you up for it?"

"Have we seen this one before?" I ask.

"Not this one."

As we round the next bend and see smoke coming from the chimney, we are glad to be home. When we step inside, we notice that Elen and Megan have been busy all day helping to make the winter's supply of candles. The pole is suspended across two chairs for the rods.

"You have been busy!" Evan says, noticing the wicks dangling from the pole.

"Burnt my fingers more than once, I have!" Elen answers, tossing her dark curls aside.

"You have to dip them time and time again?"

"That's the only way to get them the right size!" she says.

"Tiresome!"

"Sure is. But this winter you'll thank us," Megan adds lightheartedly.

As expected, our mother has supper ready, and she wastes no time in hurrying us off to wash up. She practically pushes us toward the back room, where the basins are waiting for us. This is not the first time that she has seen us arrive from the trip to the flour mill. She knows what to expect, and she's prepared for us.

"Hurry, boys. I have good news to tell."

"Oh, Mama, what is it?" I call from the back room.

"Wash that dust and grime ... and just hurry!"

I guessed it must be something important that she would let us talk about it at the supper table. She very rarely allowed much talk before the meal was finished.

As we take our places and Papa asks for God's blessings on the meal, we look across at our mother for the news. She has our attention.

"The post brought a letter from Gladys today!" she says with excitement. Mama is always happy when the post brings a letter from my sister.

"I bet the first thing she asked about was Llandon, didn't she, Mother!" Megan pipes up.

"Yes, she did ask about her beau, Megan. She is looking forward to seeing all of us, she is."

"Does she expect to be home soon?" Papa asks.

"Before Christmas, she hopes."

"Oh, I can hardly wait!" says Megan.

"It has been awhile since she was home. Not since—" Papa doesn't finish. Everyone is silent. He gets up from the table and stands at the hearth for some minutes with his back to us before he returns to the table. Everyone is intent on eating until I break the silence.

"What's for dessert, Mama?" I ask between mouthfuls.

"A surprise, it is." We all know that means something special.

"I hope its *poten dato*," I say. I watched my mother make it once. I couldn't believe that the potatoes mixed with sugar and spices could taste so good, and when she took it from the oven, the family could not wait to taste the delicious currant pudding. I hurry to empty my plate.

Chapter 9

What remained of the medieval fortress perched on the side of the hill now loomed before us.

"I see the castle now! Wow! It's so big. Let's climb the hill to get a better look."

"It's quite a climb. Are you sure?"

"Let's go!"

The remains of the spiral stone stairway are visible to us now as we draw closer. I hurry ahead of my father and then wait for him to catch up. "Hurry, Papa. I want to see inside the walls!"

"See. Over there. There are the ramparts—what's left of them!" he says when he finally reaches the top of the path.

"Why were they so high?"

"That's where soldiers positioned themselves in defending the castle. From there they could see for miles."

"The high curtain wall was once made of timber."

"Really?"

"Later would have been refortified with stone and mortar. See, you can tell. Look."

"Did families live in the castle?"

"Aye, a baron and his family. And servants and bards."

"What's a bard?"

"They were often members of the household. Minstrels who sang about our culture and kept our language alive."

"We should still have bards."

"Aye, that we should."

"What happened to them?"

"Well, according to legend, Edward the First had hundreds of them killed after the English took over in the thirteenth century."

"Why would he do that?"

"That was his way of making our people forget the past."

"Oh, Papa! Really?"

"But we never will! There's talk of bringing back the bards. There are plans to have special festivals every year celebrating our culture, all to be held in our very own language!"

"Really? Our very own language?"

"As a home, this was probably well guarded. The strongest part would have been the gatehouse."

"The gatehouse?"

"That was their defense against invading armies."

"And there was a chapel, and one of the towers was probably a prison."

"A prison!"

As we make our way through the thick tangle of bushes and vines, we draw closer to the entrance. My father explains where the drawbridge would have been and how soldiers would have hurried across it. We can see inside the walls now. We make our way over the crumbled base of what once was the stone gatehouse and peered inside the ruins.

"The walls were really thick, weren't they? Look, Papa. Look over there."

"Those stairs would have led to one of the towers."

"I want to climb—"

"No, they may not be safe. See, the top ones are crumbling."

I return to where my father is standing.

"The great hall was probably over there," he says, pointing to an area in the center of the crumbling ruins.

"It's so big! It must have been very cold in here."

"Oh, huge fireplaces warmed the rooms, and flaming torches on the walls gave warmth ... and light as well."

"Why was it called a great hall?"

Then my father explains how the long tables would have been placed with chairs for many who often joined the baron and his family to be entertained by travelling minstrels during times of peace. We stand, looking at the huge castle ruins for some minutes, imagining the family who once lived there. Then my father turns and starts down the path. "Come, Tomos. It's time we are heading home."

"This must be really old," I say, gesturing toward the ruins.

"Not as old as some. Some date back to Roman times."

"Roman times. Like you read in the Bible?" I ask.

"The very same. They had over fourteen hundred forts in Wales and England when they were conquering our county. The biggest one was probably north of here. *Tre'r Ceiri.*"

"The town of the giants?"

"Aye, it was huge. Overlooked the bay."

"That must have been a long, long time ago," I say.

"Aye, a very long time ago. The time of horses and chariots and all that."

"That's where you get the stories you tell us!" I say, laughing.

We continue to make our way back down the winding path, picking our way through the brambles that had grown over the path in places.

"I wonder why so many of the castles were destroyed," I finally say.

"A lot of them were destroyed to keep them out of the hands of the English."

"Really? Our people burned their own castles?"

"Deganwy was burned back in the twelve hundreds. Then the English rebuilt it. Then twenty years later the Welsh prince captured it and destroyed it the second time. Remember, I told you all about that awhile back?"

"Were our leaders powerful?"

"Llwyelyn was a powerful and ruthless fighter. That he

was! He died defending our nation. We owe a great debt to him."

"We didn't win the wars—"

"No, but we fought hard. Our people fought with all they had! It made us what we are today."

We are quiet for some time as we make our way back down the zigzagging path. As we near home, I look up at my father and smile. He smiles back at me.

He starts to sing. I hadn't heard that for many weeks. "*Y deryn pur ar. Bydd i mi'n was—*"

"Sing, Tomos!" he urges.

"*O! bry sur brysia—*"

When we finish the song, he looks down at me and says something I never want to forget. "No one took away our language, and we can still sing all the old songs we love. We may have given up the struggle, but the spirit of our people lives on. We are a proud people."

Chapter 10

Steffan's announcement came as a big surprise. No one was ready for such news, especially our mother. They had all been sitting around the fire and talking. I was laying with my head on the dog, not even paying much attention to what they were saying. My mother let out a gasp.

"You are going where?"

"I'm going to America," he repeats.

"America?" Mama asks. "Whatever put such a notion in your head?"

I listen as he tells of his plans. Steffan is leaving us?

"I'm going to the colonies."

"Oh no! That is nonsense!"

"Mother, I've grown tired of the quarry."

"You have a good job at Penrhyn."

"It's not the same. Things are changing there."

"It can't be that bad. Thought things were improving at Penrhyn," Evan says.

"Pennant's trying, but—"

"Come now, stay with it a bit longer. See what happens," Mama coaxes.

I notice that my father has been quiet through all of this. Now my mother looks at him with fire in her eyes.

"How long have you known about this?" she spits out.

"We talked about it at the pub last night. I understand his reasons. Perhaps it's for the best."

Ruins in the Mist

"Really? You think it best to lose another son!"

"He'll be back. It's not forever!" he says quietly.

"But you won't know anyone there, Steffan."

"Mother, some of my friends have already gone."

"How can I bear to lose another son?"

She is blinking back tears now. My father looks away. Tears are glistening in his eyes as well.

"I will be back someday like Father said. I promise you that," Steffan continues.

"But it's so far, and you don't know what to expect," Mama says as she tries to control herself.

The rest of us listen in silence. Megan is the first to speak.

"Is Morgan going with you?"

"What about your girl? What does she think of this idea?" Mama asks.

"She won't want you to go," Owen adds.

"She doesn't want to go with me, but she knows I will be back for her when she's ready to marry."

"That will be hard for both of you to bear."

"The opportunities are there, Owen. It's time to find better employment."

"I hope you're not making a mistake, Steffan."

"Vaughn and Alun have only been there a few months. Both have good jobs and money to send home."

"Pub talk, it is!" Mama says. "Talking nonsense, they are. Good jobs!"

"It will be a long voyage. Won't it cost a lot for such a long trip?" Elen asks.

"Takes probably twenty-eight days, normal travel in favorable weather. And it is costly, but I've saved enough for the passage."

"And then what?" Davydd asks.

"I'll find a job. Send money home."

"What about Owen's wedding?" Mama asks.

"That will be on the day before I have to leave. Don't worry. I won't miss that!"

"That's only weeks!"

"How will you get there?" I ask.

"The ship will leave in a fortnight ... from Amlwch."

"Will the trip be safe, Steffan?"

"These ships sail around the world, Mother. You know yourself how many have already made these trips."

"Like the Hughes. They left, and they were never heard from. What if—"

"Mother, I will be safe." I watch as he goes to her and puts his arms around her.

"You will be lonely there, you will," she says as she brushes away her tears.

"Rhys is going. Maybe even Dylan."

"And you'll see Alun and Vaughn again," Davydd says.

"Expect I will."

We watch as Mama turns and makes her way to the back room to be alone. She is muttering to herself.

The days that follow are difficult ones for her. She might have stayed in her bedchamber for the duration had it not been for preparing for Owen's wedding.

***

Our family and friends gather in the little chapel. Owen and Lynne stand up front, and the vicar says things that they repeat. I can't hear too much of what they are saying. Then the music of the Welsh harpers begins again. Later at our home friends and family toast the new bride and groom. I am allowed to stay up with my older brothers. Hugh has brought along a harp, and he draws up a chair and starts plucking at the strings. He urges the others to sing. I am glad to see my mother having a good time with all the others. She starts to sing, and everyone else joins in. She claps with all the others as Owen takes Lynne's hand and starts to dance. Gladys grabs the broom, and Elen is quick to help hold it in the doorway. Everyone is chanting now for them to "jump the broom." The music is loud. There is lots of laughter and singing. Everyone is happy. Papa has often said that a cheerful heart is good medicine.

"So your brother's off to America, eh?" one of my friends asks as we sit watching the others.

"Tomorrow morning."

"Long way up to Amlwch. How's he getting there?"

"Rhys's father will take them to the island in the morning."

"Is Rhys going to America too?"

"He is. They're hoping to find Alun and Vaughn."

The music finally stops. It must be late. I'm tired.

When everyone has left, Mama loses no time in letting us know it is time for bed. The girls had already gone up. Davydd and Evan are still asking Steffan questions before he leaves tomorrow.

"Now off to bed, all of you! Look at the time!"

I let the others go ahead. I linger on the stairs. The music is still ringing in my ears. I listen as Mama and Papa talk.

"I worry about Steffan going so far away. If only—"

"It's for the best, it is."

"We may never see him again. What if he doesn't come back?" Mama asks.

"It's best to get away. Get something better," I hear Papa tell her.

"But the Hughes. No one has ever heard from them."

"Aye, they've been gone a long time now. Probably just busy," Papa says.

"We don't even know if they even arrived. What if Steffan's ship—"

"He will be all right. Come now. It's time for bed."

"Owen looked so happy!" I hear Mama say.

"Like a dog with two tails! Come. It's been a long day."

"A happy day, Tomos, but now I'm tired, I am."

"You must take care of yourself, especially now."

They're coming. I'd better get to bed.

Chapter 11

The day after Owen's wedding my brother and his friends left for Amlwch. Mama was sad for days afterward. She even stopped her singing.

Something had changed in our home. Now three of my brothers were gone. Papa was especially quiet as he sat beside the fire at night. He didn't even want to tell stories. More and more I turned to Megan. Though Megan was not as lively as before, she had a way of making me feel better when things were wrong.

"Is Mama sick, Megan?"

"No, she's sad."

"Are you sad, Megan?"

"Yes. And you?"

"Yes. I miss Brynn."

"Maybe the fair will make us all feel better," Megan adds, her eyes lighting up.

We'd always enjoyed going to the fall fair in Bala. We'd always had so much fun. My father usually managed to buy a few more sheep or some other farm animal to bring home. It was a trip that we all looked forward to and eagerly awaited the day.

"Perhaps Mother will go with us this year," Megan says.

"Let's go ask her."

But when the time came, she did not want to go. Elen stays behind to be with her. Megan, Evan, Davydd, and I climb into the cart with Papa and head over the hills to Bala. As we slowly make our way along the winding road, we pass others as they walk. Once, we had to stop to let a drover go by with his herd, his barking dogs keeping the sheep from wandering.

We are so busy looking around that we barely notice the bumpy ride. The valleys are still green even though summer is past. We stop counting the sheep grazing in the meadows when we see a herd of goats feeding on the banks of a steep incline not far away. As he does here every year, Papa stops the cart and pulls to the side of the narrow path.

"Look yonder," he says as he holds up his hand and sweeps it toward the valley below.

We look beyond a herd of sheep and barking dogs on the roadway and follow his gaze. In the distance a waterfall is falling into the lake below it. Papa is grinning as we begin to remember all of this from previous autumns.

"The waterfall!" I say.

"That is Bala Lake," Megan says.

"We're almost at Bala," Evan adds.

"There's the old mound at the far end of town," Davydd says, pointing toward the *Tomen y Bala*.

"It's about thirty feet high and a hundred feet wide!" Evan says.

"I'm proud of you that you've remembered so much. Do you remember what it was used for?" Papa asks.

"Ancient burial tombs, I believe. From medieval times," Evan says proudly.

"That's right. It used to be more like a castle with its timbered walls," Papa explains.

"I wish that Mother could have come today. She has never come with us to Bala," Megan says.

"Your mother was born in Bala."

"She was?"

"She was? Really, Father?" Davydd asks.

"I didn't know that," Evan says.

"Figure I never ever told you that before, but she was. Her home was down in the valley."

We make our way down a steep hill and enter the valley. The autumn colors of the larch trees sparkle in the sun. Papa reins the horses to a stop once more.

"Why are we stopping, Father?" Evan asks.

"I so love this country," he says gently, still grinning.

But now we children just want to be on our way. Peddlers on foot and farm carts are passing us as they make their way to the marketplace below. We continue, and we soon join the crowd. Carts and stalls piled with vegetables and fruit share space with livestock for sale. As our father spends time talking with the other farmers and checking the livestock, we four find plenty to keep us busy. All too soon it is time to head home.

Making the steep climb from the valley—this time with noisy sheep behind the cart—we reach a level place on the road and take one last look toward the town. Through the bright color of the fall leaves we watch the valley disappear as we head for the long ride home.

Papa is grinning and begins to sing, "Y deryn pur a'r adain las. Bydd i mi'n was dibrydar—"

Megan joins him, and her voice is almost as pretty as Mama's. "O! brysur brysia at y ferch—"

We three boys stretch out, watching the clouds float across the sky. They stop singing. Then I hear Papa ask, "Do you know why they call it Bala?"

"Bala means beautiful. That's a perfect name for the town," Megan says.

"This would have made Mother feel better," she continues.

"Next year," says Papa.

"Today she would have walked to the churchyard. She needs to be alone with Brynn."

As we near home many hours later, the sun has set behind the mountains, and we are all singing so that our mother will know we are safely home. We are certain she will be waiting at the door, waiting to hear us. We are excited to tell her all about Bala.

She is indeed at the door, hands wrapped in her apron, but she hurries us off to bed soon after we have something to eat.

"Tomorrow I shall hear it all. It is late. Tomorrow it will be."

Chapter 12

Winter is late in coming. The first storm is not until early December. When I see the slate roofs white with heavy snow, I know that the festive season is not far away.

For weeks now the candles have been burning much earlier than usual, and the pitch-black mornings are certainly colder. The warmth of the hearth is even more welcome now, and my father's stories grow more and more frequent.

Outside the barren fields lay abandoned, now covered in a blanket of white. Even the barns have taken on a snug look now that the animals have been tucked in their shelters.

The paths up the mountains are now given over to the rabbits and deer. Papa says that the mountains are wearing their caps of white. Even the nearby cottages appear quiet.

The bright spot in all of this is welcoming the simple festivities of the Christmas season. The girls tell us that they are the only ones who can make the paper chains to festoon the room. They have to be perfect. That is why we boys cannot help. That's what they tell us.

"You can go with Father when he sings with the carollers tonight," Elen says.

"We don't need you here," Megan adds.

"Go play, you two. Why aren't you outside with Evan?" Elen asks.

"We're going!" Davydd says. "We'll leave you alone!"

"We have to cut and paste hundreds of links for the

chains," Megan informs us as she gathers up a handful of paper chains.

Mama is busy preparing the pudding for the big day.

"Gladys should soon arrive," she says, looking up at the clock.

"Today is the day," Elen says.

"I'll check the lane," I say as I put on my warm winter coat.

When I hold the door open too long, Mama yells at me. "Close that door against the cold!"

"She will no doubt ride from town with the post when he arrives," Elen says.

"Then she should be here soon," Megan says.

"I'll go watch for her," I say as I go out to join the others.

"She's here. She has just gotten down from the trap!" Davydd yells before I even get outside the gate. I duck back inside to let the others know. Elen and Megan throw on heavy shawls, and we run to the lane.

She looks so pretty. Her dark hair is caught up under her bonnet. The red flannel shawl over her cloak makes her look so grown up. Evan carries her valise as she picks up her wool skirt to keep it from swiping the snow-covered lane.

"She looks so fine, she does," my mother says as she watches her make her way up the path to the cottage. "Tomos, go fetch your father!"

Everyone is talking at once because we are so excited that she is able to be home for Christmas. Papa hurries from the barn with his arms open. He had been staying close at hand.

"Come sit by the fire. You must be near frozen," Mama says as she draws the rocker close to the hearth.

"Yes, it's cold out there."

"Megan, bring a throw for her legs."

"The fire will feel good. I near froze in the trap!"

"Put more peat on the fire, Elen."

The fire hisses when she adds fresh peat. Gladys waves her hand at the smoke that it causes.

"It smells good in here. You've been baking the pudding. I smell the spices."

"That I have. And a big one it is!"

"You shouldn't strain, Mother," Gladys says, looking at Mama with concern.

"It's no use to tell her. You know your mother." Papa shakes his head as he settles into his chair by the fire.

"Come, everyone," he says. "Pull up chairs. I'll tell you about *Mare Lwyd*. Tomorrow night will be the night."

"Will he come here, Papa?"

"Doesn't he always? He goes door to door, hoping to bring good luck to *every* home."

"It's a bit scary, I think," Megan says.

"I'm not scared," I say. *But I am afraid of the strange practice.*

"No need to be scared. It's just a horse skull covered with a sheet."

"What if we didn't let him in?" I ask.

"That would be unlucky, they say."

I need to be quiet so that Papa can tell us the tale.

"On the festival of the winter solstice the Celtic people placed the head of a horse on a long pole and decorated it with ribbons and mistletoe."

"Then they would dance around it wrapping ribbons around the pole," he goes on.

"What an odd way to celebrate!" Davydd says.

"For us it celebrates the end of a dark winter and the beginning of a new year."

"The *Mare Lwyd* going door to door is our tradition?"

"That's right, Elen."

"It's nothing to be afraid of, children, nothing at all," says Mama, laying the last of the hot dishes on the table.

"Come, everyone. It's time to eat and then prepare for chapel."

The carolling started a week ago. My mother always made sure she had a hot beverage ready to serve the young men as they trudged through the snow singing.

"Listen! They're singing 'The First Nowell'," Mama says when she opens the door. "To follow the star wherever it went ... this star drew nigh to the northwest—"

We watch them as they move on down the lane, listening as the sounds fade. "Right over the place ... where Jesus lay."

Tonight in the little chapel the music from the choirs seems even sweeter than it has been outside in the lane. Maybe it is because of the season. "The carols and the harps just seem to be meant for each other," Elen says.

"The voices ringing out are powerful as usual," Papa says.

"Gloria in Excelsis" is one of my father's favorites, and we sing it all the way home. We sing even louder than ever so we won't miss Steffan and Brynn.

Back home we make taffi over the open fire in the big pot like we always do on the day before the celebration. Papa reads the story from the Bible of our Savior's birth. Then he asks me to get the little hymnal from the shelf.

"The one about the nativity?" I ask as I search the shelf for the book.

"Aye, Wesley's *Hymns for the Nativity*," he answers. "The little black one."

It doesn't take him long to find the special carol. We sing this carol on the eve of Christmas every year. "Come thou long expected Jesus, born to set thy people free. Israel's strength and consolation, hope of all the earth thou art. Dear desire of every nation, joy of every longing heart."

I listen to Mama's sweet voice. I don't want it to end. "By thy own eternal Spirit, rule in all our hearts alone. By Thine all sufficient merit, raise us to thy glorious throne."

We are about to sing another carol when a few of our friends drop by to visit. Before we bid them good night, we sing "Hark, the Herald Angels Sing" together, and then we wish them a merry Christmas. *"Naldolig Llawen,"* we sing out together.

"Naldolig Llawen to you all as well," they say.

We did all the same things as other years. But I heard Mama say that there was sadness in our home that no festivities could take away. Papa reminds her that sometimes it takes work to be happy.

Winter brings more snow. The days are cold, and the nights long. Gladys has gone back to her job. Owen and Lynne visit often, for they live close by. When Papa doesn't go to the pub with Willym, he has time to tell us more stories. Mama watches the post, hoping for some word from Steffan.

Then one day a letter finally arrives. We all gather around our mother as she tears the envelope open and unfolds the single sheet. We wait for her to read.

"December 16, 1775," she reads. "Charles Town, South Carolina."

"That's been over three months ago!" Evan exclaims.

"Quiet! Let your mother continue."

"Dear Mother and Father," she continues. "I have arrived safely. Voyage was lengthy. I had only a hammock for sleeping. Charles Town is large, but think I shall like it here. Found that Alun and Vaughn are at the garrison in New York. Saw them once since we arrived. You would not recognize them in their red tunics and cocked hats. I was lucky to get on with a sea captain, travelling along the coast. Don't worry. I am well. I miss you all. Your son, Steffan."

"Thank you, Lord! He's safe. It has been so long," Mama says through her tears. We are all relieved to know that Steffan had arrived safely and was doing well.

Chapter 13

The wind is beating against the pane. The shutters are rattling against the cottage. The noise is frightening me. I sit up and rub my eyes.

We are used to the storms, that Papa says sweep in off the Irish Sea, battering everything in their path. We usually sleep right through them.

Were Papa and Mama all right?

I gather up my nightshirt and run barefoot to my parents' bedchamber just to make sure. I pause outside the door when I hear them talking. There's a dim light coming from under the door. The noise of the wind makes it hard to hear what they are saying.

"You'll be fine. I'll send Willym— Dr. Wynne."

The doctor?

That is a scream. Something is wrong.

Is Mama ill? I stand, not knowing what to do, and then I finally push open the door a crack and look in. In the candlelight I see Mama lying back on the pillow, her hair plaited for sleeping. My father is holding a cloth to her forehead. It looks as if she is in pain.

"Mama?"

My father opens the door. Then I see the blood.

"Mama, are you hurt?"

"Your mother is ailing, that she is. But Willym will fetch the doctor."

"What ails her, Papa?"

"Awaken, Elen. Quickly!"

I push open the door to the girl's chamber. "Elen! Megan!" I yell.

"What is—"

"It's Mama! She's hurt!"

They rush to Mama's room as they push me out of the way and tell me to wait downstairs.

Willym is already up and dressed, and before long everyone has made their way downstairs. Willym is out the door very quickly. The girls stay upstairs, but the others are sent back every time they lurk near her room. It seems to take so long for the doctor to come.

Finally the door swings open, and the strong wind blows snow across the floor. Dr. Wynne follows Willym into the room where we are all waiting. He removes his cloak and passes it to Evan as he hurries up the stairs with his satchel in hand.

Within minutes everyone except Elen is sent downstairs, but it is not long before she rushes down the stairs.

"Dr. Wynne wants someone to fetch Mrs. Kendrick," she says, trying to catch her breath.

Everyone shares glances that I don't understand. Evan throws on his coat and hurries out.

My father ventures up the stairs, and Dr. Wynne meets him on the landing.

"Doctor, it's not time yet," I hear him say. I can't hear what the doctor is saying.

"What's wrong?"

"Send Mrs. Kendrick up as soon as she arrives."

My father descends, saying, "She lives just down the lane. What is taking so long?"

She soon rushes in with Evan right behind her.

Everyone seems to be relieved, and I have to ask, "Not time for what?"

"The doctor will give her something," Megan says. Why don't they tell me what is happening?

We wait. My father walks back and forth in front of the hearth, his hands locked behind him.

"What is taking so long?" Megan asks as she goes to the bottom of the stairs again.

"Everything will be all right," Papa says.

"Will they make Mama better?" I ask.

"Aye, lad, they will. Come here."

He sits in his chair and takes me on his knee just like he did when I was little. I lay back against his chest. He must know that I am afraid.

"Is Mama going to—"

"There. There. She's going to be all right," he says as he pats my back.

"If only it were spring and the daffodils were on the hills. That would make her feel better Papa."

Tad gets up from where she had been laying near the hearth and flops down beside the chair. She brushes my hand with her cold nose. I stroke her head absently, hardly noticing that she is there.

Finally Dr. Wynne comes down and moves toward the door. My father meets him there. Evan passes him his cloak and hat. They whisper together. The doctor shakes his head.

"Is she dead?" I scream.

"No, lad, she just needs rest. I'll return on the morrow to check on her," Dr. Wynne says.

He puts his cloak and hat on. He says nothing more before he walks out in the early morning storm.

Mrs. Kendrick comes down. She nods to my father, and he goes back upstairs. She stops and pats each of my brothers on their shoulders, saying something to them that I cannot hear.

"Your mama is fine," she tells me. She tousles my hair, puts on her cloak, and goes out into the storm.

Elen comes down and tells us to go back to bed. She goes

up with me and tucks me in. She just tells me not to worry because Mama will be all right. No one explained to me what had happened that early winter morning. After several weeks of rest Mama joined the family again. Whatever happened, it changed my mother—that much I *did* know.

Chapter 14

Everyone was talking about the colonies more often, even more than last year. The local men gathered on Saturday nights at the pub to discuss what was happening. It was the topic of conversation in many homes as well, including ours. Skilled workers and farmers alike were being recruited for the American colonies. Everywhere families were talking. They were waiting for word from friends.

"Myles and his family are leaving next week," Willym announces.

"Aye, and I hear that the Eynon family from up the lane is on the same ship."

"Why are our friends going away, Papa?" I ask.

"A better life I guess."

"Better life!" my mother spits out. "America's got its problems too, don't forget!"

Lately Willym and my father were making more frequent visits to the pub. One day Davydd jokes about our family going, and my mother is quick to put that idea to rest. "Your father would never consider leaving the homeland, not even for a short while."

"You're so cert—"

"That's for certes," our mother interrupts.

"Papa told me he could never leave all of this," I add.

"This is our life. This is our home. No, your father would never ask us to leave all of this."

But all of that changed one evening in the spring of 1776. Gladys is home for the day. Owen and Lynne have joined us for supper. We are a bigger family again around the table. My brother and his wife announce that they are to have their first child. It is a time to celebrate. Our supper was normally a quiet time. But tonight is different. Everyone is talking—all except my father. He is unusually quiet.

I glance up at him. I watch as he pushes the food around on his plate. Then he clears his throat and makes the announcement. For a moment everyone sits stunned, hardly believing what he has said.

"What did you say?" Owen exclaims in disbelief when he recovers from the shock.

"We're going to America," he repeats.

"Going to America!" Willym shouts.

"Surely you jest!" Evan says.

"Nonsense," Mama says as her tea cup clatters to the saucer, spilling its contents. "This can wait for—"

"No, it can't wait." He takes a deep breath before he continues. "The decision has been made. We need to talk about it now."

"You can't be serious, Father," Willym says as he pushes his chair back from the table.

I look at my mother. She is pale, and her hands are still shaking.

"But I am, son. I've given it a lot of thought. I hoped that you would understand."

"We have jobs here. We can't leave!" he says as stands to face our father. The chair falls backward on the slate floor.

"Whatever are you thinking? I'll never leave here!" he says, his voice rising.

"Willym, sit!"

"No, I'll not listen to this talk!" He slams the door as he storms out.

My mother stands now and faces my father. She holds the edge of the table. She is trembling.

"Tomos, now look what you've done!"

"Father, I don't think this is the best time with all that's going on."

"Owen, that's just talk!"

"What about the troubles they're having in the colonies?"

"That's only in the north according to Ellis."

"Ellis! What does he know!"

"Davydd! That's enough!" Mama says.

My father continues to explain the situation. "The ship that is leaving in a fortnight from Barmouth is sailing to Charles Town."

"Charles Town? That's where Steffan—" Owen doesn't let me finish.

"To the southern colonies?" Owen asks.

"Aye, the same place where Steffan went. Perhaps we'll see him again," Papa says as he glances around the table.

Surely Papa doesn't mean that we are leaving here. He has told me so often that he would never leave our homeland. *Did he forget that promise?*

"Papa, you said you could never leave our home. You said—"

"I know. I don't want to go but ..." He takes a deep breath and shakes his head.

"You mean we would leave here. You promised. You promised we'd never leave here." I am close to tears.

"I know, but now it's different. We have to. It's a chance for a better life. We'll come back."

"Come back! No one comes back!" Mama says.

I didn't want to hear any more. I shove my chair back and run up the stairs. I stop on the landing and listen. My mother's voice is raised above the others.

"See what you've done!"

"He doesn't understand," I hear my father say.

"Neither do I!"

"Let's talk about it. Let me explain," my father says quietly.

I sit on the top step and listen as my father explains to the others the reasons for his decision.

"It will only be for a short time. Crops are good there."

"Father, think about what you're saying," Owen says.

"Ellis and his family are going. And the Eytons are thinking of—"

"Then they should think about what they're doing!" my mother exclaims.

"Where would we live? What about land?" Evan asks.

"We will be given land and be provided for. Reports coming from the colonies tell of nothing but good things."

"And nothing of the troubles!" Owen says.

"There are plantations where everyone can work, and food is plentiful. You've heard the talk yourselves. It sounds good."

"Talk, lots of talk. I don't know, Father. We have everything we need here," Owen says.

"Not any longer."

"Next year the crops will come back."

"I don't know. It gets harder every year. Times are tough, boys. I need help with the fields. I owe my family a better life. It's been two years now. I don't know. I just don't know what else to do."

"Father, we will do more to help. Both Megan and I—" Elen says.

"I could learn to be a farmer. I could leave the collieries," I hear Owen say. "Davydd's old enough now to help out."

"It's more than that, son, more than that."

"What is it then?"

"I don't want to lose another son in the deeps," I hear Papa say.

I notice that my mother has not been saying much. Now I hear her agree with Papa.

"No, we don't want to lose another. No, not another."

"Knowing only the ways of the deeps will only find another of your sons lying dead in the churchyard," I hear Papa say.

For several minutes everyone is quiet. The sound of the door banging against the wall startles me. Willym is back. I hear his heavy boots on the floor. Oh no! What now?

"How can you forsake your country? A *cumro* never deserts the place of his birth!" my brother yells.

"I must go, son. It will only be for a while. Until the crops come back. We've decided this is the best thing to do right now. Come with us."

"I'll not be going. Do you really think Gladys is going to go! She'll not leave either!"

"Are you sure?" Mama asks.

I hear Megan crying. I tiptoe down and sit on the bottom step. I see that Elen has her arms around her. Mama is wiping at her eyes as well. For once Davydd has nothing to say.

I don't want to hear any more. I hurry up the stairs and throw myself across the bed. My fists are clenched as I pound the bed.

"No. No, I don't want you to leave!" I cry.

Chapter 15

The decision had been made. The days following were busy ones. Gladys came home. She told us that she was not going with us.

Two large trunks were packed with the things the family would need, and Mama said the rest could wait until we returned. Willym and Owen would stay and keep the cottage in our absence. Lynne would take my mother's place, preparing meals for the men, and from time to time Gladys would get home from Morley Hall. The rest of our family was preparing to leave in just a few days.

My father and I take one last walk up the mountain path. The wild daffodils are in bloom on the hills, and I pick a big bunch of them.

On the hills herds of sheep are grazing. We hear the singing before we even see the young shepherd sitting on the side of the hill.

"Listen, Tomos. The song of a shepherd."

"Just like David in the Bible, Papa."

"Did you know that God took him from following the ewes and made him a king?"

"I didn't know that!"

"Aye, he became a very important king."

"Wow!"

"That would be a good story to read tonight, wouldn't it?" my father suggests.

On the walk back down the steep hill, neither my father nor I speak for some time. I had been thinking of this strange place that he was taking us to.

"Papa, this place ... will we like it there?"

"I hope so, son. I hope so."

"What are the colonies?"

"His majesty's colonies, the king's land. People have been setting up what they call colonies for many years now."

"Like our village?"

"I suppose so."

"I wonder what it will be like there."

"I wonder about that myself."

"Will there be lots of food?"

"Aye, it is said the crops are good. Good warm seasons for growing. There is no need for you to worry," he says as he pulls the bill of my cap over my eyes. He is smiling.

"I wish we could stay, Papa. I like our home here. Are you sad to leave?"

"It's best for now. It won't be for long. Just until things get better here."

I look at the daffodils now starting to wilt in my hand.

"I hope there are daffodils where we're going."

"We'll come home again. You will pick daffodils again," he tells me as he looks away.

"Promise?"

"Aye, that's a promise!"

Suddenly we realize we are not alone. We stop to watch the lone hawk circling overhead. Papa points to the sky.

"Look at the dark clouds coming in. That could mean rain."

"The vicar says clouds mean God is there."

"Aye, the clouds are the dust of his feet."

"Is that in the Bible, Papa?"

"Aye, that's what it says. The old prophet Nahum. That's what he wrote."

"All around us?"

"Clouds and darkness are round about him."

"Even in the darkness?"

"Aye, even in the darkness."

As we make our way down the hill we notice that the dark clouds have passed, and the sun has come out again. Then, just before we reach the lane that will take us home, my father stops and looks off in the distance. I look to see what has caught his attention.

"Look at that!" he says. The late afternoon sun is shining on the old castle ruins at the edge of town. "How could any other place be like this?" he says softly.

He lays his hand on my shoulder. "Come. Let's go home."

We walk the rest of the way in silence.

When we arrive at the cottage, our meal is ready. The girls are busy, but Mama is not in the room. Elen let us know that she was upstairs. I run up the stairs with the flowers in my hand. My mother is standing in the doorway of our room. She turns when she hears me, and I watch her wipe tears from her eyes. She smiles though when she sees the bouquet that I hold out to her.

"These are for you, Mama. They'll make you feel better."

She reaches for the wilted daffodils that I know she loves. She hugs me so tight it hurts. I turn and run down the stairs. Mama comes down, pulls a shawl about her, and goes out without saying a word.

From the doorway I watch her go up the lane. I decide to follow her. I quietly latch the gate behind me. Her head is bent as she slowly walks up the lane toward the chapel. She doesn't see me. I watch as she makes her way up the knoll. She bends down and lays the wilted daffodils on the grassy mound and then reaches over to touch the inscription on the stone.

Tell him we'll be back soon, Mama.

She gets up and pulls her shawl around her. Her head is bowed. She stops once and looks back. A mist is tumbling from the hills. I can barely make out the shapes of the stones now, but I can see that she is wiping at her tears. I hurry back to the cottage before she can see that I followed her.

No one needs to ask where she has been. Elen hugs her and whispers something that I couldn't hear.

We eat with hardly a word being said that evening. Our trunks, which are waiting by the door, do the talking for us. Tomorrow morning we will go to chapel for the last time before we leave.

As we walk toward the chapel the next morning, we hear the choirs singing. As we get nearer, Papa starts singing. By the time we get to the door, we are all singing Mama's favorite hymn. "Guide me, O thou great Jehovah. Hold me with thy powerful hand—" Still we keep singing. "Lead me all my journey through—"

After the singing the old preacher gets up and slowly moves toward the pulpit.

"It is with heavy hearts and much sadness that we bid farewell to several of our families today as they embark to find a new life in the colonies," he begins.

I hear sniffles and even a loud sob from someone. I look up at my father, and he pats my hand. The preacher is still talking. "May they take comfort today—"

My mother is dabbing at her eyes. Megan looks over at me and smiles faintly. I should be listening to what the preacher is telling us. "May they find safety on their long journey into the unknown," he says.

More sobs. More sniffles.

"I've chosen for my text today Psalm 121. 'The Lord is thy keeper ... the Lord shall preserve thee from all evil.'" He pauses, and then he goes back to reading, "Thy going out and thy coming in from this time forth—'"

By the time he has finished, I am squirming in my seat. Mama nudges me. I am glad when the choir gets up to sing. We all stand now and join in. "Blest be the tie that binds our hearts in Christian love. When for a while we part—"

More loud sobs. The choir keeps singing, "And one day meet again."

On the walk back to the cottage no one had much to say. We would miss the little chapel. We would miss the singing. But God is everywhere. That's what my pa told me.

Chapter 16

The trunks were on the wagon. The horses were patiently waiting. Willym and Owen, who had stayed home to drive us, sat up front while the rest of us made ourselves comfortable on the trunks and benches. Gladys had managed to get a few days off so that she could go with us.

That's when Tad jumps up on the wagon, her tail wagging with excitement.

"She thinks she's going with us," Davydd says.

"No, girl. Stay!" Papa says.

I watch as she gets down and returns to her place on the walk. She lies there with her head resting on her paws.

"She knows we're leaving. Listen to her whine," Evan says.

"Couldn't we take her?" I ask.

"No, Tomos, she has to stay."

I can't cry. I can't let Davydd see me cry.

I jump from the wagon and run to her, throwing my arms around her neck. I bury my face in her soft fur.

"Good-bye, Tad," I whisper.

"Come, son. We've got to be on our way."

"Long trip ahead of us today," Willym says.

I am fighting back the tears. I don't want to leave her.

I must not cry.

As we make our way up the lane, I look back at our little stone cottage and wonder how long it will be before we see it again.

It is plain to see that everyone else knows that our family is leaving today. Parry, the stonemason, and Jones the grocer come to their doors to bid us good-bye. At the weaver's shop the women stand outside the door and wave. Jones the cobbler stands in the door of his shop and waves. As the wagon rumbles over the bridge by the smithy shop, several men look after us as we pass. Before long the lane and all the familiar homes and faces are behind us.

Mile after mile passes, taking us farther from our home and closer to the coast. I am getting tired by the time we stop to have the lunch that my sisters prepared for us earlier. The tea is cold, but they drink it anyway. The horses rest while we eat.

Before we even reach the docks, we can smell the sea and see the gulls circling near the water's edge.

"It will not be much longer. We are nearing the coast. Smell the salt air," Owen says as we strain to catch our first glimpse of the ocean. Even in the gathering dusk we can see that the docks are alive with activity, and several schooners along with some smaller vessels are waiting in the harbor.

Willym edges the wagon closer, and it is then that we see familiar faces from Denbigh. On the dock several families are unloading their wagons. The Morgan family is there.

"Oh, look! There's Uncle Owen," Davydd says. "Will he be going with us, Father?"

"Aye, it appears he has decided to go. He's been undecided these past few weeks."

Elen and Megan are excited when they see their cousins.

"There's Bevan and Nevett. Oh, I am so happy!" Evan says, noticing the Eynons.

"Where's Hew and Bowen? Thought they were going," Davydd says as he looks around for his friends.

Captain Penrose is already on board the *Dolphin,* awaiting the arrival of the families who have gathered for the long voyage. The gangplank had already been lowered, and the crew is busy loading barrels unto the waiting vessel. It isn't long before we are ordered to board. Now the time has come to leave the rest of the family. Crewmen help with the heavy trunks, and we follow them, walking past bales of rope and huge puncheons piled on the crowded dock all the while waving to those left behind.

As we make our way to the waiting ship, my mother dabs at her eyes and guides me toward the gangplank. I hold on to the ropes on either side of the narrow wooden walk just as Evan and Davydd are doing. I turn for a moment to wave to those we have left standing on the dock. Willym and Owen are waving, and I see Gladys brush tears from her eyes. I am trying not to cry. I move to the rail and look back from the deck of the ship. My tears trickle down as I watch the crew pull up the gangplank and prepare to leave the harbor. I turn and see that Davydd is standing beside me. There are tears in his eyes as well.

We stand by the rail, waving until we can't see them any longer.

"It's just a blur. Our homeland is just a blur," Papa says as he gestures toward the rugged coast that is disappearing as we make our way to the sea.

All around there is nothing but water. It is getting dark. A bearded crewman quickly ushers us below with our belongings.

"There's been a mistake! We're on the wrong ship!" Elen cries when she sees what is below.

"Oh, Tomos, we must be on the wrong ship!" my mother says as she grasps my father's arm.

"It's so dark down here. Where are the lights?" Megan asks.

"They will bring lights."

"The smell. What's that awful smell? How shall we stand it?" whispers Elen.

"You'll get used to it, girls," Evan says.

While we stand there in the darkness, a sailor arrives with

two lanterns and hangs them on nearby posts so that we can see our quarters. *Our quarters! Are you kidding!*

"Perhaps it would have been better not to have seen this!" Davydd says.

"But look. These are not beds. Where are the straw mats for sleeping?" my mother cries when she sees the rough wooden pallets lining the walls of the old vessel.

"Not to worry. We shall have straw mats again soon," my father tells her.

"Remember that when Steffan went over, he had only a hammock for sleeping," Evan reminds us.

"I think I should have preferred a hammock to this!" Davydd says.

After my mother realizes that this is the right ship, she tries to make our bunks as comfortable as possible. She takes out all the covers that are in the trunks, and that first night we try to sleep sharing the two pallets that our family had been given. There is barely room to stretch out our legs. We shiver in the cold, even in our outer clothes. Throughout the night the cries of small children keep us from sleeping.

After the first few days we wonder how we will be able to endure weeks of this.

The hatch above us would be opened once a day to enable the passengers below a chance to get fresh air. We crowd on the stairs. There are too many of us all trying to get under the hatch. A few—mostly men—are allowed to go on deck. The women stay below to look after the sick children.

Some nights even the mothers cry and moan. I hear Elen and Megan whispering that their children have been taken away from them at night. I am not sure what they are talking about until one night Evan opens the hatch and comes down, crying. Mama rushes to him, thinking he has been hurt.

"What's wrong, son. What happened?"

"They just … just … just slid his body into the water," he sobs.

"Whatever are you talking about? Who's body?"

A young woman is behind him followed by a young boy about twelve or so. They are both weeping as well as they stumble down the steep stairs.

"Just like that. Third one this week," Evan says, trying to compose himself.

Mama is wiping her own tears as she tries to comfort the young mother who has just lost a son. I hear Elen whisper to Megan that it could have been any one of us. As the young woman returns to her pallet, we hear whispers of 'smallpox'.

"Mother, why are so many sick?" Megan asks as the ship pitches and rolls.

"The rough sea makes them sick."

"More likely this terrible food they've been giving us," Evan says.

"You call this food? This salt meat and stale bread? I want hot broth and fresh bread!"

"Davydd, be thankful we have it," Papa says.

"It's hard to eat with that awful smell," Elen says as she points to the bucket that is sloshing over unto the planks beneath our feet.

Several nights later, we awake to discover that the vessel is being tossed to and fro by a storm that has come up overnight. The lanterns are swinging wildly. When Evan tries to push open the hatch, he is told to stay below. He sees enough to know that the sea is fierce. The vessel is not making any headway but drifting blindly in the dark. We are in danger, he tells us.

"Walls of water are lashing the vessel ... coming right over the deck," he tells us. "No one is allowed on deck."

We huddle together, holding one another as we listen to Papa pray.

By the next day the seas have calmed, and the vessel is once more making headway.

Night after night we try to sleep. During the day Papa reads to us from the Bible—probably from memory because I don't think he could see the words. The little bit of light from the lantern as it swings back and forth is not much help. He squints. I watch as his lips move over the words, reciting the familiar verses. He doesn't need any light.

As days turn into weeks, we long for hot porridge and bacon. Mama misses her tea.

"I don't like this salt meat and stale bread," Megan says.

"I want hot broth and bread," Elen says.

"And hot porridge and—"

"Bacon," Davydd adds. "We should have brought better food with us."

"We didn't know that this is what we would get," Papa says as he shakes his head.

"Perhaps tomorrow we will be given better food ... and some tea," my mother says.

"We'll soon have hot tea again," Papa tells her. "It will soon be over. We will have good food again soon," he assures us.

"Papa, will it be much longer?"

"Evan tells me that the captain says only another week or so."

"Tomos, really? Another week?"

"We knew it would be a long voyage, Gwendolyn."

"We should not have come—that's for certes."

"You're right, Mother. We should never have come," Elen says, as she wraps her shawl tighter.

"It's too late now, it is."

"It's so cold," Megan says as she shivers under the cover. "Look at that water running down the wall. Just inches from our bodies!"

"Are you sure we have all of the covers out?"

"I checked, Elen. We have them all," our mother says shaking her head.

Water is running down the curved wooden walls and forming deep puddles. It is almost over our boots now.

"Just keep thoughts of home. Remember the peaks of Eryre. The green valleys," Papa tells us.

Was he trying to cheer us?

"My belly hurts. I'm hungry," I say.

"Son, we're all hungry. Remember the clouds."

"The clouds?"

"Aye, these troubles are clouds."

"And God is here, isn't he, Papa?"

"What's all that about?" Davydd wants to know.

"That's in the Bible, Davydd. If it weren't so dark, Papa could show you."

"If Father told you that, then I guess it's true."

At night before we try to sleep, we pray together as we sit on the edge of the hard, wooden pallets.

"We can't kneel, Papa. Look at all the water."

"God understands, son. Don't worry."

When my mother holds me close, I feel the tears dampen my face. Are they hers, or are they mine? I fall asleep with the words of my father coming to us in the darkness. How I wish we were still at home.

Chapter 17

The hatch opens, and Evan quickly made his way below.

"Soundings of thirty fathoms!"

"What does that mean?" Davydd asks.

"We're nearing the harbor. It won't be long now! We are to gather our belongings and be ready to go on deck soon."

He closed the hatch.

"Did you notice that the air is much warmer?"

"Yes, Elen, perhaps the sun is shining," Megan says a bit sarcastically.

"Sun would be nice," I say.

For a few moments we forget the hunger. We forget the many weeks of cold. Elen and Megan help fold the damp blankets and coverings that had helped protect us from the cold these past weeks. Just how many weeks, we are not sure. It doesn't take long to repack the trunk and secure the clasp. We can barely contain our excitement about finally being able to leave the ship.

Thumps and noises come from above.

Sometime later the hatch is lifted. Fresh air meets our noses. We hardly notice the gruff voice that orders us on deck. We are so glad to be leaving this dark space.

I strain to see what is ahead. The light hurts my eyes at first. Everything is foggy.

"That's sea mist," Evan tells us.

"Look at the giant fortress over there!" I shout.

"Where?"

"Way over there. You can barely see it. There, Davydd." I point to the large structure at the entrance of the harbor.

"Fort Sullivan," a young crewman tells us. "It's not even finished yet. Just the log walls up."

"So there are forts here?" Davydd asks.

"Military forts. For protecting the town," he tells us. "This will be the biggest one. Cannons will be mounted soon."

"Are they expecting an attack?" Evan asks him.

"Never know. Anything is possible. They want to be ready."

From the deck of the *Dolphin* we see what is to be our new home. According to the crew, we are getting ready to dock in Charles Town, South Carolina.

Davydd and the other boys and I push our way toward the rail to get a better look. My father comes and stands behind us, and Mama and the girls join our group as we shade our eyes and look toward the shore. Through the mist we see land in the distance. Coming into the harbor, white sandy beaches stretch before us, and overhead dozens of seabirds are soaring as if to welcome us.

"Look at the fields, boys," my father says.

"This looks good!" Evan says as he makes room for Bevan, who has pressed into where we are standing at the rail.

"Aye, that it does."

"And the houses. There are many near the harbor. We'll be living near the water."

"Looks that way, Evan."

"Oh, the homes are so ... so big, Tomos," my mother says hesitantly.

"Wow! Almost as big as castles!" I say.

"Beyond the warehouses and wharves. Look at the large homes," Elen says as she points.

"The grounds slope right to the water's edge," Megan says.

"Look at that, Mother! Look at the beautiful homes."

"Oh, Elen, I don't know. They are so big. Surely—"

"Ours will no doubt be a little smaller than that," Megan says as she looks at the big houses.

We keep looking at the town as the ship nears the dock. Tired and hungry, we are anxious to finally be getting off the ship. It has been such a long voyage.

"I can't wait to find Steffan!" Evan says.

"It will be so good to see him again."

"Mother, do you really think we will be able to find him?" Megan asks.

"Steffan told us it's a large town, but we'll find him."

"It may take a while."

The vessel inches toward the dock. The warm air feels so good on my face. I am finally getting warm.

"Look at all the vessels. Masts must be forty feet or more!" Evan says.

"Looks like a busy place. Look at all those people working."

"They're not even wearing shirts. It must be warm out there!" Davydd says as he and I press to the rail. "They're as black as coal!"

We watch as dozens of bronzed men load crates and bales to waiting ships. Barrels are being wheeled up the gangplanks.

"Wonder where they're taking all of this?" Evan asks.

"Europe I expect."

"Really, Father? That's a long way."

"The colonies have been doing a brisk trade with Europe for more than a hundred years. And most of the workers would be slaves, no doubt."

The vessel finally docks. A strong smell hits our noses.

"Whatever is that smell?" Elen says, holding her nose.

"That would be tar you smell."

"Tar? That's even worse than—"

"The buckets?"

"Yes, Davydd! Even worse than the buckets!"

We must have been a sorry sight as we struggled down the

gangplank. The woolen shawls and heavy clothing must have looked out of place in the warm Carolina sun.

A wagon is waiting to take us from the dock, past warehouses and shops, and past several taverns and odd-looking buildings.

We are taken to a large building where several other families are waiting.

"This is just temporary. Until we're taken to our homes," our father explains when Elen questions the reason for these quarters.

"What is this place?" Megan asks, looking around the building we have been taken to.

"This is a barracks. Don't worry. It's only temporary."

"This will give us a chance to find Steffan," Evan says.

"Aye, tomorrow we will check around the docks, boys."

"I must see him. I must."

"If he's here, Mother, we will find him," Evan tells her.

"We'll ask around. Someone may know of him," Papa says.

We search for days. I often go with them as they roam the streets and docks.

Finally we find an old sea captain who remembers meeting him.

"Ah, yes. I remember the young Welsh sailor. I recall he took work with Captain Hayes on the *Recovery*."

"This Captain Hayes, when did you last see him?" my father asks.

"I think maybe ... maybe a fortnight ago," he says as he tugs at his long beard and looks toward the sea.

"Is the *Recovery* here now?" Evan asks excitedly.

"No, the *Recovery* is delivering goods along the coast. Could be weeks before she returns."

"Are they gone often?" my father asks.

Looking off into the distance, the old seaman replies, "Ah, but that won't be for long, I expect."

"Why do you think that, my good man?"

"Ah, with all the trouble brewing in the north—"

"What trouble?" Davydd asks, interrupting the old seaman.

"You see, lad, there's fighting in the colonies up north."

"Really?"

"But is that not just in the Boston area?" Evan asks.

"That should not affect us here so far south, should it?" Papa asks with concern.

"Maybe not. But let's not forget that little incident at Moore's Creek back in the winter."

"What was that?"

"Loyalists against the patriots. The patriots took hundreds of prisoners."

"Was that close by?" Davydd wants to know.

"No, lad, a ways north of here. Not close, but who knows— There's been trouble up there ever since the Tea Act got them so upset."

"The Tea Act? What's that?" I ask.

"You mean you folks didn't hear about the party in Boston Harbor?"

He's laughing now, and I have to ask, "What party?"

"The colonists dressed like Indians and boarded three ships waiting to unload their cargo of tea. Dumped it all in the harbor. Hundreds of chests of it!"

"Why would they do something like that?" I ask.

"The taxes. That's what's got them so upset."

"All that over taxes. You mean all this fighting is over—"

"No, more than that. The colonists want to be free of British control."

"So this revolt will go on until they're free?" my father asks.

"Expect so. Ever since Lexington and Concord. That's what started the war up there."

"What if this unrest spreads?" our father asks.

"Time will tell. Time will tell."

"Is Charles Town prepared?"

"There's five thousand militia out on the island defending the colony."

"Out at the fort?" I ask excitedly.

"Ah, laddie. Out there." He points toward the fortress that we had seen the day we arrived.

"Heard last week the British left Boston," the old gentleman goes on.

"Where did they go?" Evan asks.

"Moved their fleet to Halifax, I hear."

"Really?"

"Hasn't been that long since they brought in troops from there. So … maybe the trouble's over up there."

"Could it be brewing somewhere else?" our father asks.

"That would be my guess."

With that, he shrugs and saunters off toward the waterfront. We watch him go—the only contact we have found that could lead us to Steffan.

"Well, boys, so much for that one."

"Let's hope we can find him again," Evan says.

"We'll just have to wait until the ship returns in a few weeks."

Chapter 18

But we didn't have weeks. Days later I sit, dangling my legs from the back of the wagon, and look back at the town we are leaving. As the wagon makes its way up the hill, I look out at the harbor and the fort guarding its entrance. We are leaving the smell of the wharves, the warehouses, and the taverns. But at the same time we are leaving any chance of seeing my oldest brother anytime soon.

As we make our way along the road, huge trees line both sides along the river. Boughs meet overhead.

"It's like a canopy in here," Megan says.

"What kind of trees are those, Father?" Davydd asks.

"Oak, I'd say. The biggest I've ever seen."

"What is that strange stuff hanging from them?" Mama asks when she sees the moss trailing from the large oak trees.

"Don't know. Perhaps that's what's called Spanish moss," Papa offers.

"It's scary."

"Oh, Mother, it's so cozy in here. Just look at it!" Megan says as she hugs her arms to her body.

"Megan! Don't make light of it. It's scary, it is."

"Is that what smells so good?" Elen asks.

"That would be the roses and magnolias. Look. They're everywhere," someone on the wagon says.

After we've traveled several miles, we notice that the houses are now much smaller than they had been in town.

Evan points out to us the large fields where many workers are busy, tending to some sort of crops. Papa hears Davydd telling me he thinks they are large gardens.

"Those would be plantations, Davydd."

"What do they grow?"

"Cotton and tobacco, I guess."

"Really?" I ask.

"How do they grow cotton?" Elen asks.

"Perhaps we'll find out."

"Father, the workers are all dark. Like the driver," Megan whispers.

"Aye, slaves. Brought here to work the fields," he whispers back.

"Look at the cabins over there." I point toward the row of crude cabins near the edge of one of the fields.

"That's probably where they live," Evan says.

"There's a smithy working in this heat. See the forge," Davydd points out.

"Probably making horseshoes," Papa tells him.

"No wonder he's working striped to the waist!"

"And another shop over there. Perhaps the coopers."

"Or a barn, Papa. See the goats!"

"And there are cows over there." Megan points to the cows grazing in the field.

"Well, look at that!" Papa says when we have gone a little farther.

We turn to see him gesturing toward the hill where a big white house sits surrounded by green lawns that stretch to the roadway. Through the tall pillars we see the many windows framed with wide shutters.

"Look at the pillars and balconies!" Elen exclaims.

"It's so big!" I say. "Looks like a castle—"

The driver interrupts me as he lifts his whip and points to the large home.

"And t'is big one where mast' live."

We just look at each other, not understanding what the driver means.

"Master? Master of what, Father?" Elen asks.

"I expect we'll find out."

We pass more fields. Shortly afterward the driver reins his horses to a stop in front of a small weathered cabin, one of three at the edge of a field.

He jumps down from the seat and comes to the back of the wagon.

"Dis' here you's new 'ome."

"Our home? Do you ... do you mean this is where we—" our father stammers.

"Yes, mist'. Sho' 'ope you like it!"

"But we were promised—"

"Don' know 'bout dat. 'Spect where we at is you 'ome."

"We were told—"

He says something about the overseer coming by to see us later, as he lifts the trunks from the wagon and waits for us to climb down. Then he gets up on the seat and drives away.

We stand there looking after the wagon, and then we turn to take a closer look at our new home.

Three wooden rockers sit on the covered porch that spans the front of the whitewashed cabin. A shutter that once framed one of the two small windows is hanging loosely.

Papa will fix that in no time.

Inside there's a large table, a bench, and four mismatched chairs. A fireplace wall separates the two small rooms beyond. I watch as my mother checks the cotton mattresses that rest on the wooden platforms.

"Straw smells all right."

Next she checks the open shelves and the window ledges.

"Someone's cleaned recently, they have."

"Guess they were expecting us!" Davydd says with a smirk.

Papa just stands looking at our new surroundings. Then

he says, "The overseer will tell us this is just until … until we get our new home."

"Don't kid yourselves. This is probably it!"

"No, Davydd. We will get a bigger place, you'll see."

"Hope you're right, Mother."

"Is this what we've come so far for?" Elen asks as she looks around the small cabin.

"It will get better," our father tells us.

"You're sure about that!" Davydd says, laughing.

Later that evening the overseer comes by. He answers all my parents' questions. Some of the answers are not what they want to hear. This was to be the only home we would have for quite some time. Papa would work for someone else—the planter, as the overseer had called him.

Chapter 19

We settled into the little cabin at Ashley Creek, many miles from Charles Town—the backcountry of South Carolina.

On hot summer evenings I sit with the others as they look out over the fields and talk about all the work that is expected of them. After a day of sweating in the fields we welcome the shelter of the covered porch.

"The overseer expects a lot from us, doesn't he, Father."

"Evan, it's his job to make sure everyone carries out their duties."

"Who owns all of this anyway?" Davydd asks.

"Some wealthy planter."

"From the big house?" I ask.

"Aye, that's who we're working for. They call us tenant farmers."

"What does that mean?"

"Means we work without pay until we pay off our passage, I guess."

"That was probably a lot for all of us," I say.

"We haven't seen the chapel yet. Where is the chapel, Tomos?" my mother wants to know.

"I'll inquire of the overseer next time."

"Chapel! How do you expect we would get there?" Davydd asks.

"If there's one, son, we will find a way to get there."

There was no chapel. Miles away there were churches, but

none in Ashley Creek. The closest we would get to chapel was listening to the slaves singing in the evenings after their work was done. "Swing low ... sweet chariot ... comin' for to carry me 'ome."

Papa says they are singing Negro spirituals. Some of the words carry over the fields. "Go down, Moses ... go down—"

We sometimes wished that we were close enough to hear all the words.

The days get hotter as the summer wears on. It isn't long before Davydd and I are running barefoot in the fields just like the other young boys our age. Evan and even my sisters work with Papa in the fields. Davydd wants to help, but he is told that he will help our mother. She needs help with the garden.

"While we're waiting for our own land, I shall plant a garden, I shall."

"What will you plant, Mother?" Megan asks.

"I'll plant sweet potatoes ... and squash ... and tomatoes and—"

"We will help, Mama," I tell her.

So throughout the summer we all work. It is hard work. And everything is so different from the ways of farming in Wales.

Even the farm animals are contained by split-rail fences zigzagging across the pastures. We think it strange, for we are used to animals being contained in paddocks and stone wall enclosures.

"I am not accustomed to working with oxen on the plough either."

"Maybe you could get a horse, Papa," I say.

"Aye, a horse would be better. I shall see. I shall try to get a horse."

I often listen to my parents talking at night when I am supposed to be sleeping.

"I wish we could go back home. I wish we had never come here."

"It's only for a short while, Gwendolyn. We'll go back."

"This is not the way I thought it would be," my mother says.

"I know. But we have lots to eat. The weather is good." Papa sounds so weary.

"I don't think I shall ever get used to this heat," Mama says.

It is easy to see that Mama only wants to go home.

One day after the corn has been harvested, Davydd, Evan, and I go to the mill with our father to see how the corn grits are prepared. Since the strange food finds its way to our table so often, we decide it will be interesting to see how it is milled here.

"If you boys are careful, you may climb the stairway today."

"Oh, we would like that!"

"Then run and tell your mother you're all coming with me."

"Be right back. Don't leave without us!" I yell as Davydd and I run to the cabin.

"I'll help Father ready the cart," Evan calls after us.

We had never gone far enough up the creek to see the mill before. We had only gone nearby to catch a few catfish. Evan, Davydd, and I like to fish at the end of a hot day and often find ourselves on the riverbank with our poles dangling in the calm water of the creek. Sometimes it reminds us of home.

"We'll soon be there boys. It's not too far now."

"I don't see the windmill yet," Davydd says.

"Oh no, there are no windmills here. The mill is powered by a giant water wheel."

"A water wheel?"

"Wait till you see it!"

"Is it big?" I ask.

"Aye, about twenty feet high. It's big!"

Before we even reach the mill, we see the giant wheel in the distance, and before long I am helping the others unload the bags from the cart. We forget all about climbing the steep stairs .We are fascinated by the workings of the mill. We watch as water from the millpond pours water into the open trough and over the top of the huge stone wheel. The miller takes time to explain to us how the whole thing works. "Now we know where our corn grits come from," Davydd says.

"And the pone?" I really like the bread that Mama makes from the grits.

"That's what she makes it from. Thought you knew that!" Evan says.

While our father talks with the other farmers, we decide to climb the stairway to the top floor, and from there we watch the huge stone turning. As the corn in the hopper drops into the hole in the huge wheel, the flour falls down the chute.

"Look how the sifter separates the grits," Davydd says as we watch.

"A lot different than at the millers back home."

"A lot of things are different here. A lot of things."

"Pa says we will soon be going home, Davydd."

"Soon? It will be years before we work off the passage."

"Says who?" I ask.

"That's what Elen said. Another two years at least."

"That's a long time. Really? Another two years?" I ask.

"And besides, where would we get the money for the passage?"

"When we get our own land, there will be money."

"Our own land, Tomos? That will never happen!"

"Father's calling. Come on. It's time to go," Evan says as he runs down the stairs.

Sometimes I walk with my father in the evenings along the creek and talk about home. He never talks about what we left behind in front of my mother.

Most evenings we all sit on the front porch. Our parents claim the two best rockers, and it is a toss-up as to which of the girls gets the other one first. The rest of us sit on the steps and listen to the whip-poor-will's song. At first Elen and Megan are afraid of the sounds. We have never heard the strange birds before.

"What is that?" Megan asks.

"Whip-poor-wills," Evan says.

"You'll get used to the sounds."

"Just one more thing to get used to, it is," our mother says.

"Like the Spanish moss hanging from the trees, Mother?"

"Oh, Davydd, that was scary, it was. Don't laugh!"

"There have been lots of changes—that's for certain," Elen says.

"I don't like changes, I don't."

And more changes were coming. The old sea captain had been right about a lot of things. This journey of ours was to take another turn.

Chapter 20

By the next summer the news reaching the Carolinas was not good. We learned that fighting had started to spread toward the south. I sit on the porch with the family, listening to them discuss the events that are taking place.

"Do you think it will reach this far south, Father?" Evan asks.

"I don't expect it will. I hear the British still have control and the colonists are doing a good job up there holding off the rebels."

"Do you think Washington's going to give up?"

"Probably not."

"Not even after his defeat at Brandywine?"

"That's all the more reason that the British not give up."

"Why is that so important?"

"They need to hold on to the colonies and control of the seas, I should think."

"But don't forget what happened at Saratoga, Father. Burgoyne lost a lot of troops there. That must have been discouraging."

"That was all because of lack of supplies as I understand. They didn't stand a chance, it seems."

As they sit talking about the goings on within the colonies and the war that seems to be getting closer, I notice that my mother hasn't been saying much. Now she lets us know what has been on her mind.

"If this fighting keeps up, do you think we will be in danger?" she asks hesitantly.

"No, I should think not."

"Even with the rebels stirring up trouble?" Davydd asks.

"Some of the colonists up there are already fighting with the regular troops," Papa says.

"Will you need to fight, Papa?" I ask.

"No, son, you don't need to worry about that. I expect the fighting will be over before we know it."

New reports coming in from the northern colonies let us know that the battles are still going on.

"Hear that the redcoats have taken Savannah. The war is not over yet," Evan says as we sit around the fire, talking about these latest reports.

"Washington probably wasn't expecting that."

"Wasn't he wintering over in Valley Forge or somewhere?" Davydd asks.

"He was, I guess. And the Loyalists had been sent home for the winter," Evan tells us.

"So now the Loyalists are back fighting the rebels, I guess."

"Suppose that's what is expected of them, Father."

By spring we learn that the British are moving their attention to South Carolina.

"There's talk of the British fleet possibly attacking Charles Town," my father tells us.

"That's good?" Evan asks.

"Aye, if they establish a base there, they should still be able to win the war."

"That *would* be good news, Father," Evan says.

It isn't long afterward that we hear that General Clinton has indeed captured Charles Town.

"He didn't give up, did he? Remember what happened the last time?"

"What was that, Evan?"

"Remember, he tried, but his ships were forced to withdraw."

"I don't remember that," I say.

"That was shortly after we arrived. Someone told me that their cannonballs bounced right off the walls at the fort."

"Looks as if they had more success this time," Davydd says.

"It was a long fight, they say, but the general finally surrendered."

"That was a major victory. Now Charles Town's a garrison base," our father adds.

"The bright red coats of the soldiers are everywhere, I hear," Evan says. "Colonists are being organized to help in the combats around here as well."

"Really?"

"What do you think, Father? Should we join the fight?" Evan asks. "They need help at the forts."

"Oh, I don't know, Evan. Perhaps it's best to just keep quiet."

"What do you mean, Father?"

"I don't know, Evan. I know we should remain loyal to our mother country. But on the other hand ... this new country deserves our loyalty. I just don't know."

"We've been here such a short time. Aren't we still British?" I ask.

"Who knows *what* we are anymore!" Davydd says with sarcasm.

"Perhaps we should support them. They need all the help they can get. Sooner this war is over, the sooner we'll be able to go back home."

"I'll go with you, Father."

"Your mother will have something to say about that, Davydd."

"I'm old enough. They'll let me go with you."

"Things should not get that bad. All right, you may go. We'll all stay together," our father says.

"They no doubt want us to help at the outposts. It shouldn't be anything dangerous," Evan tells us.

So my father and brothers decide to join the troops and help in the fight. My mother is set against the idea. My father wins.

"I didn't come here to lose everything. I'll do what I can to protect my family," he tells her.

"We'll show them!" Davydd says.

"And how are *we* going to protect ourselves while you're all away fighting?" Elen wants to know.

"You heard how the rebels attacked the settlers not far from here last week," Megan says.

"They'll not bother you here. We have nothing of value."

"They even took the shoes off the women's feet," Mama says.

"And even burned their home, Mother," Elen says. "I don't understand why they want to hurt us."

"They don't want us to side with the British. But don't worry, girls. We won't be away long."

"They won't even know we're gone!" Davydd says.

"Who are you kidding, Davydd! They'll know," Megan says.

"And in the meanwhile we could all be in danger," Elen says.

"You will be safe here. We'll make sure of that. That's why we're going."

"Tomos will be with you," Davydd says with a smirk.

"Tomos! He's barely nigh on thirteen!" Megan says. "What can he do?"

~~~

So my father and two brothers join the Loyalists, who are being trained at the fort at Ninety-Six.

Ruins in the Mist

"That's a strange name for the fort," I say when they tell us where they were going.

"It is, isn't it? It's ninety-six miles from the nearest Cherokee land. Guess that's where it got its name," Evan informs me.

There at the fort they are readied to defend the outpost and to fight the next battle. They will be fighting with the regular troops. I am left to take care of my family. I want to go with them, but I am expected to stay here and look out for the family.

One evening just before the sun goes down, I throw my old fishing pole over my shoulder and set off in the direction of the creek. Rounding a bend, I am surprised to see someone sitting on the bank, fishing pole in hand. I am not accustomed to finding anyone else here at this time of day. As I get closer, I see that it's a young boy who is probably about my own age. He gets up as I draw closer and is about to run off.

"Wait!" I call out.

He hesitates. Then he stands, looking in my direction. He stands there until I get closer. I put my hand out, but he draws back. I think he might run off.

"I'm Tomos," I offer as I put out my hand again.

I can see the fear in his dark eyes. He timidly puts out his hand toward me. Then he reaches up and removes his cap. Framing his dark face is a head of woolly hair. I recognize him as one of the young boys I had seen working in the cotton fields near our cabin.

"What's your name?" I ask.

"Jimmy."

"Any fish?"

"I ain' had one bite, Tom."

"Let's try again."

We drop the poles in the stream and wait. Still nothing.

"Ain' no use tryin' anymore today."

"Wait! Got a bite!" I say.

"An' look at dis big one!"

Before long we both had caught several catfish.

"I needs be goin' 'ome," Jimmy says.

"It's getting dark. Let's go."

As we walk back toward the cabins, I ask Jimmy how long he has been here.

"Come here on a big ship."

"How old were you?" I ask.

"Jus' a little boy 'bout one—that wha' ma say."

"You've been here all that time?"

"'Speck so."

"Living in that little cabin?" I ask in disbelief.

Over the next few months Jimmy and I become good friends. Many times I will wait for him to join me on the riverbank after his day's work is done—when he has finished filling his basket with cotton. He tells me it is better than working in the rice fields or even harvesting the indigo. Jimmy doesn't talk much, but over time he shares his story with me. He lives with his mother in one of the small cabins in the nearby fields. When he was only a baby, his mother had been sold, and because he was so young, his mother had been allowed to keep him with her. Two of his older brothers had been sold to another plantation, and their father was sold to a different master. They never saw one another again.

His story is deeply disturbing for me. I don't understand it. People don't sell other people.

If only my father was here, he could explain it to me.

I decide to ask Elen about it.

"They're brought here against their will to work the plantations."

"From where?"

"Africa, I guess."

"But Elen, that isn't fair!"

"I know, Tomos. I know. But that's the way it is. Been that way for a while, I guess."

"Jimmy might never see his family again. That's not right."

"You spend a lot of time with Jimmy, don't you?"

"We're good friends."

"Have you ever seen his mother?"

"Only once. Their cabin is on the far side of the cotton fields."

On the warm summer nights we all sit on the porch and talk. Often the voices of the slaves singing remind us of home.

"I wish we had never come to the colonies," Elen says.

"I know now it was the wrong decision, it was. But your father thought—" Mama's eyes mist as she talks.

"I miss Gladys. And Willym and Owen," Megan says as she shields her eyes from the setting sun.

"We've seen Steffan just that once in these four years. And now your father and— Oh, I'm so worried about your father and the boys, I am."

"I know, Mother, but they'll be home again soon, you'll see."

"Oh, Elen, what if something has happened? They've been gone so long this time."

"The last time it was even longer," Megan reminds us.

"Yes, I remember. So long, it was."

I get up from the step and drop down beside her rocker. I lay my head on her lap. She puts her hand on my head.

"Don't worry, Mama. Papa's brave."

"And so are you," she says as she pats my head.

"Come. It's time for bed. We can pray. That's all we can do," she says as she gets up and opens the screen door.

"If Pa were here, he would read to us. He would tell us that God will keep us all safe."

"Even Steffan."

"Yes, Mama, even Steffan."

Recently we hear that Steffan has a job with the British forces in New York and is transporting refugees to new settlements for their safety. There is little chance of seeing him again for a while, especially now with this war going on.

Chapter 21

"Is the war over, Pa?" I ask when my father and brothers return home in September after the battle at Camden.

"I think so. The general is in control now."

"What happened?" I ask.

"We forced the Patriots back when they attempted to attack the outpost," Davydd says.

"Won't they want to fight back?"

"You know they are not going to just back off. The next time it will be another outpost," he reminds us.

"Pa, what do you think?"

"Perhaps they will fight back. But we have to have faith in Cornwallis."

"I was hoping to go back with you. I am old enough now to be a drummer like Davydd."

"You're still not old enough. Besides, you would have been scared," Davydd says.

"I'm as brave as you are. Pa said I—"

"Not out there! You wouldn't be!"

"Just be glad it's over, boys," Mama says.

"I think we are all safe now that the outpost is secured at Camden," Pa says.

"At least now we will have a safe place to go if we need it," Evan adds.

"What was it like at Camden?" I ask.

"Tomos, it was a bloody battle. You really don't want to hear about it."

"Tell me about it, Evan," I coax.

My brother suggests we move outside since this is something our mother and the girls do not need to hear.

"We were waiting at the outpost. It was just after dawn when we knew they were coming."

"How did you know?" I ask.

"A scout came shouting that they were coming!" Davydd says.

"How many were there?"

"Two thousand, we were later told."

"Wow!"

"Then it was fire! Fire!" Davydd says excitedly.

"After that it's hard to know what happened. It all happened so fast," Evan says.

"Muskets cracked. Lots of smoke and flame. Shouts and cries," Davydd adds.

"What about the drummers?"

"We kept beating and beating. Louder and louder!" Davydd says proudly.

"Beating out the sounds of the muskets?" I ask.

"No, not a chance."

Our mother opens the screen door and steps out on the porch. She must have been listening.

"You could have all been killed!"

"In all the smoke I don't think the Patriots could see us!" Davydd says.

"Lucky you were. The good Lord was looking out for you."

"Where did all the smoke come from?" I ask.

"The powder explosions. Just inches from our eyes. And the smells—"

"Boys, that's enough! It's over. You're all safe. Let's talk about something else."

We soon find out that the war is not over as our father had hoped. Our hopes are dashed once more when we realize we will not be going home just yet. Even though my father's term is up, we are not free to leave. He tries to explain that to us before they have to leave for the outpost again.

"It is too dangerous to travel now. We will have to wait until it is safe. We must stay here for now."

"But I am afraid for all of us, I am," my mother says.

"While we are away, you can always go to the garrison for safety, if you need to."

"But the garrison is so far away, Father. What protection is that!" Elen says.

"The Morgan cabin and barn was burned last week," Megan is quick to add. "That does not sound too safe!"

"They escaped by hiding in the woods. How long will it be before they find out about us?" Elen asks.

"They will find out we are loyal too. We are not safe here. We need to seek refuge before it is too late!" my mother says.

"I grow tired of listening to noises in the woods. I am tired of this war," Megan says, her voice trembling. She throws herself on the cot and sobs.

Before he leaves, my father tries to explain that it is safer for all of us if they fight with the regular forces to ensure control of the forts. Evan and Davydd agreed with him. They are both old enough to know of the dangers they will face, as they once again help to push back the rebels. It isn't long before we, too, are in danger.

We move quickly, gasping for breath as we run. Megan trips, but I quickly help her to her feet. We keep looking back. We know that the rebels are not far behind us.

"Hurry! We must stay hidden! Keep close to the woods!"

"Stay clear of the openings in the trees," Elen yells as we run.

We crouch in the shadows and wait, and after what seems like hours, all is quiet in the surrounding woods. Could it be safe to go back?

"Listen. I believe they've gone back," our mother whispers. "We're safe now. Come. Let's go back."

"Elen, are you sure?" Megan whispers.

It had grown dark as we waited, listening for them to return. Now as we cautiously make our way back across the darkened field, we are aware of fire. The smell of smoke is in the air, and as we get closer, we can see that it is from a neighbor's cabin. We watch as smoke billows from the small cabin. We knew that the raiders often burned the homes after they took what they wanted. We had reason to fear what we would find.

"Oh, I am afraid, I am," Mama says as we quicken our pace across the field.

"Come, Mama. It will be all right," I say, taking her hand. Megan hurries ahead to our own cabin. We are relieved to see it still standing.

"Wonder what they took this time?"

"Everything looks all right, Mother!" Megan exclaims after bounding up the steps and pushing the door open.

"There's not much left to take. No, not much."

"How many times will we have to run for our lives? Will we ever be safe?" Elen says as she drops into a rocker.

I check to see if the little box is still under my bed. It is safe.

Chapter 22

In early October troops are being readied again. This time I am with my father and brothers when they join the other Loyalists at the fort.

It will not be long before the Patriots make their presence known.

It all happens so quickly. They are coming straight toward us. My father pushes me out of the way as the muskets keep firing. He stops long enough to reload from the powder horn that is hanging from his waist

"Stay down. Stay down!" he shouts above the noise. I fall to the ground. I can hear the rat-a-tat of the drums. I should be with them.

I can't move. My heart is in my throat. I can see others falling all around me. It is so confusing. I don't know what's happening. A tight sob fills my throat. In the smoke I lose sight of Pa. I call for him, but there's no answer.

There are lots of screams, and blasts are coming from everywhere at once. I try to get up, but I stumble and fall. I lay there crumpled in a heap. Still the musket fire continues. Even the wild hammering of my heart won't shut out the sounds from the guns.

I look up and see Evan close by, his face blackened with gunpowder. And Davydd's hands are shaking as he reloads his musket. But where is my father? Another shot. More smoke. Through the glare of the musket fire, I see my father's blackened face twisted in pain as he goes down. Evan is the first to reach him. Davydd and I are not far behind.

"You're hit!" His trouser leg is ripped open, and blood is oozing from the wound.

"It's only a graze—" he says faintly.

"More than that! Look at the blood!"

"Davydd! A bandage!" Evan shouts.

My brother is already tearing a strip from his inner shirt.

Then I notice the blood running down my own arm. My hand is covered in it. Evan tears off my tunic to check the wound.

"A deep cut. Bad enough."

"They're coming back! Stay down! Stay down!" Evan shouts when we hear more shouting and yelling.

More shots. Then all is quiet.

After some minutes we all crawl to the shelter of some nearby trees and lie there without moving for what seems to be a very long time. We wait, listening. The guns are quiet, but the air is still thick with smoke and the arid smell of gunpowder. We help our father to his feet and make our way to the path, carefully parting the bushes as we go. On the path Evan gives the signal to move forward.

I am conscious of every sound—the sounds from the woods, the sound of my own breathing.

The pounding of my heart sounds like thunder.

A twig snaps. I stop in my tracks. I realize I have been holding my breath. Terror fills me.

I feel a hand grip my shoulder. I freeze.

"Are you afraid?" Davydd whispers as he comes up behind me.

I can't speak. I am shaking.

I glance over my shoulder to make sure there is no one else following us. I stumble but then pull myself up.

Then shots ring out again.

The last thing I remember was hitting the ground and falling backward. My drum went flying into the air.

"Get up!" It was Evan rousing me from my stunned stupor. "Hurry!"

"What happened?"

"Shots. In the distance! We need to keep up with the others. Don't want to be taken prisoner."

"Are they still following us?"

"No, we're alone for now. Best to rest up ahead till dark. Then we'll make our way to the fort."

We crouch, hidden in a thicket. It is getting dark now. I force myself to close out the sounds coming from the woods. Davydd has fallen asleep. I peer through the foliage, keeping a watchful eye, unable to sleep. I can't stop trembling. I feel my father's hand on my shoulder. The trembling stops.

"Don't be afraid. God is watching over us, son. Try to sleep." Then I hear him reciting the psalm, "Yea, though I walk through the valley … thou art with me … in the presence of my enemies—"

The next thing I know Davydd is shaking me.

"We have to be moving."

I raise myself from the ground, rubbing my eyes.

"We have to go," he says.

We follow a trail through the trees to keep ourselves hidden.

"The fort … is it far?" I ask.

"Don't know."

"Which way?"

"Should be this way," Evan says as he leads the way into the moonlit path. Suddenly he stops. He looks back and motions for us to stop.

"Quiet," he whispers, holding his hand to his mouth.

We watch him as he carefully picks his steps. Then we see it. A musket is propped against a tree. He motions for us to continue. A body sprawled at the edge of the path causes us to stop.

My legs are shaky. I can barely will them to move on. I look back to make sure Davydd and Pa are all right.

After what seems to be hours we see the shadow of the outpost. "The fort's in darkness!"

"Appears to be deserted." A tattered flag flaps in the wind from atop a wooden pole. Everything is silent.

"Check the barracks," my father says. "But be careful—"

"What about rations?"

"Cleaned out. There's nothing here," Davydd says after he checks the stores.

"Let's head for home. We've got a full day's walk ahead of us."

Megan says she remembers it well. That late October day all three are sitting on the porch in the gathering dusk. She is peering off in the distance when something catches her attention. The figures that she sees approaching on the dusty road might be the rebels again, she knows. They are afraid at first. Then she recognizes us.

"It's Father!" I hear her shout as she runs toward us.

"And Evan. And Davydd! And there's Tom!"

It didn't take long for Elen to catch up to Megan. Now I can see my mother as well. She is behind my sisters as they run to meet us.

"Father, you're hurt!"

"No, girl ... it's nothing. Just a graze," he says when Elen reaches up to stroke his grimy face.

Our clothes are muddy and torn. Dried blood stains Pa's trousers as well as the bandage that is wrapped around his forehead. Evan has Pa's musket as well as his own slung over his shoulder. Davydd is helping to support Pa. My arm is in a sling. We must be quite a sight indeed.

"Oh, you are home!" I hear my mother cry before she even reaches us. "Thanks be, thanks be."

She makes no attempt to wipe the tears that are running

down her face. She tries to hug all of us at once, hardly noticing the bandages at first.

"Oh, you are all hurt!" she says as she starts to fuss over us.

"No, nothing serious. We were lucky," Evan says as the girls help us inside.

"But the blood! Oh, are you sure? Now let's get you out of these filthy clothes. And some cleaning up."

"Get some water boiling, girls! And warm the beans, Megan! There's fresh cornbread and ham hocks! They must be starving!"

The wound that my father had received was more than just a graze. He had taken a shot to the leg, but my mother assured him it would heal in time. Davydd's wound was not serious. Mine turned out to be nothing more than a deep cut and a broken arm. After my mother and sisters had bandaged the wounds, helped clean up the grime, and fed four hungry men—for now I was a man as well—we told them about King's Mountain.

"We were stormed by the Patriots."

"We didn't stand a chance."

"But Father fought bravely," Davydd says. "That he did."

"There were over a thousand of us. We should have been able to fight them off," my father says wearily.

"So many were being killed. It was bad."

"You could have all been killed," Elen says.

"Or taken prisoner," Davydd tells her.

"We all stayed together. That's what helped. We hid until they were gone," I tell them.

"We pulled Father to safety when he was shot," Evan explains.

"When Pa fell, I was really afraid," I say. "I thought we would all be killed!"

"How did you manage to escape?" Elen asks.

"After the battle we stayed hidden. So many were being taken prisoner. We didn't want that to happen."

"We made it back to the fort and rested there for a while," Davydd adds.

"Then we headed home," I say.

"It must have been scary," Megan says. Then she turns to me and puts her hand on my shoulder.

"Tomos, were you scared?" she asks quietly.

How dare she ask me that with Davydd listening.

"Megan, fighting is scary. There was a lot of yelling and smoke. It was hard to see what was going on. We were all scared." Everyone is trying to talk at once because there is so much to tell. Now we are exhausted. No one objects when our mother decides that it is time for bed. She will gladly get the last word tonight.

"That's enough for tonight, boys. Everyone needs rest now."

I am so glad to be in my bed tonight. After sleeping on the ground for these past weeks, it doesn't take long for me to fall asleep.

We are quite sure now that with winter coming on, most of the fighting will surely cease. We hope that the fighting in the back country is over. Our hope is that it will be safe to travel again—safe to go back home.

My arm heals, but Pa's leg needs more time. Even if fighting is to start again, he will probably not be able to go back.

But it is not long before we hear that reinforcements are needed at Cowpens, and our father says it is our duty to help the troops at the fort. My mother tries to keep us from going, but in the end she consents. So we make our way to the fort and prepare for the attack that's expected.

"Get some rest, men. Be ready to move out at dawn."

Early the next morning we leave the fort. All is quiet, so we stop to rest at the edge of the woods. In the silence every sound is frightening. The snap of a twig or an animal moving has us on our feet, gathering muskets and gear.

"What's happening?" I ask when we hear someone approaching.

"Someone's riding in!"

"It's a scout!"

"A company's approaching! Couple of miles away!" he yells when he reaches us.

Within minutes we are marching in the direction of the approaching company. The scout circles to make sure we are not being surrounded.

Then the crack of a musket has us on alert. From out of nowhere they are upon us. A company of Patriots emerges from the clearing unto the path in front of us.

The order comes to fire. I beat my drum louder and louder. The musket fire keeps coming. When the smoke clears, we see that the enemy has retreated. The smell of gunpowder fills the air. I see the bodies on the ground and the wounded being carried off to the side.

"Where's Davydd?"

"He's all right. Under the trees with the others," Evan says.

"Are you all right?"

"Just … just scared," I admit.

We crouch at the edge of the woods, barely daring to breathe. I feel the tightness in my throat. We wait. We dare not move. I keep waiting for someone to step into the clearing again.

"The militia could be faking a retreat, men. We'll wait before we move out," the soldier says.

Then without warning they were upon us, and as before gunfire flashes around us. Everyone is firing at once. I try to call out for Evan and Davydd, but no sound comes. Are they dead?

Finally all is quiet except for the moans from the many wounded. I wait. I am alone. My breathing is coming in gasps. I am too afraid to call out. Tears run down my cheeks. Where is everyone?

I keep pushing through the bushes. Perhaps they've gone the other way. Should I turn back?

I think I am praying. Then I hear it—a whisper.

"Tomos?"

The whisper is so low I wonder if I've imagined hearing it. It is Evan's voice.

"I'm here," I manage.

He inches toward me on his stomach.

"Quiet. Stay down," he whispers.

I crawl forward to meet him. Then we make our way to where Davydd is sitting. He is all right.

"Are they gone? I couldn't find any of you. What—"

"You must have been knocked out. We didn't realize you weren't with us," Davydd says.

"It's all over. They got most of our company though," Evan says. "Look. Bodies everywhere."

"Let's go back to the fort," Davydd says.

"Best to wait for darkness. We don't know what we'll find there. Let's get some rest."

I guess I fell asleep because the next thing I know Evan is trying to wake me.

"Wake up! It's time to go. We have to be moving."

I raise myself from the ground and rub my eyes. Davydd is finally waking as well.

In the gathering darkness, our company—what is left of it—follows a trail amongst the trees that will lead us back to the outpost. Before we even come in sight of it, we smell the arid smoke. The outpost had been burned.

"Patriots won again!" Evan says.

We learned later that the battle that General Morgan's troops had won at Cowpens would end a string of victories for Cornwallis in the south. After a clash with Greene at Guilford Courthouse in March, he moved his campaign north. Still the war went on. Greene had joined forces with Morgan. Their intent was to drive the British out of the Carolinas and to capture all of their posts, including Charles Town. The Loyalists had done all they could do.

Chapter 23

Evan bounds up the porch steps and rushes into the cabin. He is certainly excited about something.

"There's a notice up that Lord Montagu is recruiting for special service!"

"Who's this Montagu?" my father wants to know.

"Father, the word is that he comes from a good royal background and is looked upon favorably. In fact, he was governor here until about six years ago."

"Really? Does it say what this special service is ... or where?"

"Not really, Father. It says that 'the regiment to be raised and commanded by Right Honorable Lord Charles Montagu is to fight against the enemies of King George the Third.'"

"It sounds like something important is brewing, I would say. So no one knows where?"

"No, there are no details, but everyone seems to be excited about it. They think it may be good."

"When is this recruiting to take place?"

"Montagu has been recruiting for months now."

"Something big by the sound of it!" Davydd says.

"So are you thinking of enlisting, Evan?" my father asks.

"I think it could be a good thing, Father. Perhaps you should consider it too. You know how things are here right now."

"Guess my leg has healed enough. Perhaps I should."

"I'll enlist with Montagu!" Davydd says, getting up from his chair and pulling it closer.

"Let's enlist, Father. It would get us out of here."

"I hear that the troops have pretty much left the Loyalists to fend for themselves now," Evan tells us.

"Well now, I'd have to think about it," my father replies slowly.

"Father, I think it would be best. Especially now," Evan persists.

My mother has been listening without saying anything, but I can tell by the look on her face that she is not happy about this recent bit of news.

Is the thought of another separation too much for her?

"Oh no. Not again!" she finally says.

"But Mother, this time will be different."

"How will it be different, Evan? We will be left alone again!" Elen says.

"No, Elen, listen to this! The notice says that anyone who signs up for three years is promised good pay, proper clothing, and free quarters."

"And after that, what?"

"After the peace takes place, they are free to return to their homes."

"Oh no, Evan! Not another three years. Your mother wants to go home now."

"But Father, families are going along with the regiments. We would be together."

"Really? We could go along?" Elen asks.

"That's what the notice said. I read it myself."

"Could be just more promises, Evan," Pa says.

"Do you think so?"

"You see where those promises got us."

"But Father, you know they'll not let us go anywhere now with this war going on. Perhaps this is our best hope of getting home sooner."

"How many men is this Montagu fellow looking for, Evan?"

"Well, already two battalions have been put together from the prisoners that were on the ships in the harbor, and he's recruited more from New York."

"Then I fear it is too late to sign up."

"Another battalion is being readied. Loyalists like ourselves who are volunteering to support the empire."

"Anything will be better than fighting off the rebels here. Aye, perhaps we should consider—"

"Since we've been left to protect ourselves, now that the forces are focusing their attention to the north again, perhaps this is the best thing to do."

"They don't seem to care what happens to us here now," Davydd says. "I'm for signing up!"

"Then first thing tomorrow, let's go see what all of this is about."

"What about you, Tomos?" Davydd asks. "Think you're old enough now?"

"I'll sign up with you."

The next morning we get a ride with a farmer friend who has decided he wants to find out more about this special mission. He, too, wants to get away from all of the fighting here.

The recruitment papers are signed. We are told very little—only that the mission would be in a British colony. We hope that it might be New York. From what so many are saying at the garrison, that appears to be the safest place to be now.

My mother looks up from her packing and reaches up to tuck a lock of hair that has loosened and fallen across her face. I can't help noticing the tired look on her face. For days my sisters have been helping to pack our few belongings before we head for the barracks at Charles Town.

"Those old trunks are probably getting as tired of travelling as we are," I tell her.

"They're about worn out—that's for certes—just as I am."

Ruins in the Mist

"Mama, maybe this will be the last time," I say as I touch her hand, causing her to pause and look up at me.

"Do you really think we might soon be going home?"

"If we go north, we'll be that much closer to home," I tell her. "That's good."

I went out and picked up my fishing pole from the porch. Evan and Davydd are sitting there and talking. "Going fishing?" Davydd asks.

"My days for going to the creek will soon be over. Want to come along?"

"No. Think not. Jimmy might be there to keep you company."

But when I arrive at my favorite fishing hole, there is no one else there. I was hoping that Jimmy *might* be there. After about an hour I have only one catfish to show for my efforts.

By the time I get back to the cabin, the others have gone inside. I sit on the step, thinking about my friend—the only one I have made these past five years. I am going to miss him. I must go and see him one last time before we leave Ashley Creek. How can I tell him I won't see him again?

I get up and go inside. I reach under my cot and pull out the little box that held all of my possessions. What should I take? I pick up the little tin toy that Gladys gave me that last Christmas … and put it back. Next I pick up the little book Pa taught me to read when I was only five. I finger the blade of the small knife that Owen gave me before we left home. There are several small trinkets and not much else. I look at each again, and then I choose the one thing I treasure most and slip it into my trouser pocket. I replace the box and hurry outside.

I wasn't expecting to find my mother there.

"Oh, I thought you were in the garden, Mama!"

"We've already finished picking what is ready. The rest will stay for whoever moves in here."

She looks out over the fields, her hand shielding the setting sun from her eyes. "I don't know why we ever came here, son. This has been a bad choice, it has."

I give her a hug and then reach up and touch her hair just before I step from the porch.

"Where are you going, Tomos?"

"Just off to find Jimmy. Got to say good-bye before tomorrow."

I run down the path and past the row of whitewashed cabins. In front of one a young woman is singing as she souses clothes up and down in a tin washtub. At another, clothes are draped over the nearby bushes to dry, while a woman stands over a blackened kettle that hangs from a tripod over a low fire. With a stick she pokes at whatever is in the pot.

I hurry across the fields to the little cabin. I keep looking for Jimmy. He should be finished with work by now, but I see that he's still in the cotton field with his mother. Their workday had not yet ended. She looks up when she sees me approach. Jimmy lays down his basket and looks at his mother. She motions for him to go. He runs to meet me, and his mother follows us to the cabin and joins us on the step. She wipes the sweat from her face with her apron. Her young, dark face looks so sad.

"Wha' brings ye her' boy?"

"I have to say good-bye."

"Mus' ya go?"

"Yes, my family ... my family is leaving."

Why is this so difficult?

"Where you reckon you'll go?" she asks.

"Don't know exactly."

"Sur' 'ope ye come back," Jimmy says.

"We'll be going back home. After the war."

"You sho' 'bout leavin', Tom?" I see tears in his big dark eyes.

"We have to leave in the morning."

"You sho'?" he asks again.

Ruins in the Mist

"I hope you find the rest of your family," I say, looking at his mother.

"Reckon they don' know we's alive."

"Maybe someday you can go home," I tell her.

"Reckon dis here is ou' 'ome," Jimmy says.

"We's slaves. Mast' bought us," his mother says. "Dat's why we ain't going 'ome."

I try to say more, but the words won't come. There is something in my throat that wants to stop the words. Jimmy's mother sees that I have removed something from my pocket.

"What do ye 'ave there, son?"

"Just a little book I want Jimmy to have." I hold it toward her, and she reaches out and touches it gently.

"La' sakes! Just look at that!"

She has no way of knowing how much it meant to me.

"But he can't read. My Jimmy never learn' to read."

"Maybe someday he will learn," I answer as I look into her sad face.

"Someday ... I 'ope 'e will 'ave learnin'."

"I'm 'fraid he don't 'ave nothin' for you," she continues.

"Oh, that's all right. I just wish ... I wish you and Jimmy could come too. I wish you could both come away with us to tomorrow."

"We's not free. We 'ave to stay here. Mast' always been good to us ... 'deed 'e is."

"I will miss you both. I will ... I will—" I'm not able to continue. Tears are threatening to spill. I must not cry.

"You go. I'm skeered for ye. Jus' be careful. We will worry 'bout ye." She wipes at a tear that has rolled down her cheek. "Lawd' 'ave mercy on ye all."

I reach out and press the little book in Jimmy's hand. My fingers linger on the dark hand of my friend, and then my eyes fall on his dusty bare feet. I look up at him and see that tears are running down his dusty face.

"You are my friend. I'll never forget you," I manage to say.

Jimmy just stands there, looking at me. I'll never forget the look on his face. He is making it hard for me to say good-bye. I wonder if I will ever have another friend like him. I almost wish we were not going away. I hope they will be all right and find their family someday.

"Well, chil'en, it's getting' dusk."

"Yes, I must be going." I reach for her calloused hand. She holds mine for a moment.

"S'pose ye won't be back. No one comes back," she says sadly.

I feel the tears that are threatening to spill. I have to get away from here.

"Good-bye. I've got to go," I manage at last.

I run across the fields. Tears are blinding my eyes. I find myself at the creek. I sit there. For how long, I'm not sure.

I hear singing coming from the cabins in the distance—some old spiritual that someone is singing from memory. I am going to miss this. I am going to miss Jimmy. I am torn. I want to leave, but I don't want to leave my friend. As I sit there on the riverbank, thinking of the past few years and all the things that have happened in our lives, my thoughts turn to home. Questions crowd my thoughts. *Will we ever be free to return? Are we not just like Jimmy? Are we not slaves as he is? What will this new move mean for us?*

I notice that it is getting dark and realize the others will be waiting for me. I get up from the riverbank, knowing that Jimmy will come here alone now. I will not be here to share any more stories as we wait for the catfish to bite. I slowly walk back toward the cabin in the gathering dusk. My heart is heavy.

Later that evening my father does his best to answer the questions I have about the slaves.

"Shiploads of them were brought here after being separated from their families."

"Why, Pa?"

"To work the plantations in exchange for a place to live and food for their table."

"But is that right? Someone bought them. They can't even leave."

"No, it's not right. No man should own another."

"Jimmy doesn't even know where his father is. Or his brothers—"

"That's sad, son. So sad."

"Do you think they will ever be free? Jimmy's mother doesn't think they will."

"Let's hope that someday it will be different." I wait for him to continue. Surely he has the answers.

No matter how much my father tries to explain it, I still don't understand it. Why are we free to leave? Why can Jimmy and all the others not leave if they want to? What will happen to my friend and his mother?

All that answers me is a lone whip-poor-will and the chirping of the crickets in the warm southern night.

Chapter 24

At dawn we begin our long trek toward Charles Town. In the early morning light the trees cast shadows across our path, and every sound from the woods makes us jump. We had been warned that an ambush was possible at any time. Soon it will be light, and the danger will be even greater. We had been told how important it was to leave quietly and to leave at the first light.

I look back toward the cabin that has sheltered us these past five years. With its hand-hewn beams and rough walls, it has managed to keep us safe. Now from the wagon it looks even smaller as we make our way out on the dusty road and head toward the garrison. The last time my family had been in Charles Town was when we had been moved to the cabin to await our own land and home—which we never did get. The land that was granted to the landlords by the king was never passed on to the tenants and servants. It seems so long ago.

Soon the little cabin is only a distant speck lost in the vastness of the fields around it. The blackened shell of a neighboring cabin stands as a reminder of the dangers we are leaving behind. Even at this early hour workers are already in the fields harvesting the crop that is ripe for picking. We are leaving the row of cabins—even the one where Jimmy lives.

We drive by the big two-storey house with its shutters

Ruins in the Mist

and broad verandas all around. We see the gardens that are lush with blooms and the magnolia trees. And there's the big church that we never visited. As the wagon makes its way toward Ashley River Road, the scent of jasmine is in the air.

I had forgotten the threat of ambush until noises in the woods cause Joe to suddenly bring the wagon to a stop. The trusted old slave had been chosen to take us to Charles Town with our belongings. He puts a warning finger to his mouth, cautioning us to keep quiet.

"Do you think it's the rebels?" Megan whispers.

"Oh no. I'm afraid, I am," Mama says timidly.

My father picks up her hand and holds it.

Even old Joe seems to be afraid.

"Be quiet," Evan whispers. "Be very quiet."

We sit there for some minutes—although it seems much longer. Finally old Joe decides that it is safe to continue on our way, but we continue to watch the shadows. Every sound catches our attention as we resume our journey.

Hours pass, and my father keeps on telling us that it shouldn't be much longer. Before long we see that the houses are getting much bigger, and that means that the town is near. The danger is over.

As we near Charles Town, the great oaks on River Road form a canopy overhead. The moonlight is filtering through the moss, and the trees are casting their shadows over the road. Mama looks up at the trees. Knowing what she is probably thinking brings a smile to my face.

"I shall miss all of this," she says quietly.

"At first you were afraid of it, Mama. But now you know."

"Yes, now I know. That's the way it grows."

After hours of bouncing over the rough road, the moss swaying in the warm breeze is welcome. The strong perfume of dogwood blossoms is in the air as we rumble over the cobblestones toward the town. The long journey will soon be over. The damp, salty air lets us know we are nearing the coast.

At the barracks we are given shelter while the companies are readied for the mission. Little is known as to where we are going. Meanwhile, it gives us boys a chance to explore the busy docks and look around the town. Everywhere men are unloading heavy crates and barrels from the many vessels at anchor. We watch as bales of cotton and hogsheads of indigo and tobacco are loaded onto waiting vessels bound for Europe. The towering masts of the ships in the harbor are quite a sight.

One day after spending some time about the wharves, I walk ahead, leaving Evan and Davydd to talk with a couple of soldiers in British uniform. A stiff breeze tugs at my light coat as I make my way along the dock. I stand looking out over the harbor, remembering the day we came here. Has it really been more than five years since that day?

"Father, ships are being readied for Montagu's regiment," Evan tells him when we return to the barracks.

"Where did you hear that?"

"Davydd and I were talking to a couple of British soldiers in town," Evan says.

"Did they say when?"

"They think they are to be sailing soon."

"Oh, that will suit your mother fine. It's time. The girls are getting anxious."

"Aren't we all!" Davydd says.

"Any word where they are taking us?" Pa asks.

"Not for sure. Some are thinking Halifax or New York. No one is sure."

"That would be great. Might give us a chance to see Steffan again."

"One thing's for sure—the fighting is not over wherever they're going," Evan says.

"That's not good news."

"The word is that the garrison is in danger of attack wherever it is," he continues.

"So this regiment is being taken there for reinforcement, I would say."

"Yes, Father, that would be my guess as well," Evan says.

Chapter 25

Within days, five hundred recruits along with families and even a few servants board the *Argo* and the *Industry*, and we set sail from Charles Town. It isn't long before it's clear that the ship is not headed north.

"We're headed southward," Evan says.

"So we are not headed for Halifax. That would be north, wouldn't it?"

"You're right, Davydd."

Meanwhile Evan talks with some fellow recruits who had overheard some of the crew talking. They appear to have some information about what is going on in the West Indies and our reason for going there.

"We're headed to Jamaica for duty. The garrison there is in danger of attack! They say it's serious."

"Evan, where is Jamaica?" I ask.

"Not quite sure. In the West Indies somewhere, I guess."

"Who would be attacking it?" Davydd asks.

"It's a British colony, but the word is that Spain is trying to reclaim the island."

"And what was that they were saying about the French?" Davydd asks.

"The French have shifted their attention to the islands as well. They've had a fleet in the area for over two years now."

"They've already taken over a nearby island. That can't be good," Evan continues.

"Then it's no wonder the British are nervous," Pa says.

"Having Spain to reckon with was enough. Now France too," Davydd says.

"Now with the French being such a threat, there is fear of a French invasion," Evan explains.

"Aye, they probably want to capture all the other islands," Pa says. "And with a strong naval fleet it's going to be possible—that's for certain."

"Then our job will be to defend the garrison?" I ask.

"It would appear so," Evan answers.

Jamaica was indeed south—some 450 miles south of Florida. Unlike our last voyage this one is more pleasant. The warm ocean winds and warm temperatures have us looking forward to what might lie ahead. We are allowed on deck each day to enjoy the sun and to watch the flying fish flashing like small silver arrows. Standing at the rail in the evenings, we watch the beautiful sunsets settle over the many islands.

"Megan, watch the company you keep!" Davydd says when he sees our young sister talking to one of the sailors we had talked to earlier.

"Ah, no need to worry, laddie. The young lady is in no harm!"

"Looks like you might be getting a bit too friendly," Evan says, walking in their direction.

"What's he telling you anyway?"

"Stories of Captain Kidd and Blackbeard," Megan answers.

"Like to hear those stories myself," Davydd says.

"Me too," I say as I join them. As he points out locations of wrecked pirate ships and buried treasure, he tells us stories that are hard to believe.

"Just legends?" Evan asks.

"No, really happened!" the sailor says.

I'm not sure whether I believe him or not.

The farther south we sail, the warmer the August sun gets. The wind is with us, and we are told that before long the ship will enter the Windward Passage. As the *Argo* makes its way to the bay where we are to anchor, dozens of seabirds follow the vessel.

The sun is shining as the vessel slips past Port Royal Cay and rounds Gallows Point. Sheltering the harbor at Kingston, the Palisadoes will be our destination—the sheltered side of the spit protecting us from the sea.

"Look at all the trees!" I say as the vessel gets closer to shore.

"Lots of those on the island! Miles and miles of them!" we are told.

There are palmetto trees everywhere. When we are finally ashore, I can hear the rustling of the fronds as they sway in the gentle breeze. The air is warm.

We are settled into our new quarters at Rock Fort. The fort, we were told, was one of several on the island. It is a large fort with stockade walls, a blockhouse in the center, and barracks along the back and one side. Sentries stand watch in the gun towers at each corner. The fort is entered by a wide gate that faces the harbor. My mother and sisters join the other women and children in the family quarters—a row of buildings nearby. We are issued uniforms. My red jacket is worn and a bit faded. It hangs nearly to my knees. I roll the sleeves back. Having uniforms is something new for us. Then, muskets, fifes, and drums are given out. I am to be a drummer.

Our regiment is assembled. A burly sergeant steps forward.

"Attention!" he yells.

"Your regiment is known as the Duke of Cumberland Regiment. You will be ready to defend our positions at a moment's notice."

I could hardly wait to try out my drum. I dared not look down at it now. Everyone else was looking straight ahead.

"An attack is imminent. The greatest threat will be from the French fleet. However, the first attack will be a land attack to test our forces."

Ruins in the Mist

"Every fort on the island is ready. This will be no exception. Now return to barracks. Dismissed!"

That is our welcome to the island.

The weeks that follow are filled with drills and training. The drummers are reminded of the different sounds that will alert the soldiers and relay the commands to them. We march every day and wait for the night watches to be given out. When my turn finally comes, I join two other soldiers in one of the gun towers for the night.

Inside the stockade all is quiet. The moon is bright. I look toward the family quarters and wonder how my mother is taking this recent move. I hope my family is comfortable enough in their small quarters.

Two days later at dawn the piercing notes of reveille awaken me. It seems as if I had just fallen asleep. Before we know it, we are out again. I am getting tired of all this marching. There is nothing much else happening. Everything is quiet—no sign of any attacks.

"We'll make camp tonight. There's rumor of a possible attack," the sergeant says at the end of the day. "There's a company at the point lying in wait," he goes on. "Keep watches through the night. Arms ready."

"Drummers, be ready! Now get some rest. Be on your feet at first light."

I bed down beside Pa and Davydd. Evan is with the watch party that is posted. Davydd is asleep within minutes. But he can sleep through anything. I must have finally fallen asleep.

At dawn the next day we are ready to march. All appears quiet. At noon we stop to rest. I unstrap my drum, and muskets are dropped to the ground. I throw myself down beside the others. A watch is posted.

"What was that?" I am on my feet in an instant.

"That shot came from the fort. A sentry ... firing a warning. We're going back, men."

"Drummers, take your positions!"

I tighten my drum before I strike up the rat-a-tat with the others.

Back at the fort we find out that it is another false alarm—one of many that will keep us alert during our marches over the next few months. The actual attacks never come, even though we learn that other islands around us are being invaded by the French.

The nights are the worst. I lie awake, listening and waiting. I realize I am not a very good soldier. *Has Mama been right all along? Are we too young for all of this?*

"Pa, what's the reason for the fighting down here?" I ask as we lay in the barracks one night.

"Same as in the northern colonies."

"What's that? The taxes?"

"Aye, the same."

"What do they have to pay taxes on?"

"Everything that's shipped from here, I guess."

"I don't understand why France and Spain are involved, Pa."

"Probably saw the war as an opportunity for revenge," Evan says.

"Revenge? Against whom?" I ask.

"Britain. That's why they have so many troops here."

"There's good news. I hear that the French fleet has headed north again," Davydd says.

"So that probably means that something is brewing in the colonies up north again."

"Aye, probably is. Doesn't look like the troubles are over yet."

Much later we hear what the French fleet has been up to. For us here, it appears that the danger is over. We patiently wait for news, but none comes. We are all getting anxious to be taken out of Jamaica. Surely there is no reason to stay here now that the danger is past. We want to go back home.

Chapter 26

The news shocks us. After months of waiting we are finally hearing what is going on. A report has just reached the post. According to the report the news is not good.

"Men, the news is not good. But the war looks like it may be coming to an end," the commander informs us.

"Greene has been successful in driving the British out of all the southern colonies. He has been regaining the forts one by one. Cornwallis was hoping to make Virginia his center of operations," he says. "That did not happen."

"A couple of months ago he decided to use Yorktown as his base, which would be a reasonable choice since the British fleet has nineteen ships based in New York." He pauses and then goes on, "But then deGrasse's fleet was ordered to take control of the seas not only here but to support Washington in his operations." He clears his throat and goes on, "When our fleet was sent out to support Cornwallis, the French fleet intercepted them, causing so much damage that they had to return to port."

We wait for him to continue.

"That's when the French fleet, aided by Washington's army, sealed off the bay, allowing the army—some seventeen thousand—to surround Yorktown. It was bad for our general. He didn't have a chance. He couldn't hold off the heavy bombardment."

Whispers go through the company.

"Where was the British fleet?" one soldier asks.

"Let me explain, soldier."

"They were off on another mission and did not return in time to aid Cornwallis. When they heard what was taking place, they set sail for New York, but they arrived too late. The general had already ... already surrendered."

"Surrendered! You mean he just gave up!" another soldier exclaims in surprise.

"Yes, soldier, he had no hope of escape. It is said he made a poor judgement call and was cut off by the French fleet. He had to surrender—him and eight thousand of his men."

So now we know why the fleet has left and headed north.

"So what—"

"Permission to speak, soldier."

"So what will all this mean for us?" the young soldier asks after he is granted permission. The soldier's question is one we are all asking.

"Men, it looks as if the war may be coming to an end."

I can hear the sighs of relief that go through the company.

"So will we be leaving here?" someone ventures to ask.

"We will just have to wait and see. Have to wait for orders. Dismissed!"

We return to the barracks, not quite sure what to expect next. Everyone sits in groups and discusses what is happening.

"Do you think it's really over?" I ask.

"Sounds like the war in the north is about over. But ... I don't know."

"Sounds that way. But the threat from the Spanish and French fleet is still there," Evan says. "You can tell by the way he talks, even though he didn't come out and say it."

Evan is right. There will still be more fighting. We are not going anywhere for a while yet.

The French fleet has started capturing other British islands all around us with the intent of eventually capturing Jamaica. deGrasse's large fleet attempts a rendezvous with the Spanish fleet in the spring of the next year. The British fleet arrives and saves the day, sailing through the broken French line of battle with a daring maneuver that guarantees the safety of its fleet. We watch later as the captured ships are brought into the harbor. The attempt to invade the island is a disaster.

"That was one brave move!" Davydd says.

"Certainly was. That was a daring maneuver. Sailing through the broken French line like that," Evan agrees.

"Who was he anyway?" I ask.

"Admiral Rodney. He proved he knew what he was doing."

"That was a gutsy move. He saw his chance and took it," Davydd says.

"After all, deGrasse had over thirty ships, and then with the dozen Spanish ships that had joined him, he must have felt quite confident."

"Probably thought he had nothing to worry about," Davydd says.

"Aye, but he wasn't counting on the thirty-six British ships that arrived!"

"Just proves that Britain is still a force to be reckoned with, Father."

"Wonder what they thought when Rodney brought the captured ships into the harbor," I say.

"Look at them! He captured four of them and destroyed more," Evan reminds us.

As we look at the ships now anchored in sight of the fort, it is a reminder for us of these many years of nothing but war. And now after months of waiting, it looks as if we might finally be going home. It is our father who raises our hopes one day when he tells us what he has heard from a fellow soldier.

"Thousands of Loyalists are being transferred to New York."

"Finally!" Davydd says. "What now?"

"They are waiting there to return to their homeland."

"I guess Britain's hold on the colonies is over," Evan says.

"Savannah has been evacuated. Charles Town will be next," our father goes on. "That means there will be no place for us there, if that happens."

"So they'll have to let us go home," I say.

"Aye, looks like we'll all be going home soon!"

"Mama will be so glad. And the girls as well!"

"Let's go tell them," Davydd says.

"Not so fast. A treaty will need to be signed before everything is final," our father points out.

"A treaty? How long will that take?" I ask.

"That could take some time," Evan says.

Chapter 27

In the spring a treaty is signed, giving the colonies what they want—their independence. They had severed themselves from the British Empire. But where did that leave us? We wait day after day for some word as to our fate. We surely cannot stay here. We know that if Charles Town is evacuated, there will be no place for us there. Every day we keep an ear for any word that something might be forthcoming. We wait for orders.

Then one day we are mustered and informed of the latest developments.

"Britain has been ordered to withdraw all its forces from the colonies. They have to be out before December."

As we walk back to the barracks, our hopes are high after we hear the details.

"Sounds like they have quite an undertaking on their hands," our father says.

"That doesn't give them much time. I understand there are still thousands to be evacuated," Evan says.

"And what about us here in Jamaica?" Davydd asks.

"Looks like Montagu's troops are in trouble. I don't know."

"What do you think Montagu will do?"

"I don't know, Davydd. It certainly puts the battalions in a bad place."

"Why do you say that?"

"If we can no longer return to Charles Town—"

"And we can't stay here," I interrupt.

"Don't worry, boys. Montagu will find a way. Come now. Let's tell the rest of the family the news."

※

"Really leaving?" Elen exclaims.

"Are you sure?" Megan asks.

"It's time, it is," Mama says. It has been a long time since I've seen her so happy. One day in late October the soldiers are gathered and disbanded. We are told to be ready for evacuation. It does not take long to gather the few belongings we have, and then we wait. We are all anxious to finally be leaving here.

"What is taking so long, Tomos?" my mother asks Pa.

"It should not be long now, Gwendolyn."

"I will check around tomorrow and see what I can find out," Evan offers. "There's a lot of activity around those two ships in the harbor. That could mean something."

"Those are Montagu's vessels. The *Argo* and the *Industry*," Davydd says. "I heard the fellows talking."

"Those ships have been in the harbor since last week. Something is going on," I say.

"Maybe they are being readied for us," Elen says.

"They probably are," I tell her.

"I hope it's soon, I do," my mother says. "I do so want to be going home," she continues. "I want to see Owen and Willym. And Gladys. Oh, I miss them so. Do you really think they are getting ready to take us out of here?"

"Oh, I should think that's what they're planning. What else can they do?" our father tells her.

"But what if they send us back to Ashley Creek?"

Ashley Creek? I wonder if Jimmy is still there. Perhaps—

"Oh, I don't think they will go back there, Gwendolyn. It would be too dangerous."

"Are we still in danger, Father?" Megan asks, grabbing hold of his arm.

"Not to worry, girl. Montagu will see that we're safe. That he will. He will take us to someplace safe."

The two ships are indeed being readied for our passage to safety. We watch for days as supplies are transported from the fort to the ships waiting in the harbor.

One December day in 1783, we board the *Industry* and sail out around the strip of land protecting the Palisadoes. We are finally on our way, but we still have no idea where we are going. They have told us very little, but we know that some of the Loyalists have already been able to return to their homelands. That gives us hope.

As the ship leaves the dock, we stand on the deck and watch as the fort fades into the mist. We are seeing for the last time the palmetto branches gently swaying in the warm breeze.

"Do you think we're going home, Father?" Megan asks.

"I believe we are. Some think we are headed for Britain. No doubt that's where Montagu will be going."

"He'll want to return home now that the war is over," Evan says.

"Oh, I shall be glad to see Gladys again," Megan says as she and Elen share a hug.

"And Willym and Owen. I am so excited!" I add.

"What about Steffan? Do you think he will get back home too?"

"Aye, now that the war is over, he'll want to return home. He may even be there before we arrive."

"Do you suppose Morgan is still waiting for him after all this time?" Elen asks.

"Difficult to say. She told him she'd wait."

"But she didn't know it would be this long," Megan says.

"These past seven years have been ones we all want to forget," our father tells us.

"We've been lucky, Father. With the fighting and all. Nothing too serious," Evan says.

"Except for Father's leg," Megan says.

"That's healing nicely, it is," Mama says. "You boys have been the lucky ones. You had nothing more than a few cuts and a broken arm."

And a few nightmares.

As we stand looking back at the shrinking island—now just a blur in the distance—I listen to Megan and Elen talking. "What do you think Gladys is doing? It has been so long since we have heard anything."

"Nothing since leaving Ashley Creek."

"It's been over two years now."

"Yes, I know. It will be so good to see her again."

"And to see what Owen and Willym have been doing."

"Owen and Lynne no doubt have another child by now."

"Probably more."

"I wonder if Willym ever married."

"You know our brother. Probably not!" They laugh. I haven't heard them laugh together for quite some time.

Before long we are taken below to the dreary quarters that we will share with hundreds of others. We are so excited to finally be going home that we don't even complain.

***

After the first week I notice that the air is getting colder, and Mama pulls out all the shawls and coverings we have in order to keep warm. At night we huddle together and try to sleep. Sleep does not come easy. The girls are sick, and Pa has terrible bouts of coughing that he has trouble controlling.

The motion of the vessel and the smells of the buckets cause us to long for the fresh air. Lucky for us during the days—providing the weather is good—we are allowed to take turns going on deck for a short spell. One day when Evan and Davydd take their turn on deck, they overhear some of the crew talking.

"They are taking us to some British colony."

"Back to Charles Town?" Megan asks.

"No, someplace safe ... by what they're saying."

"And it's cold wherever it is—that's for sure!"

"Where do you think they are headed, Evan?" my father asks.

"Definitely north by the feel of it!"

"So no word exactly where?"

"Maybe the military base in Halifax. That's what they're talking about on deck."

"Is that far?" asks Megan.

"Some distance yet, I should think."

"Do you think we will ever see Steffan again?" my mother asks.

"I'm sure we will," my father answers.

"He's probably gone someplace safe by now," Evan says.

"Probably be waiting for us in Halifax."

"And then we can all go home together," Mama says. Even in such conditions as these, I detect excitement in her voice.

For weeks now we notice that the wetness dripping from the sides of the old vessel has turned to frost. It is harder and harder to keep warm. The constant creaking as the vessel strains against the wind makes it difficult to sleep. Papa's coughing leaves him weak and gasping for breath. Mama looks even more tired than usual. The wisps of gray hair falling around her face make her look much older than she really is. She pulls her woolen shawl even tighter about her shoulders.

"Oh, how much more of this moaning and crying can we stand?"

"The children are sick, Mama," I remind her.

"Can't something be done for them. They need help."

The ship creaks and groans even more now with the storm that is raging. I can hear the waves crashing over the deck above us. The noise of the sails whipping under the force of the gale sounds like thunder. I can see terror in the faces of those around us as they sit on the bunks holding on to one another.

Some of them listen as my father quotes bits of encouragement. I watch as my mother tries to help the other mothers who are trying to comfort their crying children. I know why they are crying. I am cold and hungry too.

Our coverings are so worn and tattered that they do little to keep out the cold on the stale straw beds that we share. It has been days since anyone has been allowed on deck. We have no idea what is going on.

"Why do they keep us from going on deck for air these many days?" Megan wants to know when Evan and Davydd come below after finally they are allowed to go on deck for a few moments.

"The weather is not good," Evan says.

"They could at least open the hatch a bit," Megan says.

"Not now, Megan. Later perhaps."

"Oh, for just a little fresh air."

"It wouldn't be safe to go up now."

"Why not?"

"The seas are really rough. Swells are high. Waves are crashing over the deck."

"With your father feeling so poorly it is best we stay below—that's for certes. Look at him. He needs a doctor soon," our mother says.

I sit down beside him and tuck the worn covers around his shoulders. I lay my head on his shoulder.

"Papa, let's pray. That always helps."

"Aye, son, let's pray. God is with us even here ... in our darkness."

Evan knew that the crew could not open the hatch now with the water that was spraying across the deck. It wasn't long before water was seeping around the hatch and dripping below. Water was sloshing around our feet.

"Your father needs a doctor soon. If only we had hot porridge for him. That would make him feel better."

"Hot porridge would make us all feel better," Elen says.

"I can't even remember how long it has been since we had last tasted hot porridge," Megan says.

"How long has it been since we even had a proper meal?" Elen asks as she shivers under her cover.

"A meal? Why we haven't even had proper rations for days now!" Davydd says.

"Come now, children. Let me read something to you. Here ... listen to this." We watch as our father squints in the dim light and the lantern swings violently on the post. "Can't find the place. But it says, 'Thou art my hiding place; thou shalt preserve me from trouble.' God is looking out for us. He is with us. Even here. 'The Lord on high is mightier than—'" The coughing stops him. Then he continues, "'Mightier than the noise of many waters, yea than the ... mighty waves of the sea.'" He falls back against me, exhausted. "'The sea is his ... he made it.'"

"It's hard to see that now with all of this," Mama says. "But it's true, it is."

Everyone is quiet for some minutes, thinking about the words that Pa has just quoted.

"Surely it will be warmer where they're taking us. Not since leaving our home in Wales have we felt such cold," Elen finally says. "I would give anything to be back there now," I say, holding the cover up over Pa's shoulders.

Chapter 28

Halifax, 1783

A sudden lurch and then the sound of wood scraping wood has us fearing the worst. We listen to the sounds coming from the deck above us. The hatch is flung back. Water pours over the stairs. A young sailor comes halfway down the stairway. A blast of frigid air comes with him.

"Be ready to leave the ship. Gather your belongings!" he shouts.

As he prepares to close the hatch, he is met with shouts and angry words.

"Let us out of here!"

"What's the wait? We have had enough of this."

"Get us out of this rat-infested hole!" someone yells.

"When will we be allowed on shore? We've been down here long enough!"

"Wait. It won't be much longer," the sailor answers as he closes the hatch.

My sisters help Mama fold the covers to put them back in the trunks. They are damp and smelly. The clasps are secured. We wait. Finally after what seems like hours, the hatch opens again, and another sailor barks the order. "Single file. Hurry. All on deck!"

Some rush toward the narrow stairway, pushing in their attempt to be rid of the confines of the damp hold that has held us prisoner these past weeks.

"I said single file. No pushing!" the burley seaman shouts.

We wait our turn as soldiers and their families make their way up to the deck, slipping and stumbling on the dark narrow stairway. Evan and Davydd help Pa up the slippery stairs. He is barely able to stand, and it is all they can manage to keep him from falling. I help Mama up to the deck. A fierce wind whips at my face and tears at my flimsy jacket. I am glad now that we had wrapped a cover around Pa.

Nothing could have prepared us for what we would face this cold, December morning. An overnight snowstorm had blanketed everything, and the wind is bitterly cold now.

"Everything is white!" exclaims Megan.

"And it's so cold." Elen says as she draws her woolen shawl closer. "What have we come to?"

The harbor is filled with vessels, and even in the cold the smells from the docks meet our noses as we wait to disembark. The smells of tar and the stench of rotting fish are strong, but not nearly as strong as the smells we have endured on this voyage.

We follow as the trunks are carried down the gangplank, holding our coats and shawls tightly about us against the bitter wind and snow. On the crowded dock we make our way past coils of rope and smelly barrels as we are led away from the vessel.

We are taken to wagons and carts that are lined up on the dock. Our trunks are loaded, and the sick are helped on the wagons. Then we begin the ride up a steep street. We see clusters of narrow houses lining the rutted street as we make our way from the crowded docks. The smoke coming from the chimneys is a welcome sight on such a cold day. Just thinking of a warm shelter is almost enough to make me forget the cold as the wagon rumbles over the cobblestones. The horses strain as they move toward the hill.

"Looks like another garrison. Look at the walls," Davydd says as he points toward the huge fort that was now just above us.

"Look at the walls," I say.

"Surely ... surely that's not where ... they're taking us," Elen says fearfully.

"Not another garrison!" Megan says. "I thought they were taking us home."

"Look at the tents and huts on the hill yonder."

"Who could live in tents in this weather?" Davydd asks.

"They promised us proper shelter, they did!" Mama says.

"That they did, Mother. We will soon be warm and have a good meal, you'll see," Davydd says as he draws her shawl tighter around her shoulders.

"I hope that the shelter will be warm for Pa's sake. Look at the way he's shaking," I say. I can feel him shivering as I keep my arms around him, trying to shield him from the blowing snow.

"A warm place is what we all need ... after this," Elen says, shivering.

We are not prepared for what happens next. The wagon comes to a stop in front of what was to be our new shelter. A young soldier jumps from the wagon and lets down the tailgate, waiting for us to get off.

"This is where you want us to stay?" Evan asks in disbelief.

"The huts are all taken. More will be more built in a few days," the soldier explains.

"But this is a tent!" Elen says, her voice rising as the young soldier goes on explaining about the town being unprepared for such an influx of refugees.

"Everything is taken. There is nothing else available. I'm sorry."

Elen was not to be quieted so easily. "It is winter! Surely you don't expect us to stay here!"

"It is only until something else is ready. Probably by next

week," he continues. I could hardly believe what he was saying. It was December, and we were being asked to live in a tent on the side of a hill exposed to this weather. After what we had just come through, it was all so overwhelming.

How can this be happening?

Now it was time for my mother to have her say. Surely this young soldier would be no match for her.

"But my husband. He's sick ... see. He can barely stand. We cannot stay here! The long voyage has been hard on him."

"Where are the beds?" Ellen asks as she looks around. The soldier points to the pallets that have been piled with fir boughs and covered with heavy, rough coverings of some sort.

My sister lifts the covering and looks in disbelief at the boughs underneath. Then she turns to the young soldier.

"Surely you ... you don't mean ... you don't mean these are our beds?" she asks.

"Balsam boughs are softer than spruce. The needles are not so sharp."

My mother was not ready to give up yet. She stands before the young soldier and tries again.

"My Tomos must have a cot. He has been recently wounded as you can see. He must have a cot."

Surely the young soldier would understand our situation.

"I'll see what I can do," the soldier offers before he makes a hasty retreat. Would he return?

Within a short time two men arrive with a cot and extra coverings as well as some warm coats and boots. More wood was piled near the crude stove that is expected to keep us warm. I watch as my mother examines the fire-blackened pot that sits on top of the stove that had once been a steel drum. In a wooden crate nearby there's a tin teapot and several plates, mugs, and a few pieces of cutlery—our kitchen cupboard.

On the backside of the garrison grounds behind the fortress, our tent is one of many. The small huts that have been built to house the incoming refugees are all filled. They apparently were not expecting us—the late and final arrivals.

Throughout the next few weeks we try to adjust to these cruel conditions. Often at night the blowing snow drifts up around the tent, and the canvas snaps in the wind. The freezing rain is even more chilling than the snow. Food is scarce. The gnawing ache of hunger is with us throughout the long, cold days. The hot tea that my mother keeps boiling to keep us warm helps, but we yearn for a hot meal.

"The charities are doing what they can to supply rations," a soldier tells us when we ask about the scarcity of food stuffs. "I'll try to get more rations to you soon."

"Oh, that's kind, you are," my mother says. "I know you will do what you can."

We do what we can to keep warm. We pull the makeshift beds closer to the little stove, which is our only source of heat, and we pretend that we have enough food, even though our stomachs tell us otherwise.

My father is feeling a little better now that he is warmer. He was not coughing as much, but I can see that he is not himself. He is so frail. He tries to keep our spirits up by telling us stories and reminding us that in the spring we will be going home. He reads the familiar passages from the old Bible, and we talk about how things will get better soon. He reminds us that God will take care of us and bring us all together again soon.

We also know that we have to find Steffan. "He must be somewhere in this town," Evan says.

"But where? Almost every day since we've arrived, we've searched for him."

"The answer's always the same. Check the docks," I say.

"It's a big town, but we'll keep looking. He must be somewhere," Evan says.

Ruins in the Mist

My brothers and I spend many days checking the ships as they come in, asking questions and keeping a watchful eye for Steffan. We had been told that he was making trips to Roseway on a regular basis, so the docks are the best place to watch. Finally after several weeks we find him. He is anxious to see the rest of the family, and we excitedly lead the way. As we all make our way up the hill to surprise the others, snow is falling, making our trek more difficult. By the time we reached the shelter, we are covered in snow, and the icy air is making it difficult to breathe.

When I go to pull back the tent flap, my brother stands there aghast.

"This? This is what they gave you?"

"It's all they had, Steffan."

"This will never do!" He ducks under the canvas and steps inside.

What a reunion this is. None of us had seen Steffan since we had left South Carolina.

"Oh, Steffan, I am so happy, I am," Mama says through her tears as she hugs him.

My sisters hug him, and then he looks at the cot that has been drawn up near the old barrel stove.

"Oh, Father, you are ailing. And look at this place they've given you. This will never do. I've got to see what I can do to get you out of here. You'll all freeze to death."

"Please don't leave us here, Steffan. Take us home," Megan pleads as she holds unto her older brother. "Please say you will get us home!"

"I will do what I can, but now is not a good time."

"Why is now not a good time, Steffan?" Elen asks. "I thought the war was over."

"No captain will take the risk of transporting passengers before spring."

"You have a ship, Steffan. You could get us home," I say.

"My ship is much too small for an ocean crossing even in the best of weather."

Steffan takes a closer look around the tent. There isn't even a place for him to sit.

"I must see what I can do to get you into a hut. This will not do. Father, you need care."

"Why are they keeping us here? We were ... promised better ..." Bouts of coughing keep him from continuing.

"This is the safest place right now."

"At least take us with you to Roseway. Anything would be better than this," Elen says.

"Hundreds were taken to Roseway. There's no room there either."

"We can't stay here. We can't."

"I'm going to see what can be done. I'll do all I can to get you passage in the spring," he says as he lifts the tent flap and disappears into the swirling snow.

Throughout the winter my brother sits with the British soldiers whenever he can, hoping to find out what is planned for the hundreds like us stranded in this forsaken land. He tries to find answers to why we are not given better shelter and when we will be provided for as promised. His questions go unanswered, and his concerns are not addressed. The only success he has is finally getting us moved to a vacant hut. It was a small improvement but not much.

One day in February he brings us the news that Lord Montagu has died. The harsh weather was too much for the young commander. "What will become of us now that he's gone?" Davydd asks.

"Someone else in command will take over his duties."

Chapter 29

Throughout the long, cold winter we suffer endless days of hunger and long nights with the wind whipping at our flimsy shelter. We watch the snow build up in drifts around the door of the small hut we have been blessed with. Cold blasts of wind blow through the cracks and bring with them snow that settles on the floor near the walls. All through those dreadful days we look forward to the warmer days of spring.

"Do you know what today is?" Steffan asks one day as he sits by his father's cot.

"We don't even know the date. We've lost track of time. What is the date?" Megan asks.

"March the first."

"*Dewi Sant Day!*" I exclaim.

"If we were home, we would be having Mama's hot *cawl* and—"

"Fresh bread and butter," Davydd says, interrupting Megan.

"Don't remind us. Best we forget our special day. We don't need to be reminded of *cawl* and bacon and fresh bread," Elen says.

There is much sickness and death among the Loyalists during the winter. We keep hearing the dreaded word *smallpox*. We know it isn't good. As dusk settles over the camp, the familiar sound of the wagon making its way over the frozen ground can be heard.

"There goes the death wagon again."

"Picking up the poor, wretched souls who haven't made it through another day," my mother says sadly.

"There it goes, making its rounds."

Who is the cart taking to the burial grounds this time?

My own father lay very ill upon his cot. His condition has worsened since we came off the ship, and we fear for him every day. At night we listen to his wheezing and the coughing that rattles his feeble body. I pull the covers tighter around him, hoping in some way to protect him from the cold. When I pull a wooden crate to the side of his cot and bend over to talk to him, I can smell the rotted straw that is his bed. As I watch his chest rise and fall in his effort to breathe, I realize how very ill he is. As he tries to talk, his feeble voice dies to a whisper. Often a fit of coughing interrupts what he is about to say, and he sinks back, overcome with exhaustion.

"Let your father rest now, Tomos. He needs his rest."

"I won't talk, Mama. I need to sit beside him," I answer. "You will feel better soon, Pa. The days will soon get warmer. You will feel better," I whisper.

But he only continues to get worse. Pain racks his frail body, and his cough worsens. My mother sits by his side and coaxes him to drink the hot broth that she has made from the last of the small pieces of meat that we were given last week.

"Oh, if only we had a hunk of wholemeal bread. And some cheese. That is what your father needs," she says.

"When will they bring us more food? There is nothing left," Elen points out.

"They promised us more today."

"And the tea is gone, Mother," Megan says as she replaces the lid on the can.

"Already? Then save the leaves, Megan."

"The leaves? The ones in the pot?"

"Just add more water. Make it last until tomorrow."

"Hope we get some butter this time and some sugar for the tea."

"Butter! We don't even have bread to put the butter on!" Davydd says.

"They will bring us more bread, you'll see. There are still a few small pieces left," Mama tells us.

"It's so stale!"

"I'll pour—"

"There is no tea, Mother, and there's no bread and no sugar either. Face it! We're starving!"

"Davydd, we'll get supplies today. We will. Here, have this bread."

"Without sugar? No way!"

Mama passes me the piece of bread that she had soaked in the weak tea. I pass the plate back to her.

"You can have it, Mama. I'm not hungry. I can wait."

I hear her whisper, "Thank you, God, for this food. Keep us another day ... we pray."

Davydd mutters something before he goes out.

"I hope there's oatmeal when the supplies come. Your father would eat hot oatmeal."

"Listen to him. That cough is getting worse, Mama."

It hurts so much to see him like this. I've got to do something.

"He hasn't eaten now for two days, Mama," I remind her as I sit by his cot.

"I know, Tomos, but your father just needs rest. He will be all right. You will see."

"He needs food."

"He ate a little yesterday," she says.

"That was just a few bites from the stale bread with hot tea poured over it."

"If we had butter and sugar for it, he may have eaten more," Megan says.

"Your father likes the *siencyn te*. Perhaps tomorrow they will bring sugar for it."

Rations arrive the next day—such as they are. Mama insists on saying grace as always.

"Davydd, go fetch the doctor."

"Mother, we sent for him yesterday."

"But he still has not come! Davydd, go find the doctor!" she insists.

"I'll go again. Perhaps this time he will be able to come—"

"Hurry, Davydd!" Elen says as she pushes him toward the door. "Tell him he must hurry!"

"Evan, go find Steffan. You must find Steffan!" Mama wails as she hands my brother his heavy coat.

"Tomos, you should go with Evan—"

"No, Megan, I am not leaving Pa," I interrupt. "I am staying here."

I rest my head on the rough cover and feel his chest rising and falling as he attempts to breathe and my mother wipes the sweat from his brow.

I hear her whisper, "Lord, help my Tomos. We need him, Lord." Her voice breaks. "We need to go home together. Please make him better. Amen."

Megan comes over and puts her arms around Mama. She looks up at my sister and says, "It's all we can do. God will hear my prayer."

"Would it help to read from Pa's Bible, Mama?"

I reach for it and pass it across to her and then rest my head on the edge of the cot, waiting for her to read. I wait. After some minutes I look up.

"I can't read," she says as she lays the old Book on the covers.

"Pa, the doctor is coming. You will soon be feeling better."

"Tom ... Tomos—"

"Yes, Pa, I'm here."

"Tomos—" My father moans and tries to speak, but he is too weak to talk.

"Pa, don't talk. The doctor will give you something. You have to get better."

"Tomos, let your father rest," my mother whispers from the other side of the cot.

"Mama, he needs to know that we will be going home soon," I remind her.

"Father, it's Megan. You have to get well. Steffan is going to arrange passage for us. We'll soon be going home."

I notice that he is trying to speak again. But his breathing has become shallow, and the words won't come. I lean closer to try to hear what he wants to say.

"Not ... for ... for ... me," he finally manages. "Promise ... promise me ... you will ... go back—"

"Pa, we're all going back together. We will go home. We will climb the mountain paths again and gather daffodils in the springtime like we used to do."

"Promise ... me, Tom...you will ... go back. You need—" He is too weak to continue.

My father closes his eyes. I bend closer to hear what he is trying to say. His voice is weak and barely audible. He is gasping for breath.

"See it, again ... Tomos—"

"I promise you, Papa, I will go back." I make no effort to stop my tears.

"Where is the doctor?" my mother cries "What is taking so long!"

Pa shudders and gives a gasp. I throw myself across his limp body and hold onto him as if to keep him with me.

"You can't die, Papa. You promised me! Don't leave me. Don't leave me."

Elen pulls me away as Mama slumps to the floor beside the cot. Megan helps her up and guides her toward a seat.

The door flings open, and Davydd follows the medic into the hut. We all stand back and watch in silence as he goes to the lifeless form. Mama is the first to speak.

"Is he going to be all right? Can you give him something? Is it the miners' disease, doctor?"

Was he going to tell her it was probably the dreaded smallpox?

"I'm sorry. He has passed on already. I'm sorry."

I break free of Megan's hold and fall across the lifeless form on the cot.

"No ... no ... no," I cry through my sobs.

"No ... no ... Not my Tomos! I can't bear it. I can't," Mama cries as Elen leads her to a seat and sits with her. The medic takes me by the shoulders and moves me away from the cot. He pulls the cover over my father's face. Then he picks up his bag and starts toward the door.

"I will send word." Then he is gone.

I wipe the tears that are running down my face. My mother and sisters are crying loudly.

I look at the covered form on the cot. I drop to the ground and throw myself across his body.

"Papa ... Papa ... don't leave me— Don't leave—"

I can't stop the sobs.

"What will be next? First Brynn ... and now your father. Oh, what shall we do? It is all too much, it is!"

"Mother, everything will be all right," Elen says through her own tears.

"No, Elen, it won't be all right. We've even left your sister and brothers behind all these years."

"Oh, nothing will be all right again. How can this happen? He shouldn't have left us ... oh—"

"Mother, try to calm yourself!"

"Davydd, how can I calm myself? Whatever shall we do? We're left alone in this desolate place far from home. Your father is gone—" Her sobs take over.

Megan goes to the door and looks out. I know she is looking for Evan and Steffan. It is almost dark when the two arrive— too late to see Pa before he died.

I guess what I am feeling at this moment is more anger than grief. How could my Pa just up and die? How could he leave us all alone, especially now? I wipe my eyes angrily with my sleeve.

"Don't be angry, son."

"Didn't God know that we need him!"

"God will take care of us," she says through her tears.

Tonight the cart stops in front of our hut. I try to hold back the sobs as two men lift the body of my dear father unto a stretcher and prepare to carry him out into the dark night.

"Where are you taking him?" my mother asked through her tears as she reaches out and tries to hold on to the side of the stretcher.

"They must not take him away!" she cries as Megan and Elen hold her back.

No answers are given. My father is being taken off into the night. I stand at the door and watch the cart rattling over the rutted and muddied ground until it is out of sight. Tears are running down my cheeks. My dear papa is gone. How can I ever live without my papa?

I turn to Elen and let her hold me until the trembling subsides. It is as if my world has suddenly turned upside down. The sounds of sobbing break the silence in the hut.

Later that night Steffan explains to us that our father will be given a proper burial, but that is little comfort. When Mama's tears finally cease, she will be the first to try to comfort us—her children.

"We will be all right. Yes, we will be alright. Your father would want all of you to be brave—that's for certain."

"Why did God let our Pa die?" I ask.

"We do not have the answer, son," she answers gently. "God knows best."

"We should never have left our homeland. Father didn't

really want to leave. It broke his heart to leave his beloved homeland," Evan says as he fights to hold back the tears.

"We should have stayed with the others. We never should have come here to the colonies," Elen says. "We should have done more to keep this from happening." Her voice breaks.

"Father was always so happy there. We should still be there," Megan says. "We never should have come to this terrible place!" She buries her face in her hands and sobs uncontrollably. Steffan tries to comfort her, but her tears continue.

"Whatever will we do without Father?" Davydd finally says.

What will we do without him?

Chapter 30

How we managed to get through that horrible winter I'll never know. We often went without food. Many days we longed for a hot meal, even for a bowl of hot oatmeal. The rations seemed to be getting scarcer each week, and in order to make the tea last longer, my mother used less each time she made it. April brought cold rains. The hut leaked, and we got used to drying out the bedding every morning.

One day a soldier makes his rounds and tells us we will soon be taken from this place, but he cannot tell us any more than that, just to be ready. We hope we will be going home. It should be safe on the seas by now. The winter storms are over.

Our hopes are high. We wait, but still there is no word about what is going on. To pass the time, Davydd, Evan, and I spend a lot of time around the docks. There are many schooners and brigs in the harbor every day, coming and going, loading and unloading goods. We wonder where they might be going as we watch them roll the heavy barrels up the gangplanks and then leave the harbor for the open sea. We watch as they sail out around the island and finally out of sight.

"Soon we will be boarding one of those ships. Soon we will be going home again," Evan says.

"I wish ... I wish Pa was going with us."

"I know. I wish he was too," Davydd says.

"Father would want us to go back home," Evan reminds us as he looks out to sea.

"But we'll be leaving Pa here," I tell them. "How can we leave and go home without him?"

"He would still want us to go back," Evan says. "That's what he would want for us."

"I'm glad we are finally going home," Davydd says.

"It shouldn't be long now."

"Did you notice all the activity around the garrison this week, Evan?" I ask.

"Looks like something's going on."

"Some of those who came with us have already left," I say.

"I don't see the *Industry* in the harbor anymore. I wonder what became of it?" Davydd asks. The ship that had brought us here in December is nowhere to be seen.

"Oh, I heard that after Lord Montagu died, his ships were taken back to Britain by some of the family," Evan tells us.

"But then ... how will we get home, Evan? If we had known, maybe we could have—"

Evan interrupts me. "It's going to be all right, little brother," he says, giving me a hearty slap on the back. "There are lots of other ships. Just look at the harbor! I'm sure Steffan is looking out for us."

True, there are other ships, and one is being readied for us. Steffan comes in one evening and gives us the news, but it is not the news we are hoping for.

"The *Content* is being readied. Provisions are being taken on. It expects to sail in a few days."

"At last!" Elen cries. "At last!"

"Are they taking us back home, Steffan?" Mama asks.

"Of course they are, Mother!" Megan says, looking at Steffan. "Tell us they are!"

My brother has to break the disappointing news to us. Our hearts are set on going back to Wales. Now he is telling us that will not happen.

"Not right away, Mother. But you will all be looked after."

"What do you mean? Not going home?"

"You mean we are being taken somewhere else and not back to Britain?" Evan asks.

"That is what I hear at the garrison. Captain White is preparing to take those that survived the winter to a settlement a few days' sail from here."

"But that is not what we want, Steffan! We want to go home!"

"I know, Mother, but for now perhaps this is best."

"Steffan, you know that we must go back. We must!"

"Mother, we will go back—just not now. It would take money for the passage, and we don't have that."

"We will find a way!"

"Are there others already there, wherever they are taking us?" Elen asks.

"Yes, since last year settlers have been going to Chedabucto, and there's a small settlement there."

"But Steffan, if we have no money and no land, how shall we live?"

"Mother, all of that has been taken care of. Land and provisions are being supplied."

"But for how long?" Evan asks. "What? More empty promises? We don't need more of those!"

"Three years, long enough to get established, and the land is good for farming."

"Three years! You mean it will be another three years before—" Evan interrupts my mother.

"Well, I won't be going. I'm no farmer … and don't want to be one. I'll be going home on the first ship that will take me!" he exclaims.

"We could go back and work the mines, Evan. They would take us!"

"Yes, Davydd. That's what we'll do. We'll go back and work in the mines."

"Enough, boys! You know we have to stay together now."

"But Mother, we don't want to stay here any longer. We want to go home."

"We all want to go home!" Megan says.

"Where do you think you'd get the money, Evan?"

"Mother, we'll work for our passage. We'll find a ship that needs extra crew."

"Our minds are made up. We're going back," Davydd says with determination.

"What about you, Steffan. What are your plans?" Evan asks.

"I'll go with the family and help out until Tomos is old enough to take over,"

"Old enough! Why, he's almost sixteen!" Davydd says.

"Don't you want to go back? After all, it's been a long time."

"I know, Evan, but the family needs me here to help them get settled. And besides, I have a job. They depend on me. I'll stay."

"So the rest of you are just going to accept this? Not even try to get home?"

The following week several wagons arrive to take us to the docks. Those who had survived the winter with us at the garrison are leaving as well.

I help my brothers lift the old trunks on the wagon. The spring thaw has turned the roadway into deep ruts and mud, so it's a relief to reach the part of town that has cobblestones on its streets.

"I'm not sorry to be leaving this town. Look at the mess on the streets!" Elen points out.

The open gutters are filled with garbage, and rats are a common sight in the muddy streets. Barking dogs compete with the laughter that comes from the doorways of salons and brothels. Even in the daylight the houses and alleys look dreary and bleak. Steffan has been warning us for months to be careful, especially at night. That's when press gangs roam the streets. I won't be missing any of this.

"I hope wherever they are taking us, it will be safe to walk on the streets," Megan says.

"Streets! You expect to find streets? It could be even worse than here!"

"Davydd, that's enough!" Steffan says.

"It hasn't been safe for you girls to walk alone around here—that's for sure," I say.

Ever since coming here, my sisters have been warned to stay off the streets. Even my brothers and I don't feel safe unless we are together. I am not sad to be leaving this town behind.

Chapter 31

On the docks we bid a tearful good-bye to Evan and Davydd. Mama wipes at her tears as she clings to them.

"Don't worry about us, Mother. We will be all right," Evan says as he hugs her. "We will get back home and save money to get you all back with us. You'll see."

"Oh, I do hope we can be together again. Take care of Davydd. Stay together. Stay safe."

It is breaking my heart to see my mother have to say good-bye to two more of my brothers.

"Mother, we will be all right," Evan says as he hugs her tightly. "I'll take care of Davydd. Won't let him out of my sight!" he says, laughing.

It is time to go. Steffan helps Mama up the gangplank as Elen and Megan follow behind. From the deck of the ship we wave to Evan and Davydd, standing on the dock below.

We are taken below. I know what to expect. We are getting used to such conditions. *All these old vessels must be the same, I thought. The same narrow bunks strewn with straw and covered with rough coverings.* As uncomfortable as these are, they are an improvement over what we have had in the hut these past four and a half months.

This will be a short trip, we are told, providing the wind is favorable. No more than a few days if the winds are brisk. For that we are grateful.

"I have sailed along this coast long enough to know he's

right. Shouldn't be more than four days at the most," Steffan tells us.

"Have you been to Chedabucto before?"

"No. Just as far as Canso."

The *Content* makes its way northeast along the coast. During the days I spend most of my time on deck with Steffan. He is acquainted with some of the crew. They keep us informed of our progress and point out the interesting places along the coast. The shoreline reminds me of Wales. Steffan tells me that there's almost two hundred miles of shoreline between Halifax and Chedabucto.

"That's Quoddy," a sailor says, pointing off toward the rugged shoreline.

"Why do they not sail closer to the coast, Steffan?" I ask.

"Rocks everywhere. They have to be careful."

"Big enough to cause damage?"

"Oh yes. There's been many a shipwreck along these shores, I've been told."

"See that inlet over there" Steffan says, pointing. "That's Necum Teuch. And we'll soon be passing by Ecum Secum."

"What funny names!"

"Mi'kmaq names. Encampments where the early traders met to barter for furs."

"Really! Indians! Are they still here?"

"Yes, apparently so. Some of the earlier Loyalists encountered them when they first arrived. They have their headquarters near Canso."

On the third day when Steffan and I are on deck, he tells me we are about forty miles from Canso.

"There's Cape Mocodome at the entrance to Country Harbour. Another Mi'kmaq encampment."

"Looks like a big harbor."

"The deepest there is in these parts. It has welcomed many a seafarer over the years."

"Early explorers came here way back in the sixteen hundreds," he goes on.

"Really? Sounds like a lot happened around here."

"Yes, I've heard a lot of stories since I've been here."

The air is getting damp. I pull my coat tighter.

"Shouldn't be much longer, should it?"

"No, but it's getting dark, and the fog is thick. That will slow the vessel tonight."

"How far is Chedabucto from here?"

"Not far. Should be there early tomorrow if the wind favors us."

"It's getting cold up here. Better go below now. I'll be down in a bit."

"Megan, you should have been on deck earlier! A crewman was telling me about John Paul Jones and what he did here in Canso just a few years ago."

"Who was John Paul Jones?"

"An American privateer. Determined to destroy as many British vessels as he could."

"What did he do here?"

"Back in seventy-six he attacked the town twice, destroying over fifteen vessels the first time. And then three years later he attacked again, this time raiding some nearby villages as well."

"Wow! Is he still around?"

"Guess not."

"Sounds like he was to be feared. Was he always a pirate?" Elen asks.

"Apparently not. He once was a well-liked British commander before he joined the American Navy. In fact, during the recent war he was considered a hero."

"Sounds like quite a guy!"

"Takes all kinds, I guess."

"Hope we don't see any more of him around here!" Megan says.

"Expect not. Now that the war is over."

"Steffan told us to get some rest. He'll let us know when we get close to our destination. I see Mama's already asleep."

Chapter 32

Chedabucto, 1784

On the morning of May 16, the hatch opens, and Steffan descends the steep stairs.

"Are we near, Steffan?" I ask.

"Waiting for the fog to lift before proceeding into the bay."

"Then it will be soon, it will?"

"Won't be long now, Mother. The wind has been brisk. We've made good time."

"Will we soon be able to go on deck?" Elen asks.

"Soon. Help Mother get things gathered. I'll let you know when we're ready to anchor."

Less than two hours later, Steffan is back. I help my mother up the stairs, and for the first time in days she and my sisters breathe the fresh air and escape the darkness of the ship's hold. The sun is shining. It feels so good to feel the warmth of the sun after the long cold winter we have just come through in Halifax.

As we edge closer to the shore, we see that a small settlement is already there. Houses have been built close to the shore. But on the hills on either side of the bay, there is nothing but forest.

"There are ruins of some sort over there," Megan says, pointing. She has my attention.

"Ruins? Really?"

"Those are the ruins of the old French settlement," Steffan tells us. "There was a fortress there at one time."

"I miss the castle ruins at home in Wales don't you?"

"Yes, I do Tomos. That's what our country is about. They're reminders of what made us who we are today."

"I hope we get to see them again soon," I say. "I really want to go home again, don't you?"

"We'll get home again. But for now we'll have to stay here until we can get money for passage."

"Will that take quite a while, Steffan?" I ask.

"Best to be content with this place for now. We'll get home as soon as we can," he tells us.

"Look at all the trees!" Megan says as we watch several rowboats leave the shore, making their way to the vessel.

"Over there on the hillside is probably where we will make our new home," Steffan tells us as he points to the sloping hills, heavily treed, reaching to the water's edge. "That's where they'll probably settle us."

"Oh no ... surely we won't be way over there!" our mother cries. "It's nothing but trees!"

"How could we live there?" Megan asks. "I don't see any homes, do you?"

"Not yet, we'll have to build our own. Why look at the trees. There's no scarcity—that's for sure."

"Who will cut the trees for us?"

"Megan, don't worry. We'll be given tools to cut the trees, and the logs will build our homes."

"A log house?"

"Yes, Mother, a log home—with logs that Tomos and I will cut from the land. We'll build it ourselves."

Rowboats transfer us from the vessel to the shore with our belongings. The regiment along with the few women and children who have accompanied us, stand on the hillside and watch the vessel leave.

"So they're just going to dump us here and leave?" Megan asks as we watch the ship sail away.

"A tent and a few rations. That's it?" Elen asks, not believing our situation.

"It's just until they get everything worked out," Steffan says, "They'll need a bit of time."

I watch as my mother drops wearily to one of the old trunks. She shakes her head and looks around. I see the tears that are running down her cheeks.

"I don't believe it, I don't. How could they—"

My sisters are trying to comfort her. I don't believe I have ever seen her looking so forlorn.

⁂

A month after arriving in Chedabucto, our regiment—what is left of it—is mustered. Only about half of the disbanded soldiers decided to stay and wait for their land grants. I guess they decided they would have better luck somewhere else.

"We are tired of waiting too," Elen says when she learns some have not waited. "It seems that's all we've been doing these past eight years."

"I know, Megan. Another wait can hardly bring anything worse than what we have already been through."

"I hear that the land grants are to be given out in a few weeks," Steffan says.

The grants are given out. Not everyone is satisfied with their lot, but I take the one hundred acres that would have been granted to my father, and we decide to stay. What else can we do? We would have preferred grants closer to the water, but we have no choice.

The dense woods before us make our hearts sink. However can we make a home here? The very thought of it is daunting. We hardly know where to start. Our land is surrounded by dense forest and the only means of getting to where we chose to settle is over a narrow trail. After being without a proper home for so long, the idea of actually having one is something we would have to get used to.

"If this is to be our home for now, it's best to accept it, it is."

"Mother, we may never get home to Denbigh."

"Don't say that, Elen. Don't say that."

"How can you still think we might get home? It's no use. We've been waiting for too long."

"We can't give up. We can't. We have to get home again."

Steffan and I work long hours. The axes hardly see any rest those first few months, and gradually the lot starts to take shape. Once we had enough space cleared for the cabin, the actual job of building fills our days. With hammers pounding and axes peeling and notching logs, a cabin starts to take shape.

"There's Mama and the girls coming with lunch. Are you hungry?"

"Sure am! We've been working hard this morning."

"Someone should have warned us about these pesky insects!" I say as I keep swatting at the blackflies that seem to have taken over the hillside.

"I'll set fire to that other heap of brush. The smoke should help," my brother says.

"I hope so. Along with the smoke from the stumps, we should be able to get the day in."

I watch as my sisters lay out a lunch of bread and cheese along with nice hot tea.

"We bought fresh water. Come, boys. Let's eat."

As they did every day, they would sit on the hillside, swatting flies and watching us prepare the logs. When they grew tired of the smoke and blackflies, I'd see them heading back to the tent.

"Smoke too much for you?"

"No, you can send some of it our way," Megan says as she skips down the hill, picking her way amongst the stumps.

Summer is coming to a close. The cabin needs to be completed soon before the colder weather sets in. The roof is on, and another week will see the windows in. I can see that the girls are getting excited. They've been taking advantage of the warm days to wash the covers and heavy shawls in the stream and then spread them on the grass to dry. Soon we will have to replace them. They are becoming threadbare from all the use.

My brother and I listen to them at night on the other side of the blanket wall before we fall asleep. That usually didn't take too long. We are always so exhausted from the hard work that even our swollen, itching faces don't keep us awake for long.

"They'll have the inside wall finished this week."

"Then we can move out of the tent."

"They have to build the bunks first, Megan."

"Sure will be nice to get off the ground."

"Mother do you think we'll be able to get fresh straw for the mats?"

"Steffan and Tomos will get fresh straw. And build shelves."

Finally the small cabin is ready, but Steffan and I still have a lot to do. The horse and few chickens we had been given need more than the lean-to, and the farm implements we have been promised will need to be stored from the weather. Fences need to be built to contain the animals, and firewood needs to be cut and hauled. "There's a lot to do before winter sets in," I say as we finish our supper.

"Good thing Mother and the girls do what they do," my brother says.

"Next week we'll start building the barn."

"The trees over there on the west hill should give us some pretty good logs, I should think, don't you?"

"We can just roll them down the hill. Be a lot easier," I tell him as he makes himself comfortable near the hearth. I join him there, and we talk for some time about our plans for the barn.

"Time we were getting some rest. Another long day tomorrow."

The next morning when we head for the pasture, Elen is already splitting kindling on the big stump at the side of the cabin, and Megan is bringing another pail of water from the spring. We recently put up a line between two poles for them to dry the clothes. Perhaps today is washday.

Later that evening when we come in for supper, I remind Megan that it is getting too cold to keep the tin tubs outside.

"If you keep them inside, the water won't be so cold for washing up." She just laughs at me, but the next day they are on the counter.

The first winter in Chedabucto is a challenge. About the middle of November the first snow comes. The wind blows it around in drifts and piles it up against the cabin door.

I awake early one morning and look around the darkened cabin. A sliver of light is peeking through a crack where the moss chinking has fallen away from the logs. *I must fix that today*, I think.

We are kept busy with keeping enough logs cut for the fire, and with Elen and Megan's help, we manage to get through the winter.

Chapter 33

Over time the barn and outbuildings are enlarged, and we even add another room to the small cabin. My mother gets the garden plot she has been hoping for, and on the hillside amongst the blackened stumps, fields are cleared for planting and grazing. Harvest time is hard work. The girls help bury the vegetables in straw in the cold cellar. The endless stooping with the sickle results in many nights of aching backs.

As time goes on, the hardships and struggles seem less severe. Grief and sorrows are now a part of our past as was so much else. We try to put the longing for home aside. We work hard to make a home here for now. My father would have been proud of what we had done.

If only the flashbacks would go away.

Many nights I jerk awake, my screams waking my mother.

"It was just a dream. Go back to sleep."

"It seemed so real. The guns and the noise."

"It will all go away, it will."

"I hated the war, Mama. I tried to be brave, but—"

"Shhh— Go back to sleep."

My mother is right. In time the flashbacks and memories fade.

One evening as we relax in front of the fire, Steffan tells me of his plans. "I'm going back to work."

"Does Mama know?"

"Not yet. Now that the work is done, I need to be going back to sailing."

"Where will you go?"

"Captain Lewis has offered to take me on as mate. He travels along the coast, delivering supplies."

"I know how much you love the sea."

"Perhaps someday I'll have my own vessel."

"The captain was here just a couple of weeks ago, wasn't he? When will he be back?"

"He expects to be back in Canso in a fortnight. I'll meet up with him there."

"Canso's quite a ways. How will you get there?"

Mama and the girls come in from picking berries.

"Get where?" Megan asks, catching the last of our conversation.

"Steffan's leaving."

"Leaving?"

"I'm going back to work, Mother."

"What about your brother. How will he manage without you?"

"Mother, he's old enough now to take over the farming. He's—"

"He's only a boy, Steffan!"

"He's almost eighteen. He can take care of things quite well," my brother says as he lays a hand on my shoulder. "Just look at how he has grown."

"We'll miss you. What will you be doing?" Elen asks.

"Delivering supplies. I'll be in Canso quite often. I'll visit when I can."

Chapter 34

The next four years see a lot of changes for our family. I watch as our community grows. A church has been built in the village, and stores along the waterfront bring in the supplies we need.

Each Sunday I hitch the wagon, and we make the four-mile ride to the church. It had been so long since we had even been able to do that. Elen married a few months ago. I expect Megan will be next. Already she is making plans to leave us as well. She teases me, telling me I will be next.

"Tomos, you need to find a wife!"

"I don't see that happening anytime soon. Did you notice how few young women are around here? You know how few arrived here with us!"

"What about that pretty girl you've been eying at church on Sundays?" Megan teases.

"Megan, surely not in the chapel!" my mother says in disbelief.

"Couldn't miss it! He's struck on her."

"You mean the young girl from the cove?"

"Yes, that one. Didn't you see them making eyes at each other Sunday morning?"

"It's about time he married—that's for certes."

I listen as my mother and young sister plan my future for me.

Perhaps they are right. Perhaps it is time to ask Mary to marry me.

Since we arrived here, my mother's health has failed, and now that my brother has left, I am the only one left to care for her. No matter what else I do, I still need to take care of her. She will always have a home with me for as long as she needs.

When Steffan has a chance to visit, which is not that often, he tells her about the town of Shelburne, a place he visits often.

"Oh, tell us more. It sounds like a nice place to live. Maybe we should go there."

"Oh, I don't know, Mother. I think this is the best place for now. Things are not so great there any longer. The sawmills are busy with the trade to the West Indies and all, but a lot of people are moving away."

"Is that because of the damage from the recent hurricane, Steffan?" I ask.

"In part. I expect it will take a while to rebuild all the wharves and warehouses."

"I know Megan would go with me. And you are there often, Steffan."

"No, Mother, they are settled here now. You can't leave Elen."

"I know Elen and Tomos have to stay here. Oh, I can't leave them, but I just want to go—"

"I know you are not happy here, but perhaps in time you will learn to like it."

"I just want to go home, Steffan. I'll never like it here. Never!"

I hope that all of that will change for her. It is difficult to see her so sad. Often she sits alone in the darkness. When I try talking with her, it seems I can do nothing to cheer her. Megan tries cheering her and tries to interest her in other things. No matter how much we try, it is always the same.

"We should not have come here. We should have gone back."

"Mama, it's too late now. We can't go back," I try to reason with her.

"Why can't we leave?" she pleads.

"Mama, it costs more than we have. And the passage is long. Don't you remember?"

"I know it was long, but I would like to go back."

"Like Steffan said, in time you may get to like it here."

"No, Tomos, never!"

The winters in Nova Scotia remind us of the winters we had in Wales—cold winds and snow. I learn to hunt partridge and rabbit for the pot and how to bank the fire to make it last through the night. The smell from the chimneys is so woodsy compared to the peat we were accustomed to back home in Denbigh. When the wind whistles between the cracks and snow piles up outside the door, I often wish for the warmth of the Carolinas.

But no longing is so great as that for my homeland. My mother is not alone in her thoughts of home. Often after a day's work I will join her as she sits by the fire. Sometimes neither of us say anything but just sit deep in thought. When we finally share what the other is thinking, it is usually about our family back home.

"Tomos, I miss your brothers so. Do you think they are all right?"

"Yes, Mama, the last news from them was good. They are working the collieries."

"I'm glad they got to go home, but I miss them so. Oh, I do wish we could have all gone back, I do. Why did they make us stay here?"

"Try not to think of that right now. Perhaps someday Steffan will make arrangements for you to go back. He said he would try."

"It's been so long now, Tomos. I fear I shall never go back."

She is quiet for some time. I watch her as she absently rolls her hands in her lap. I wish there was something I could say that would ease her pain. I know she will probably never see the rest of her family. With her failing health and the distance between us, it is not likely to happen.

"Do you remember our home?" she says. "You were so young. I thought that—"

"I remember a lot about it, Mama."

"Do you remember how Brynn teased you when you were little?"

"And Davydd too!"

"I had to put him in his place more than once!"

"Yes, you no doubt did! And I remember how Pa and I walked along the paths in the hills and how I picked daffodils for you in the spring. Pa and I had good times together. I've been remembering those times. I think of him a lot."

"I think of him a lot too."

"I remember all the old castle ruins that we used to visit. And all the stories he told."

"He taught you a lot about who we really are, didn't he."

"He taught me that we have to be brave. No matter what happens."

"Your Pa was…was a special—"

"When he died—" A sob catches in my throat. "I tried to understand why God would let that happen."

"I know. But your Pa taught you to believe that—"

"That God knows what he's doing. Yes, Pa taught me a lot."

I watch her as she slowly gets up from the chair.

"I'm going to bed now, son. *Nos da.*"

"*Nos da,*" Mama."

I love the way we still wish each other good night in our own language.

She makes her way up the narrow stairs to her room.

I sit there deep in thought, watching the flames flicker around the large log in the fireplace. It reminds me of the times I've sat at my father's knee, listening to the stories he told me as a young boy. I still remember those times. How I miss him. I wish I could walk the mountain paths with him just like we used to. I can still hear his voice telling me tales of knights and castles. My father's wish—his dying wish—that I go back haunts me. I made a promise. I know that I need to go back someday.

My mother's voice startles me. "Why are you sitting in the dark, Tomos?"

"Mama, I thought you had gone to bed. It's late."

"Couldn't sleep. I have been thinking, I have. When will Steffan return?"

"He said he should return by Christmas, Mama. Why?"

"I think I should go with him the next trip, Tomos."

"Why, Mama? I need you here. And besides, Steffan is at sea most of the time. You would be alone."

"I've been thinking. You will marry soon."

"But that will not be until after Christmas. You don't have to leave because of that."

"It will be best. You don't need me here now."

"But Mama, it's already been decided that you will share our home. We don't want you to leave."

She is quiet for some minutes and then she reminds me of the day I first met Mary.

"Do you remember the day she noticed you for the first time?"

"That I do!" I say, laughing. "That's been over two years ago."

I first meet her at the little church in town. She is sitting with her family, which always sits on the opposite side from where our family sits. That Sunday morning I catch her looking my way but when I manage a slight smile she quickly looks away and her gaze returns to the hymnal she is holding. Megan nudges my arm and whispers in my ear. "She's noticed you!"

My eyes go back to the book I'm holding mouthing the words, but my mind is somewhere else. After the service ends, Megan steers me toward where the family is standing and introduces me. After that I try to see her as often as I can. I know that her brothers certainly approve. They are always trying to put us together during events at the church. I have sometimes been invited for a meal at their home.

The family came here from Pictou ten years before we arrived. Mary, herself is the fourth of eight children and has a brother my own age.

Chapter 35

I remember that night—the night I asked Mary to be my wife. As I wait in the small parlor, I am glad for the loud ticking of the clock. I don't want anyone to hear the pounding in my chest. I am sure her father can hear my heart beating because it's so loud.

"Tomos," he says in his thick Scottish accent. "Sit. Mary will join us shortly."

I am glad he's doing most of the talking. I finally find the words to ask him the all-important question. He tells me he's delighted that I should be the one to ask for her hand in marriage.

~~~

When she walks into the room, I see she is wearing a blue frock and her dark hair is gathered up in a matching ribbon. She looks so young—even younger than her nineteen years. She takes my breath away—and my voice too—for when I go to speak, no words come.

"Hi, Tomos," she says in her soft voice. I am glad someone can speak. Finally I am able to find my words.

"The cart is ready for a ride. We should be going."

"Oh, it's such a lovely evening, could we walk instead?"

"Of course. Get a wrap. Could be cool along the water."

She takes my arm, and we walk along the road near her

home. I am right—the air along the cove is cool and crisp, but the sky is bright with stars. As we turn to retrace our steps some time later, I stop and take her into my arms. There in the stillness of the evening, with only the stars as my witness, I ask Mary to be my wife. I am glad the horse knows the way home. My mind isn't on the long ride but rather on the beautiful girl who has just promised to be my wife. I have lots of time to think of the future. I know that Chedabucto will be my home from now on.

Mary and I are married not long after the new year in the little church where we first met. The church is crowded. The organ sounds, and Mary walks up the aisle where I wait. Our families are sitting in the front pews, and for a moment a surge of sadness comes over me when I realize my father is not here to take part in this big event in my life. Nor are any of my brothers, except Steffan. My bride looks lovely wearing her mother's ivory wedding gown, her dark hair arranged with long ringlets down the back. I hardly hear what the preacher is saying. I guess he is praying and wishing us well. I remember repeating after him, "I, Tomos, take you Mary. With this ring I thee wed." I guess the rest doesn't matter. I feel her beside me as we walk down the aisle.

Back at her parents' home friends and family come to us well. When the time comes for toasts, most are in Gaelic, and I need someone to translate for me.

"*Olamaid deoch-slainte!*"

"*Meola naidheachd!*"

"They are saying *congratulations* and *let us drink a toast*," Mary's brother whispers.

"Thanks, George. I really have no idea what they're saying!"

"*Go mbeannai Dia duit!*"

"And what was that?" I whisper, again hoping George will come to my rescue.

"That was, 'May God bless you.'"

Finally my brother gets up and lifts his glass. His toast I *could* understand—the language of my people. "*Lechyd Da!*"

The look on my mother's face tells me that today is a happy one for her as well. She walks toward me, and I know that what she is about to say is for me alone.

"Tomos, your papa would be so ... so happy. If only he could have—"

"I know, Mama. I know." I reach down and wipe a tear from her face.

She looks at me and smiles. "I am so happy, I am. Be happy as your father made me happy. Have a happy life free from sorrow," she says as she dabs at her eyes. This time her tears are mixed with laughter, and I know that she is truly happy for me.

Amid the music and well wishes of our family and friends, Mary and I begin our new life together in the home I have built on the hill.

I am glad that my mother has decided to stay for a while to help Mary settle into our home. She will want everything to be done the way we've always done it. I can hear her now. "This is the way we've always done it back home."

They get along fine, and my mother finds out that her presence is welcome, especially when Mary finds out we will be expecting our first child.

Chapter 36

A strong gust of wind blows snow into the room when Mary holds the door open for me.

"There's a blizzard blowing!" I say as I stomp the snow from my boots.

"Reminds me of the storms we had back home. We couldn't get over the hills for months when they came," my mother says.

"Listen to that wind!"

"The storm is getting worse," I say.

"You shouldn't be out on such a night as this! We kept watching for you from the window," Mary says.

"The animals need looking after. I need to be out. Surely you know that."

"Is the snow deep?" my mother wants to know.

"Knee-deep already. It will be drifted in to the barns by morning, I fear."

Throughout the winters howling winds and drifting snow are no stranger to us. I discover that if the snow isn't too deep, it is perfect for tracking deer. Mary's brothers introduced me to the practice of hunting, which is still totally new to me.

Now I am going out for the first time on my own. I take down the rifle from its rack above the door, load a shell in the chamber, and drop several more in my pocket.

As I strap on my snowshoes, my hands tremble in anticipation. I cradle the rifle in the crook of my arm as George showed me and grasp the rope of the toboggan with the other. I set off across the fields to the nearby woods. I figure that with the fresh fall of snow that came overnight, it should be easy to pick up a trail. I walk for some distance, pulling the toboggan. No signs. No droppings. There is nothing. Then just as the sun is getting low and I think about turning back, I spot them—fresh hoofprints. I know it is a fresh trail by the way the hoofs are cut into the snow. The tracks are crisp, and I can tell by the way the snow has been kicked up behind the hind track that the game is near and is walking rather than running. I quicken my pace, eager now to follow the trail. I have to be quiet. The game must not be aware of me. Then a whitetail jerks, and a buck leaps from a clump of spruce. He stops to listen. I drop my mitts and raise my rifle slowly, barely making a motion so as not to alert the buck to my presence. It is a perfect shot. I let the butt rest against my shoulder. I turn up the bolt head and slide back the bolt. I sight down the barrel and wait for just the right second. I pull the trigger, steadying myself against the recoil that I knew would come. The shot rings out. The buck drops. I place the rifle on the toboggan and make my way across the clearing to where he lies. I slit its throat and then struggle to get it strapped to the toboggan. A trail of red from the hollow in the snow to the toboggan proves that I, too, can bring down a kill. Dusk is upon me by the time I arrive home with the heavy load. My father would have been proud of me.

Our first child arrives. She has her mother's dark hair and blue eyes. My mother is more cheerful than I have seen her for some time. So much is going on that perhaps she doesn't have time to think of her own longings.

Megan, too, has married, and Elen is expecting her first child.

Just about the time that Anna is ready to walk, another

daughter comes along. This one we name Zipporah, and the following year Elizabeth is born—the same year that both Megan and Elen each have a son.

During these first few years it is easy to persuade my mother to stay to help Mary with the little ones each time she is expecting. And besides, she is enjoying each of her grandchildren. Each time Mary and I have another child, I am a bit disappointed, for I want a boy who will grow up to help with the chores. Still another girl arrives. Jane is a delight, and my mother decides to stay in order to help with our growing family; however, it isn't long before I can tell she is again growing anxious. Even the patter of little feet cannot keep her, as much as she loves her grandchildren. She is talking of going with Steffan once again. She keeps asking when he will be coming. This time I know I should let her go.

They leave, and I stand looking after the schooner that is slipping away from the wharf. I finally sit on the wharf and watch until the vessel becomes just a speck on the horizon.

I drop my head to my knees and close my eyes.

How could she leave? We have been through so much together.

My mind drifts back to that day—the day we were dumped on the shore and left to make a new life in a strange land.

There are times when the past wants to undo all the good things that have happened in my life since then. Sometimes I feel as if I don't belong here at all, that I should be somewhere else. But then I think of what my father would say if he were here. He would tell me to look for God's purpose in all of this— to see the buds on every tree in the spring, to see the sun after the clouds have passed, and to see the rainbow after the rain. He would tell me to embrace the life I have been given and to treasure the memories that are such a part of my life.

Chapter 37

Life in Chedabucto has been good. It has been ten years now since Mary and I married. Thus far we have been blessed with four girls before a son arrives. My long-awaited son, John, is born one winter night, and even though we fear for his survival, he grows into a healthy baby. I am a proud father. I have the son I have been waiting for. Then three more girls bless our home. By now the older girls can help with Suzanna, Sarah, and Marie. I had hoped for more boys who would grow up to help on the farm. The days in the fields are exhausting, and I know I need help. But John is not quite ten. It will be a while before he is much help.

The horse hitched to the wooden plough turns over as many rocks as it does soil, I'm sure. Land clearing is a difficult task. I learn to cut grain with a sickle and sow seeds by hand. Then there are supplies to pick up in town. I can't expect Mary to do any of that. Her days are busy enough with caring for our young family. I decide it is time to start teaching John how to be a farmer and how to handle the horses.

"John, would you like to go to town with me tomorrow when I pick up the supplies?"

"Oh yes, I would like that!"

"You can help me load the wagon."

"Father, do you think we might get a treat? And bring one for the others?"

"We'll see. If there's a little left over. Yes, maybe a small treat."

"Then it's off to bed. All of you. Your father is tired. He's had a long day." With that, Mary ushers the little ones to the stairs.

The next morning as promised we harness up the youngest of the horses and set off for town. As the cart rattles over the rough road, we try to talk above the din. Sometimes I can barely hear what he is saying.

"I'd like to go fishing again … one da … y … y … soon," he manages to say.

"That's what we'll do. When you are finished with your schooling next week."

"Did you like school?"

"Never went."

"Never … never went to school?" he asks with surprise.

"No schools when I was a boy. Not where I lived. Church schools in the south but none where I lived."

"Wow! No school. How did you … learn?"

"My pa taught us. Stories from the Bible. No schoolmaster could have taught me what Pa did."

"Did he teach … teach you to read?"

"First time when I was five. A little book that I kept for years."

"What else?"

"He tried to teach me to read the Scriptures."

"Is that why … why you read to us every night?"

"Yes, I finally learned. Your grandfather wanted that for me."

As I think about how my father taught us, I hope, too, that I will be able to teach my own children. I am reminded of one of the first verses he ever taught us. "That from a child thou hast known the holy scriptures which are able to make thee wise unto salvation through faith … which is in Christ Jesus."

I pause and think of the responsibility I have to see that my young son is taught as my father has taught me.

Not always is the chore of picking up provisions so simple. During the winter the snow is often too deep for the horse and sled.

"Some of our supplies are running low. What are we going to do?" Mary asks one evening.

"I will go on snowshoes and carry what I can. Perhaps next week I will be able to get through with the horse again."

"I wish it wasn't so far. Do you think you can manage?"

"I'll finish up the barn chores and be ready to go before noon."

"I will be glad when John is older. He'll be a help to you."

"God should have blessed us with boys ... not—" I realize too late what I am about to say, and I'm glad when Mary interrupts me.

"Oh, don't say that. The girls are already a big help to me."

"The next one will probably be a boy, Tomos," she says, hoping to cheer me.

I hope she is right. I am getting tired of waiting for another boy.

The icy wind slices through my old woolen coat, and my feet and fingers are numb. I try to follow my earlier tracks, but the blowing snow has covered them. My snowshoes sink into the soft snow, making the walk more difficult. I bend my face against the bitter wind that is lashing the clothes about my body and stinging my face like sharp needles. I pull my cap even lower over my ears. The weight of the pack on my back only adds to my discomfort. The wind is whipping the snow in drifts across the frozen fields and unto the roadway in front of me. It is difficult to see where I am going, and with darkness coming on, I have no way of knowing whether or not I am still following the road or if I am in some field. In the darkness the dim lights in the windows let me know I am still on the road. I keep moving, hardly even feeling my legs. They are numb.

Ruins in the Mist

As I get nearer to our home, I realize that the wind has made a slight crust over the snow, making the walk a little easier. I am glad for that. Not only are my legs aching, but my whole body is weary from the long walk. My face is numb from the biting wind and snow.

When I finally reach home hours later, I see that Mary has left a lamp burning in the window—my beacon in the snow. The younger children are already in bed. They waited up for me as long as they could. Mary removes my boots, while the older girls help remove my wet clothing.

"Your mitts are frozen stiff!" Jane says. "And your teeth are chattering!"

Later by the fire Mary breaks the news to me. I don't think I am ready for it.

"We're going to have another child."

"Oh, that's wonderful!" I know that's what she wants to hear. "Perhaps this should be the last one Mary. Perhaps nine will be enough."

"You're right," she says, laughing,

"We have a good family," I say absently. I concentrate on the burning log that has just dropped, sending up a shower of sparks. Mary keeps talking, but I hear little of what she is saying.

"John will soon be able to do more to help … and the girls do what they can … the barn chores. In time they will do even more."

Mary probably senses that I am too tired to talk any longer. She gets up and announces that she is going to bed. Without saying anything more, she slowly makes her way up the stairs.

In June, our second son is born. Tommy—as his sisters call him—has lots of attention. He will be the one who will carry on the family name.

Try as I might, I cannot forget the promise I made to my father as he lay dying, and that promise has haunted me all these years. I know the time will come when I will have to find a way to return to my homeland. The yearning—the *hiraeth*—is great, but with each spring the longing has lifted as planting crops and fields has demanded my attention. But now the more I think about it, the more I realize that I have been unable to think of little else these past few months. I must return to the place that my father and mother loved so. They never wanted me to forget my homeland. These long winter nights leave me with too much time to think.

The chime from the clock brings me back to the present. The flames have died down, and only embers glow on the hearth. The old collie comes over and rests her head on my knee. Does she sense what I am feeling? I get up and make my way to the stairs. I will take the journey soon.

Spring arrives, and with it comes the blackflies and mosquitoes that pester me as I clear the rocks and trees from the pasture land that I am getting ready to fence. I have decided it is not suitable for planting. Instead, it will make good pasture for the cattle.

I have plenty to keep me busy, but John is not about to let me forget my promise to take him fishing.

"The ice is out, Da!"

"That means—"

"The salmon are in!"

"Get the poles. Let's go!"

"There's the log bridge. We're almost there!"

He runs ahead of me, and I call to him, "Be careful, son. The water's deep. Especially at this time of year."

He has his pole dipped in the water before I reach the bridge.

"Watch it! The logs are slippery. Don't fall in!"

John has a nice catch to present to his mother when we return. This scene will repeat itself whenever we can take a break from the chores. These days are special to us. They remind me of the days I spent with my father when I was his age. Like me, he is interested in the stories I tell him when we are together—except John is interested in the stories of the Indians who camped along the river.

"Have you ever seen them?"

"No, John, they were here long before we came. No one sees them anymore."

"I wonder where they went. I would like to see them."

"Some of the roads we use here were once their paths. They traveled for miles on foot and then used this river for their canoes."

"Did they live here a long time?"

"Yes, quite a while, so people say."

Throughout the summer John helps me in the fields, and Elizabeth and Jane tend the gardens, bringing in the vegetables for the big pot of *potch*.

As the summer draws to an end, they help as we store the extra crops for the long winter ahead. On the day that we take the last of the vegetables to the cellar, we notice that it looks like rain. I am pleased that everyone has been helping to get them stored. Now we can get inside before the rain comes.

We watch as the sky darkens. The wind comes up, and it starts to rain heavily. I rush to the barns to make sure the animals are secured. This is going to be no ordinary shower. I am soaked by the time I get back inside.

"It is good that the crops are already in," Mary says as she rocks the baby's cradle with her foot.

"Rain is pelting down!" I say as I throw off my wet coat.

Suzanna and Sarah watch from the window.

"Look at all the stuff flying around outside!" Sarah says.

"There goes the roof off the henhouse, Da!" I rush to the window where John is peering out.

Part of the roof is flipped back. The hens will be terrified. "I hope the roof holds on the barn."

"Do you really think the roof is in danger of blowing away," Mary asks with concern.

"It should hold. I should have fixed the back side earlier though. It needs repair."

There's a crash. It frightens the children, who move quickly from the window. I peer out and see that a large tree near the fence has snapped and crashed to the ground. The house shudders each time the gale bears down upon it.

Then silence. It is still raining, but the wind has subsided. "I need to check the damage." Mary meets me when I return to the house, fearing the worst.

"One side of the barn roof is torn off, but the animals are safe. I've moved them to the small barn for now."

"What about the chickens?" John asks.

"They're all right. They were in the other part. I closed off the doorway."

"And there's a large tree fallen near the east pasture and another one close to the fence at the rear garden. And a lot of branches strewn around."

"So the house is all right?" Mary asks anxiously.

"It looks fine. I'll check it again when the rain clears."

"It could have been a lot worst."

"That was a hurricane, I would say."

We find out later that the great gale has caused a lot of damage in town, especially along the shore. Waves crashed over the wharves, and vessels at anchor had masts torn away under the force of the wind. Roofs had been blown away, and vessels—not protected in the bay—had been lost. In town our little church lies in ruins. We learn that a nearby community has been flattened by the gale that had been felt along the entire length of the eastern shore of Nova Scotia. There were reports of many vessels being destroyed and people losing their lives that fateful day in 1811.

Chapter 38

The time has finally come to tell her.

"Mary, there's something we need to talk about."

She stands, waiting for me to continue.

"I need to go back to Wales." I see the shock on her face.

"To stay?" she asks. Her voice is barely a whisper.

"No. No. Just a trip."

"It's so far, Tomos, whatever ... whatever are you thinking!"

"I need to. Please try to understand."

"I don't understand. It's been so long since you left. You don't even know if your family is still there. Why now after all this time?"

"I promised."

"You promised what?"

"I promised my father ... that I would return to our homeland someday."

"But your father's gone, Tomos. That was a long time ago."

"You don't understand. He was dying. I promised." Mary comes and wraps her arms around me. Neither of us says anything for several minutes. "I blamed him for so long." I find myself taking a deep breath. "I was so angry."

"Blamed him for what?"

"For leaving. For dying. For leaving me." I hesitate. "He shouldn't have come to America."

She walks away and sits in the chair opposite me by the hearth.

"Your father did what he thought best for the family at the time. Don't blame anyone for that."

I think about what she has just said.

"I don't understand what that has to do with this idea about going back now," she continues.

"It was a promise. I've never forgotten it. He was dying, Mary."

Now we are both silent. She looks away, staring into the fire.

Then she looks up at me. I detect a slight smile on her face.

"It's all right. If you need to go, I won't stand in your way. Do what you need to do."

I wrap my arms around her and tell her I love her.

"Do you understand why I have to go, Mary?"

"Yes, I know you have to go. I know you'll never be content until you do."

"Thank you for understanding."

"I see how tortured you are with all of this weighing on you. You have to do it."

"It's a longing. Like we call it back home—a *hiraeth*, a homesickness."

"I know. I see how you sit. Ever since Christmas … you've been so far away."

"Mary, I'm sorry. I—"

"Plan your trip. Go back home. Everything will be all right here."

I wonder why I deserve such a woman as Mary.

Throughout the long winter months I often spend time alone thinking of the trip. After the children have gone to bed, I sit with the collie at my feet and think. I try to remember where I had lived as a boy. Try to remember what my sister looked like. And my brothers. I close my eyes and try to remember. There are images, but are they real?

I remember the walks I took with my father. The nights in the *hafod*. The castle ruins. The stories.

The falling log wakes me from my reverie. It is time to go to bed.

~~~

"You are late today. Expected you long ago," Mary says when I arrive from my latest trip to the village the following week.

"I took time to watch the vessels being unloaded after I picked up the supplies."

"Oh, I do hope the merchants got new shoes and calicos today!"

"Do you need new shoes already?" I ask, knowing all too well that she does.

"I'll take you along next week when I go to pick up lumber."

As promised, I take Mary to town to get her new shoes and calicos for the dresses she is making for the girls. When we walk into the general store, the merchant is unrolling bolts of cloth for one of the town's ladies to inspect. Mary waits her turn.

"Look at this fine English lawn," he says, taking a bolt from the shelf behind him.

"Just came in on the ship a few days ago." He reaches for another bolt and places it on the counter.

"And look at this fine cloth. The finest indeed."

I watch as Mary runs her fingers over the expensive goods.

"This here's a bargain. Only—"

"Yes, I know. But calico will do … a few yards for dresses for the girls. Let's see— Five yards will do for now."

"And I'll be needing a paper of brass pins."

As the order is being wrapped, Mary walks around the store. I sit on a wooden keg by the door and watch her as she peers at the expensive goods in the glass case. Someday I may be able to buy her a pretty silver comb for her hair and even some of those pearls.

~~~

"Tomos, what takes you to town so often?" Mary asks one day. "Isn't it about time to be getting ready for the fall harvesting?"

"It's still too early for that yet. There's still some growing time left yet."

"Spending time around the wharves, are you?"

"Oh, I visit with the seafarers. Watch them load and unload. They are a friendly bunch!"

"Are there many ships in?"

"There were five in yesterday. It's very busy now with the timber trade and all."

"Is that just here?"

"No, the seafarers tell me that the harbor at Arichat is busy as well."

"Remember the last time Steffan was here. He told us that Halifax is always filled with ships as well."

"Guess it's because of the war. It's busy everywhere. And besides, there's a great demand for lumber in Britain right now. Ships are going back and forth all the time."

"No wonder it's busy!"

"But I hear that—" I stop short of telling her that those very ships are now travelling in convoys to avoid being attacked by the Americans.

She doesn't need to know that, especially now.

Since Madison declared war on Britain, safety for the ships has been a real concern.

"So the lumber from here goes to Halifax and then gets shipped to Britain?" she asks.

"Yes, it's a busy time—that's for sure," was all I said.

I also didn't want to tell her that I had been inquiring about passage to Britain. The prospects looked good. In fact, just yesterday one of the captains assured me that he could get me to Halifax. From there it should be easy to get a ship to take me the rest of the way. But he did suggest I wait till spring.

I could take the trip and be back in time for the planting season.

"Mary it's time to think about the trip back home," I tell her one evening when we are alone.

"I was thinking you would soon be bringing that up again."

"Yes, for months now I've been thinking of it a lot."

"So you really plan to take such a trip now with the war on?"

"No, Mary, I'll wait till spring."

"And what about the planting?"

"I'll be back in lots of time for that. Can't do much before late May anyway."

Evenings after supper I spend time with the children and then sit for hours after they have gone to bed, thinking of the family I left in Denbigh so many years ago. I only remember them as young boys. And Gladys—will I even recognize her? It has been so long. Davydd and Evan are all grown up now as well. I wonder if Owen and Lynne still live in our cottage. And Willym—Ma was always so upset when he had more than one brew at the pub. I remember that. Sometimes he would wake us when he came in at night. Pa tried to talk sense into him, but he wouldn't listen. Perhaps he married and settled down. It will be a great feeling to step into the cottage again and be taken back to when I was a boy. I can barely wait.

Chapter 39

"Do you think I'll have any trouble getting out of Halifax?"

"Not at all," Captain Newman says. "No trouble to get a ship to Britain, if that's where you're headed."

"Do you think it's safe now with the war and everything? What about the Americans?"

"You couldn't have picked a safer time, my man. The British have control of the seas now."

"Are you sure? What about the privateers?"

"The whole coast is blockaded. The only route possible for them to get at Upper Canada is over land."

"So you're saying we are not in danger from the American fleet."

"Not with our own privateers out there! They're doing a great job!"

"Really!"

"Why, there's a packet out of Liverpool that's to be feared! They've captured dozens of vessels."

"So you're saying there's a lot of action out there along the coast."

"The privateers are busy. They're doing a great job keeping our shipping lanes safe."

"My wife, she will worry if—"

"No need to worry—that's for sure! It's a great time to travel."

With all my work and making plans for this trip, I haven't

been paying too much attention to what is going on with the war. It seems far removed from our locale. I *do* know that Chedabucto is the headquarters for the militia and that with the experience of the officers in charge, we are no doubt in good hands. And besides, now with the fort at the entrance to the harbor, our own town is protected as well. War is the last thing I want to think about, although the news reaching us from time to time is disarming. Brock does a good job in Upper Canada, defending the country from the Yankees until he is killed at the Heights in the fall. There hasn't been much else happening

Before dawn I am at the wharf. I seek out Captain Newman and bid good-bye to my neighbor, who brought me to town. Standing on the wharf amid the barrels and rope, I look back toward the steep hill from which we have just come and wonder how long it might be before I will see it again. I don't have long to think of that. The *Sally* is waiting, already loaded and ready to leave the bay. Several other schooners are waiting as well, their masts blending together in the morning mist.

As I lean against the rail, I survey the shoreline and the town we are leaving, so unlike the scene that greeted my family almost thirty years ago. Memories of that day are fading, but I still remember the forest of trees that lay before us as we stood on the shore.

Now there are warehouses and stores along the waterfront and houses built along the roads going up the hill. A sizable town has grown up. I watch it all recede as the schooner makes its way to the bay.

For the first time I am able to get a close look at Fort Point, the fortress that has been built at the entrance to the harbor.

"The old French fort," a sailor says when he sees me looking in the direction of the fortification.

"But that's a British flag—"

"And British guns!"

"Those buildings I see probably house the militia now."

"They do. The town is well protected. Look at those cannons!"

"Cutler's in command, isn't he?" I ask.

"Yes, along with Marshall. Did you know this is the only fortification east of Halifax?" he asks.

A brisk breeze catches the sails as we head toward Canso. Standing on deck with the crew, they point out several small islands. They have stories to tell about the islands and inlets along the route.

"There's Grassy Island Fort," a young sailor points out. "Years ago the British had a garrison there and later built the fort."

"Was it ever attacked?" I ask.

"The French sent an expedition out from Louisbourg and destroyed the settlement."

"When was that?"

"Back in the 1740s, I think."

Upon leaving Canso, the seas become choppy, and the crew fights to keep control of the vessel.

"Got to keep watching for the hidden rocks," a sailor says. "There's a lot of hidden danger along these shores."

I knew—from Steffan's trips to Chedabucto—that the trip to Halifax could take four to five days, all depending on the weather and the winds. The captain says we are making good time on this one. As the afternoon sun is getting ready to set on the fourth day, the crew announces that the port is near, and within the hour the schooner has found a place at the crowded docks. I watch as a sailor edges his way along the yardarm and others scramble up the rigging to furl the sails.

On the busy docks I soon realize that it is not going to be an easy task to find someone to answer my questions. Finally I find a seaman who agrees to take me along the following day on his return to Barmouth.

"Be leaving at daybreak," the bearded seaman says in his deep voice.

"I'll be ready. I will find a place to lodge for the night, and I'll be here early."

"Come with me," he offers. I am glad for the offer. The town is swarming with seamen, and I really didn't know which way to go.

"I never expected so many people," I say as I gesture toward the crowds swarming the street.

"Halifax is the base for the British Navy, my man. Lots going on here right now."

"Oh yes, that's right. With the war going on."

As we make our way up from the docks, my new friend wants to know if this is my first time in Halifax.

"No, I was here before. Many years ago. I suppose a lot has changed since then."

"If it was more than a few years ... yes, I suppose it has."

"It was—let me see—thirty years ago. That was back in '83."

"Must have been a young chap then!" he says as he slaps my shoulder.

"Yes, I was not even sixteen when my family spent the winter here. The ship arrived here in December from Jamaica," I tell him.

"You must have been the last of the disbanded soldiers to arrive that winter. I heard they had it rough."

"We're lucky any of us made it through. It was terrible."

"It must have been."

"I wish I could forget it, but to this day I remember it. It was here that I lost my father. Took ill on the trip up ... and then with the cold and the hunger. It was too much."

He keeps talking and asking questions, as we continue to make our way along the busy street, pointing out things to me and explaining about the war that is going on.

"Got to be on your toes now with the Yankees wanting to blockade the shipping and all."

"Do you think they have a strong enough force to worry the British?" I ask.

"Not a chance. Did you take notice of the fleet in the harbor!"

"I hear the privateers around here are doing a good job protecting the coasts as well."

"Good thing for us."

"What do you think? Is the war going to last much longer?

"Probably soon be over."

We turn a corner and duck into an alley.

"This way. Follow me. Got to know your way around here," he says as I follow him through the darkened alley. "Got to know how to dodge the women. They're on every corner," he says, laughing. "Brothels everywhere," he adds, seeing my questioning look.

"Brothels?"

He then explains to me about the sinful practices that have taken over the town.

We find a comfortable room above one of the many taverns, and after a hearty meal I, too, fall asleep, listening to my new friend's loud snoring.

The timber-laden vessel leaves the harbor early the next morning for the ocean crossing. To pass the time, I spend a good part of the days on deck, talking with the crew. Most of their idle talk is about the war in Upper Canada.

"It's too bad about Brock being killed. He was doing a great job," one sailor says.

"I hear he had even convinced the native people to join forces with him," another says.

"Yah, the Shawnee leader … what's his name?"

"Tecumseh."

"Did you hear how Brock often bluffed the enemy? He was a bold one!"

"They say he had a great reputation for quick thinking," the sailor says as he tugs at a rope.

"He was one to be feared—that's for sure."

These sailors appear to know a lot about what is going on. I listen as they continue to talk about the well-liked general.

"Wonder who will take his place?" I ask.

"Haven't heard. There hasn't been that much going on this spring in Upper Canada."

"Guess the Yankees turned their attention somewhere else," a sailor says.

"I heard someone say they tried to capture Montreal," another adds.

"Really? That wouldn't be good," another answers.

"That would cut off Britain's supply line, wouldn't it?" I ask.

"Sure would."

Chapter 40

One day many weeks later I am standing at the rail, looking out across the vast expanse of water. The sky is clear. I spot something in the distance that catches my attention. Sitting high atop a rocky neck of land and jutting into the bay, I see the outline of a massive fortress.

"That's Criccieth Castle you're seeing in the distance."

"What a sight!" I say.

As we sail even closer, I see the twin towers of the gatehouse and the walls extending beyond.

"Built in the thirteenth century, I guess."

"Was it Welsh?" I ask.

"That it was. Built by Llewelyn the Great."

The view is lost now as the vessel moves into a sheltered bay. The water is calmer here than it has been all day, for the seas have been rough for the past few hours. I see the faint outline of land in the distance through the fog.

"Docking soon!" a sailor announces.

"Are we arriving at Barmouth?" I ask.

"No, this is Tywyn. Barmouth is full with so many taking shelter from the weather."

He notices my concern and is quick to put my mind at ease.

"We'll be able to continue on to Barmouth tomorrow when the weather improves."

"Get some sleep. The cove is sheltered here. Should be a quiet night."

I go below and sleep. The next morning I awake to the sound of clunks and thuds coming from the deck above. The crew is preparing to leave the port. I go on deck for what will be the final day of the voyage. The crew informs me that it will not take long to get to Barmouth—a few miles up the coast, providing the wind is with us.

By early afternoon I have secured a room at *the Sloop Inn* and have a hot meal. The inn is crowded with seamen, and I want only to get some rest before the long day tomorrow. The fresh sea breeze coming through the open window is welcome, and the noises from the docks soon fades as sleep overtakes me.

Dawn is just breaking when I awake to the sounds coming from the docks as the many vessels in the harbor prepare for the day. The floorboards squeak as I make my way to a table. The innkeeper serves a breakfast of thick bread slathered in butter with lots of bacon and cheese. It brings back memories— when my mother made breakfasts such as this.

I know I shouldn't tarry too long. I need to be on my way. I have waited so long for this very day. I step outside and look around. There is a steep mountain behind the inn, and on its slopes are cottages that one can reach by steps up the hillside. The harbor is calm, and the docks are indeed busy at this time of day. I need to ask directions. After all, I am a stranger here. I walk back inside.

"What's the best way to Bala?"

The innkeeper leads the way to the door and takes me outside. He looks off in the distance.

"Where you want to go is yonder." He points in the direction of Dolgellan.

"Are you riding?"

"No, I'll be walking."

"That's going to be quite a walk. The coach goes that way ... but that's not until day after tomorrow. But you will find a fair number of inns along the way."

"I'll take my time. I've waited a long time for this."

He looks at me, questioning my statement. I explain why I'm here.

"Some of the path is not so good though. Rough and a bit narrow. But it is the shortest distance to Bala. Aye, it will save you time, it will," he continues as I follow his gaze.

"Thank you for your kindness," I reply.

"Do you need someone to go with you?" he asks.

"No, I'll be all right."

The innkeeper was right. The path is winding and steep in places, and before I have gone very far, I realize that this is going to be a task that I am no longer fit for. I remind myself that I am no longer the young boy who left these hills back in '76. But the views are spectacular. That is enough to keep me plodding around the next bend on the narrow path. From time to time clearings reveal tidy cottages with their rough stone walls, small windows, and thatched roofs. Some sheep are grazing in a paddock enclosed by stone walls at another homestead. The tranquil surroundings bid me stop and take in the scene more closely. I lower myself to the ground near the edge of the path, and it is then that I notice it.

I get a whiff of something in the air. It is the smell of sweetbriar and honeysuckle that is pleasant in the morning air. I could have stayed there, but I know I must be moving on. As I take one last look at the fields below I find myself asking, *Have I been here before? Could I have walked here with my father years ago?*

Chapter 41

Then I see it—the remains of the giant fortress perched on the side of the hill. It holds the ghosts and stories of centuries past. It is easy to see that the stonework dating to Roman times has withstood the centuries well. I strain to hear the murmurs of minstrels, the voices of its people—my people. I wait for the sound of the music, but none comes. I hear nothing but the sigh of the winds.

If I move, will it disappear?

The moment comes—the moment I have planned for so many years. I had sent no message. No one is expecting me. I stand entranced. From somewhere back in time the memories come as I look at the scene before me. What I see takes me to another time. The years slip away. I am a boy again. This is my home, and the memories unfolding now are the reason I am here.

Much earlier today as I climbed the steep path from the inn, I stopped often to take in the views along the way. Now as I stop once again to rest on an old stone wall, an opening through the trees presents a clearing. I get up and move toward the edge of the path to peer down the deep valley.

I might have remembered some things from long ago, but I didn't remember such beauty as this. The fields, which are divided by stone walls, the green meadows, the gently rolling hills, all are backed by the spectacular Aran Fawddwy Mountains. Washed in the late afternoon sun, their white peaks are reflected in the glistening lake below.

Was this the way it looked when my Celtic ancestors first reached its shores centuries before?

This has to be Bala Lake. And there to the north is the market town of Bala. That strange mound at the end of town has to be the *Tomen y Bala*. I remember my father telling us the story of the Tomen when we came to the market here. Strange that I would recall those details after all these years.

Off in the distance in the shadow of the ruins on the craggy cliff, an old church steeple reaches toward the heavens. Cottages dot the hillside, some probably abandoned years ago just as my mother's was. I wonder how many of her friends remember her. If I was close enough, would I see them still standing in the doorways, shawls wrapped around themselves, waiting? Waiting … for what? Maybe for their friends to return—

The barking of a dog startles me. A voice calls out, "Good day, my friend."

I turn to find a collie inspecting me cautiously, as is an elderly gentleman in shabby country garb, resting on his walking stick. The man looks me over as the dog sniffs the old brown satchel on the ground beside me. I stretch forward to take the gnarled hand that is stretched toward me.

"Good day to you," he repeats in the familiar Welsh.

"Good afternoon, sir," I reply in his language.

Squinting into the late-day sun, his face relaxes now. His leathered skin tells me he has spent many years walking these mountain paths. Like me, he no doubt thought he was alone up here today.

"Which way are you bound?" And before I can answer, he says, "I don't believe I know you."

"Tomos."

"Bryce, myself. You're not from here."

"Well, not anymore."

"Then where now have you come from?"

"The port at Barmouth. Two days ago."

"Your family once lived in the Bala valley?" he asks, pointing with his walking stick.

"So I *was* right. This is Bala. My mother once lived here before she moved to Denbigh to marry my father."

"So you were born in Denbigh?"

"That's where I'm headed."

"That will be too far before dark. Aye, much too far."

"Oh yes, I know. The innkeeper at *the Sloop Inn* thought that with the drovers on their way to market tomorrow, I might get—"

"You'll get a ride as far as the Wrexham crossing—that's for certain."

"Is there an inn nearby?"

"*The Cross Foxes.* About two miles that way." He raises his walking stick and then points it at me.

"Tomos. What was your father's name?"

"Tomos Jones, the farmer."

There is no mistaking the smile that wrinkles his face now.

"That's a very common name in these parts. For every ten Welshmen, 'tis said one be Jones. Truth of it is I'm one myself."

"Really!"

"You can't throw a stone in Wales without hitting one," he says, laughing.

"Jones the farmer's son." He thrust his hand toward me again. "Jones the smithy."

"A blacksmith. That has been a while," I say, looking at the old gentleman more closely.

"Aye, quite a while."

We both laugh heartily. It seems I've known him much longer than I have. He lifts his stick and points toward the setting sun.

"Must be moving along. It's getting late for me." He whistles for his dog, and they set off down the path. I watch as they move around the bend. I see that the shadows are closing in along the wooded path. I need to be on my way as well.

As I hurry along the path, a rustling stops me. I see that it is only a hedgehog waddling for refuge in the nearby hawthorn bushes.

Twilight has bathed the surrounding countryside in its glow by the time I see the sign pointing to *the Cross Foxes*. It is a welcome sight. I don't feel so young anymore. My joints and muscles are aching. Someone should have told me I was getting too old for such a trip. But then would I have listened?

Yes, there it is—just the other side of a narrow arched bridge. I could have easily missed it in the gathering darkness, mistaking it for one of the other cottages along the roadway. A hot meal and a much-needed bed are only moments away. When I see the crowd out front, I wonder if there will even be a vacancy. Several wagons and drovers are preparing to take lodging. I make my way through them to the door of the vine-covered inn and push it open.

I lean back against the heavy door. A friendly collie meets me and sniffs at my trouser legs. I drop my satchel and take a quick look around the room. Huge beams cross the low ceiling. It takes a moment to adjust to the dim light. The lamps have not yet been lit. The only light is from the fire glowing from the large chimney corner. The fog of smoking pipes adds to the dimness of the space. The musty smell of the burning peat fills the room. The smell is one I vaguely remember from somewhere.

The innkeeper's wife greets me and leads me to the chimney corner. "Come sit and rest. You surely look tired."

"It has been a long day."

"Have you walked far?"

"Since morning—"

"Since morning!"

"But how did you know I was—"

"Ah, the dust. It's easy to see you've been walking."

I drop wearily unto one of the empty settles. She brings me a mug of water.

"A room will be readied for you. The evening meal is soon ready," she says as she gestures toward the tables that have been set.

She throws more peat on the fire and pokes it with the fire iron, causing it to hiss before she hurries off with my satchel.

Several other men are sitting near the fire, talking and smoking. From their dress I assume they are locals, perhaps even drovers. I listen to their conversation as the innkeeper goes about lighting the room. The local dialect is one I understand, having wanted to keep the language of my people. It doesn't take me long to discern that they are indeed on their way to Wrexham.

A stocky man about my age who is wearing yellow-brown breeches and gaiters comes in and takes off his woolen coat. After he hangs it on a hook behind him, he motions for me to join him with the others.

"Come, my friend." He pulls another chair toward the table to where the others have moved and waits for me to sit. Being Welshmen, they start asking questions.

"Where are you from, my good man?" one asks, emptying the last of the *cwrw* from his mug.

"I don't believe we know you," a farmer drawls as the smoke from his pipe drifts upward.

I open my mouth to speak, but it is to no avail.

"Are you on your way to market?" another asks.

"You are not one of us."

Maybe not one of the locals but certainly one of them.

"I'm two days off a ship at Barmouth," I finally get a chance to tell them.

"From across the sea?"

"From where now did you come?"

"My home in Nova Scotia."

"From the Americas? All that way?"

"Yes, it's a long journey."

"You're far from home. What is it that brings you here?" a farmer asks.

Far from home? No, this is my home.

"What brings you here from so far?" a young drover wants to know. "It's not common for someone to come from so far."

The questions keep coming. *Can they not see how weary I am?*

"I'm on my way to Denbigh. I was told that I may be able to get a ride for part of the way."

"Aye, I'm going that way," a farmer offers.

"There's room on *my* wagon for one more," another adds.

"I'll take you as far as the crossing. It won't be far from there," the first farmer says.

"I'll be ready. Thank you."

"I must be leaving early," he says.

We leave the warmth of the fire and take our places at the tables where the tantalizing smells await. The innkeeper and his wife bring baked salmon swimming in pools of rich butter, carrot pudding, thick slices of bread, and chunks of cheese. This they wash down with more foaming *cwrw*.

After we eat, they again take places by the fire. The talking continues. The pipe smoke mixes with the smoke from the fire, filling the room with a thick haze. Before long the talking stops. I'm not sure whether it's due to the lateness or if it's the effect of the brew, but I welcome the quietness.

The clock announces the hour. It's time for them to find their way home or to their rooms. I watch as the fire burns down to glowing embers. The large chimney corner reminds me of the huge ones in the old castles.

The innkeeper approaches and shows me to a small room just beyond the main room. "This is all I have left. With the drovers everything is taken."

"This is fine. I am so tired I could have slept there by the chimney corner."

He leaves, and I breathe in the fresh woodland scent before

Ruins in the Mist

I close the window. The late spring air is refreshing after the smoke from the farmer's pipes in the outer room.

After I wash up at the pitcher stand, I fall unto the soft straw bed and pull the cover up. Sleep comes easily. The events of the past few weeks fight for presence in my thoughts, but soon sleep lays claim to the many thoughts crowding my mind.

Chapter 42

I awaken to muffled voices and for a moment forget where I am. I had been sleeping soundly, but now the birds are chirping in the early dawn.

I dress quickly and head with my satchel to the outer room. The farmers and drovers are already gathering for breakfast. They know how important it is to get an early start. The farmer who had offered me a drive—Hew Bellis as I had learned at supper—is about to sit down. A broad smile crosses his face when he sees me.

"Come sit, my friend," he calls. "You're up!"

"I'm a farmer too. Accustomed to getting up early."

The innkeeper's wife brings eggs, lamb chops, and bacon accompanied by freshly buttered bread and a roasted cheese dish that is familiar to me. As I bow my head to pray, Hew is silent.

"Should be doing more of that myself," he says when I look up.

"Long time since I've had *caws pobi*," I say as I taste the delicious cheese dish. "My mother used to make it often."

"No Welshman should ever go without it, no matter where he lives."

We quickly finish eating and hurry outside. I hold the horses while Hew harnesses them. The herd of sheep are gathered behind the wagon, the sheepdog keeping them in their place. I climb unto the raised seat beside him, and soon we are on our way, joining the other wagons with their braying herds.

"What's your business in Denbigh today?"

"No business, sir. I want to visit the place where I was born."

"Why is that so important that you would come so far?"

"The *hiraeth* got too strong. I had to come."

"How long have you been away?"

"Thirty-six years," I tell him.

"Thirty and six is a long time."

"Too long."

As the horses trot steadily toward Wrexham, the bleating of the sheep breaks the silence of the morning.

The slow, steady pace of the horses gives me a great chance to take in the beauty of the countryside. A wide expanse of hills gives way to valleys already turning green in the spring sunshine. I get a slight whiff of sweetbriar on the grass and bracken-clothed hillside. We pass fields enclosed with stone walls where sheep and cattle graze.

Hares occasionally cross in front of us and scurry for cover in the hedges along the roadside. Rounding a bend, we come upon a young farmer taking his herd of sheep across one of the many narrow double-arched bridges. Like the others, it is built of rough stones and covered with moss. As we wait, I watch the majestic waterfall tumbling down the side of a steep cliff nearby.

"Look at the way the sun hits the water!" I remark to Hew.

He shrugs and reminds me that he sees this often. I find myself wondering how my father could have left all of this. Is this what I have been missing all these years?

Time passes quickly, for Hew likes to talk. There was one thing my father taught me—Welshmen like to ask questions. By now I have learned a lot about him, and he knows all there is to know about me. By midmorning we have reached the crossing. One old wooden sign points toward Wrexham, and another points north to Denbigh. He reins the horses to a halt.

"I would gladly take you farther, but must be getting on

to market," he says as I gather my satchel and drop it to the ground. I climb from the wagon.

"Don't forget your walking stick," he says, throwing it down after me. "You're going to need it. The walk will be steep from here."

"Is there an inn?"

"There's a small inn. Three miles over the mountains. *The Shepherd's Inn.*"

"In the shire?"

"Near the castle ruins. You can't miss it," he says as I step back to let the sheep go by.

"Thank you for your kindness, Mr. Bellis."

"May our paths cross again, Tomos. May you find the family you seek," he calls out as he urges the horses on again.

"May God prosper you," I call out to him as he moves on down the narrow road and disappears around the bend with his herd.

I am almost sorry that the wagon ride has ended. It has saved a lot of walking for me. Although Mr. Bellis has asked a lot of questions, he has been most cordial. I have enjoyed our conversation.

Mr. Bellis was right. The walk up the mountain path is truly steep. I have to stop often to rest. A *hafod* with a herd of sheep grazing nearby reminds me of the times spent in the summer hut with my father when I was young. Off in the distance I see the ruins of a large stone castle when I stop to rest. The signpost that I passed not long ago let me know I was in Ruthin. So that would be the remains of Ruthin Castle. Rested now, I get up and continue on my way. I still have a long way to go. The recent signpost told me I still had almost eight miles to go before I reach the shire.

I notice that the trail has become narrower and the trees more dense. Through a clearing I see the mountains in the distance. They appear shrouded in a purple mist even though the sun is shining.

The winding climb finally ends when the trail levels off. It has taken most of the afternoon to come this distance. I am not young anymore. All this walking is difficult for me. I rest once more on a crumbling stone wall before I continue my descent. I could have stayed longer, but I see the shadows have lengthened across the path. Darkness will soon claim what's left of the day, and I still have several miles to go, according to Hew.

The climb down is easier. I quicken my pace as I make my way toward the shire. I am reminded of times when I was a boy sharing walks with my father. I'm sure it's his voice I am hearing now in the rustling of the trees—the music of the mountains.

Even now as the day's shadows fuse into the coming darkness, it grows difficult to see far ahead. The trees seem to close around me. I am glad of a clearing when it opens up. I walk to the edge of the glade and look to the valley below. I've waited all these years to see that valley.

The distant mountains are faint outlines now, and I can just make out a small river running through the vale. There on the steep hill is the outline of the castle ruins that Hew Bellis spoke of earlier. I stop to look at the ancient gray fortress with its massive walls towering high above the town. I know that under its shadow is my final destination.

Worn by time, the ruins now shrouded in the shadows once offered protection for my people. The very name of this town means *Little Fortress*. It has withstood invasions, attacks, and takeovers by the English. For a brief time in the thirteenth century our people rose up and took it back.

A narrower path branching off to the left of my path leads to what remains of the castle's entrance. I'm tempted. I stop and look, but I'm too weary.

The stark limestone remains of once-powerful gatehouses and towers serve as a reminder of the giants that once were and are no more.

Chapter 43

It is not long before I reach *the Shepherd's Inn*. It is small—hardly more than a large cottage—but it is a welcome sight. I want only a good meal and a comfortable bed and not a lot of talking.

When I push open the door and see several locals sitting deep in conversation, I know my day is not yet over. After a hearty meal I move to a chair by the hearth, and it is not long before I see that the men are intent on drawing me in to their conversation.

"You are from away?" a farmer drawls.

"You are not known here," another says, eying me critically.

"I have come from the coast three days ago."

"What brings you here?"

"I'm hoping to find my brothers and a sister," I explain, hoping that will satisfy them.

"Where do they live?"

"Last I heard they were living here in the valley."

"And what's your name?" When I tell them my name, an elderly gentleman gets up, resting on his stick, and comes over to my chair.

"You mean Tomos the farmer? I knew your father before he moved away," he says. "A farmer if ever I knew one!"

"I knew him. He left a long time ago," another farmer says. "So many left—"

"And never came back."

"So sad. So many left when the crops failed."

Ruins in the Mist

"If only they had waited," the farmer says.

"The land came back, it did," the old gentleman says as he takes another puff from his pipe.

"So you still have family here. A brother you say?"

"Four brothers and a sister."

"Farmers in the valley?" a younger farmer asks.

"No, all miners. I'm not sure where though. It's been a while since I've been in touch."

"The mines are not doing so well now since—"

"Since that last accident," another adds.

"After that, a lot of the miners went south for work," the younger man says.

"Do you know who lives in my parents' home now?" I finally get a chance to ask.

They look from one to another, shaking their heads.

Oh no. They must remember something.

They are quiet for a moment. Then the older gentleman remembers something.

"Owen Jones lived there for some years, but—"

"He's my brother!" I say excitedly.

"He, too, has moved on," another interrupts. "Not sure who lives there now."

"Perhaps one of the others. Do any of you ever see Willym?"

"Willym! Is he your brother?" the younger man asks.

"Yes," I answer." Do you see him?"

"Used to see him in here a lot ... but it's been a while."

"Quite a while now," another offers. "Aye, a while now."

These fellows are not much help. I want to know who lives there now.

"The cottage, how will I know it? I don't remember how it looked," I say.

"You can't miss it. It's just in the vale yonder from here, it is," the old farmer says.

"Sits between two stone-bound fields. Barn's off to the left. Ivy covers the front of the cottage," the young man adds.

"My mother was always reminding me to close a gate," I say, laughing.

"Aye, there is a gate. Probably still painted white as always," a farmer says as he lifts his mug.

"To family!"

"To family!"

One by one they yawn, get up, and leave. I am left to the quietude. The lamps have been turned low, and now the glow from the dying embers is the only other light in the room.

Walls darkened from years of smoke surround me. I notice a stack of books on a table near a small bookshelf, and I cross the room to examine them. It's hard to see the titles. *Historie of Cambria*, *The Natural Daughter*, and a few others. Disinterested, I go back to the comfort of the hearth for a few more minutes.

The only sound is the ticking of the old clock. Gazing into the few remaining embers, my thoughts turn to the events of these past few days. Since I got off the ship, so much has happened. I have walked where my father once walked. Tomorrow I will be back in the home where I once heard my mother's sweet voice singing and where I listened to my father's stories around the fire. The good times—the times when I was a boy.

I wonder if it has changed much since we've been gone?

Does Willym live there now?

Where did Owen go? What about Evan and Davydd? And where is Gladys?

Will they even recognize me when I come to the door?

Memories crowd my thoughts. Scene after scene flashes before me. I no longer smell the peat from the fire.

Darkness surrounds me. I hear laughter ... and voices. And there's singing—

Chapter 44

The next morning I stand not far from the ancient ruins, looking down over the valley—the valley where I was born. Now I understand why my father wanted me to come back, why he had wanted me to see all of this again. This place belongs to my people. This belongs to me. The very thought fills me with emotion.

"Pa, I've come home," I say aloud. "I've kept my promise."

I quickly make my way down the winding path from the hill, taking in the awesome beauty of the place. The mountains in the distance are just poking through the mists as the morning sun bathes the surrounding hills with its brilliance. I have waited so long for this moment. Now I am finally here. I am afraid that if I close my eyes even for a second, it might be a dream.

I quicken my steps now. The cottage should not be far. Will I remember it? The silence is the first thing I notice. Where are the children who should be playing on the lane? And the cottages. I cannot help noticing how forlorn some of them look—as if no one even lived in them—with shutters askew and roofs sagging. A dog barks and runs toward me as I make my way down the lane. I stop to scratch his head.

A few locals stop what they were doing and wave as I continue on my way. Are they wondering who this stranger is, carrying the old satchel, making his way through their shire? They whisper among themselves. They wave, and I wave back.

Jones the grocer appears to be closed. As I cross the bridge, I notice that the cobbler shop sign is hanging crookedly.

I walk past the little chapel and then turn to look back. I am tempted to retrace my steps and open the door but decide that can wait for later. Now I want to find the cottage. I am anxious to see my family. I quicken my pace.

It looks familiar—yes, that has to be the one. Just as the locals told me last night at *the Shepherds Inn*—fields on either side that are enclosed in stone walls—only now many of the large stones have fallen to the turf below and are buried in the tall grass and weeds that have overtaken the fields. Whoever lives here now isn't doing any farming by the looks of it.

Now I'm not so sure that this is the right place. There's no smoke coming from the chimney. Overgrown ivy covers the stones on the cottage walls, and the gate is stripped of its paint. Now it swings on its hinges—not latched as it should be. Remnants of a tattered gray curtain flutter through one of the broken windows, and I can't help noticing the shutter that hangs from one hinge. Weeds are growing up the wall and in through the broken window.

"Where has everyone gone?" I realize I asked the question aloud.

I stood there and looked at the desolation.

I slowly walk up the cobbled walkway and through the tangle of weeds, making my way to the door. I pause and lay aside my walking stick. My hands are trembling as I reach to take the door handle. I knew there was no need to knock. There would be no one to answer it. The door creaks as I push it open.

The smell of emptiness is what greets me inside. Dust and cobwebs fill the corners. The windows are wearing masks of black dust. A shaft of sunlight pierces through the layer of dust on a broken windowpane. More dust covers the old table, and when I touch it, I am overcome with a longing for something I have known. I stand there, trying to remember what it was.

The giant hearth is now cold, and an old iron pot has been left hanging, forgotten when the last owners had abandoned it as they did with the old table and a few other furnishings.

I hesitate as I reach the stairs. I think I hear voices. I speak, but it isn't my voice. It appears to belong to someone else. "Is anyone here?" I say aloud. No one answers. It is the echo of my own voice. Was I expecting to hear my mother's voice?

I can smell the dust now on the narrow stairs as I make my way to the attic rooms above. I duck a cobweb that tries to reach out and grab me as I reach the landing. It is now that a flood of childhood memories come rushing back. My eyes mist when I reach the room I had shared with my brothers. There is the alcove where Davydd slept. The memories are coming back. The memories of being here as a child. The laughter. The tears. My mother calling. Now the rooms are silent. Only cobwebs fill the corners.

I close my eyes and try to imagine my mother standing there. A wave of memories engulfs me. How long I remained there—lost in my memories—I do not know, but I hear a voice coming from below. This time it *is* real.

"Who's there?" a woman's voice calls out.

I make my way down the dusty stairs, and the woman standing there reminds me of my mother. I know before she even speaks that I am seeing my sister after all these years. There is no need for her to tell me who she is. The likeness is striking—the same dark hair and eyes—a younger version of my mother.

"I'm Tomos," I finally manage. She appears to be in a state of disbelief.

"Tomos!" she cries, running to meet me. I press her face to mine as she throws her arms around me. She finally pushes me back.

"Let me look at you! I can't believe—"

"It's me. Do I look the way you imagined I would?"

"Look at you. You were so young. You've come home

at last!" she says through her tears. "You were only a child when—"

"You look the way I remember Mama looked years ago," I tell her through my own tears.

"Are you alone?"

"I am. It's only for a visit. I have to go back. There's so much— What happened?" I say as I gesture, overcome at the emptiness around me. "Where are Owen and Willym? I thought they would stay—"

"They had to move south for work."

"What about Evan and Davydd? When they came back, they were supposed to stay—"

"Mostym closed. There were a couple of explosions there. The last one was seven years ago. They wouldn't go back after that," she says. "So many were killed in that one."

"So the mines are closed here. What about at Flynt?"

"There's been nothing at Flynt now for over twelve years. Evan and Davydd worked there for few years before they came back to Mostym."

"Why did you not come back, Tomos? We all waited. We've waited all these years for you to come home."

"I will tell you all ... later. There is time later," I say absently as I try to form a picture of what might have been here.

Gladys watches me as I move throughout the room, touching the rough stones on the hearth and running my fingers over the dusty shelf where my father always kept the treasured family Bible. Could the old chair sitting so forlorn by the cold hearth be the one my father sat in? I picture my father and mother sitting there. In the back room I can almost see my sisters as they wash the dishes and scrub the blackened pots. Two old tin tubs in a corner take me back to when Willym and Owen and Brynn washed up after a day in the mines. *Brynn— Brynn's gone—*

"Tomos!" My sister's voice brings me back to the present.

"I'd like to look outside," I tell her.

Ruins in the Mist

"I'll go with you. Everything is the same, you'll see."

I take one last look around the room. Then I fasten the latch as if closing the door can keep the past within.

But everything is not the same. We pick our way through the high weeds on the way to the barn and outbuildings. The barn door is open. Old pieces of farm machinery stand waiting for someone to put them to work again. A mouse scampers across the floor and makes for the pile of unused straw in the corner, not happy about the intrusion. The sun coming through the dusty window casts beams of yellow light through the cobwebs that hang from the low beams.

A flood of memories comes to me. My father's laugh. The first time he put me on the horse. The times he let me follow him in the fields. Stepping in the tracks he made in the snow. Gladys lets me stand there, lost in my memories. Finally I turn to her, breaking the silence.

"We can go now. There's nothing here anymore."

We slowly walk back toward the cottage, and I look up at the sagging roof and crumbling chimney where moss has made its presence known. I pick up my walking stick and satchel and make my way toward the gate with Gladys. I latch the gate—without my mother having to remind me to do so. But it doesn't stay latched. I lean against it for a moment and then let it swing open again.

"What happened, Gladys? Why did someone not stay in the cottage?" I ask as we make our way to her home, which isn't far from the old cottage. A dog barks and runs to meet us. I reach down and stroke his head. I remember the dog we left behind so many years ago.

"What happened to Tad?" I ask.

"She lay at the gate, waiting for days after you all left."

"Waiting for us to return?"

"Just laid down and died one day."

Gladys and I talk well into the late afternoon. I learn that my sister married Llandon three years after we left for America and had three children. Of course, the first questions Gladys has are about the rest of the family.

"How's Mother? It's been so long since there have been any letters. I wondered—"

"She's been with Steffan for years now. She's failing. You wouldn't know her."

"Suppose she gave up hope of coming home."

"She gave up hoping long ago."

"If only she could have come with you this trip," my sister says quietly.

"Oh, she's much too feeble, Gladys. The trip would have been too much for her."

"What is Steffan doing?"

"Steffan is still working. He has his own ship now. Still lives in Shelburne."

"Poor mother, she has had a difficult life. I miss her so much."

"And Pa, you heard about what happened to him?"

"Yes, when Evan and Davydd returned, they told us about Father and the terrible winter you had after you got to Nova Scotia."

"Did you not get her letter after he died?"

"It reached us long after you left Halifax."

"Mail takes so long ... months even."

"For so long we had no way of knowing where you all were. The last word was after you settled in South Carolina. Then nothing more until the boys returned home. We couldn't understand why you didn't all come back then."

"We couldn't. There was no money, and there were so many waiting to get out of Halifax."

"Didn't you have a choice?" she asks.

"We had to go wherever we would be provided for."

"We were so worried. We didn't know what happened to you all."

"I know it was a really bad time for us as well. We were in desperate situations."

"Yes, Evan and Davydd told us all about the war. You were all soldiers!"

"Yes, even before we were old enough."

"Were you scared?" she asks.

"Probably," I tell her, laughing. "You knew that Pa was wounded quite badly in the fighting?"

"Yes, do you think it had anything to do with him dying?"

"No. I believe it was from the extreme cold and lack of food. We came close to starving—all of us."

"Oh, it must have been terrible!" she says. I watch as she brushes a tear from her eye.

"We try to put it all behind us. We try to forget."

"You probably never will," she says. "How did you ever get through such dark times?"

"Pa kept us going. Reading and praying. He wouldn't let us give up hope even in the worst of times."

"He was a good father, wasn't he? I miss him so," she says.

"That he was! The best! We had good times together."

"He always taught us to trust in God, didn't he? Remember how he was always quoting the Scriptures?"

"That's what I remember about him. Even when we were facing such hardship, he reminded us about God being with us. I remember we had this thing about the clouds."

"The clouds?"

"Yes, when I was young, he told me that our troubles are clouds and that God is above the clouds."

"That's interesting. Wonder where he got that from."

"Since I've been reading his old Bible, I've found it in Psalms. 'Clouds and darkness surround him,'" I tell her.

"If only Father had not made that decision to leave, we might all be here together—"

"He told us that he had no other choice," I remind her.

"But we know now that it was not the best choice. If he had known what lay ahead, he certainly would not have gone."

"I've asked myself many times why he did it." We were both quiet for a moment.

"Do you hear from Evan and Davydd often?" I ask.

"Once in a while a letter will come, but not often. Perhaps we could get word to them that you are home. Yes, we must! I know someone who will be going down to Powys this week. We'll send word to them that you're here."

"And what about Willym?"

"He gets up more often on account of Bronwyn's family being here. They're expected here this week. Bronwyn's mother is quite ill."

"So he finally married Bronwyn, did he?" I ask.

"I didn't think you'd remember her," she says.

"I don't. Except what Davydd used to tell me."

"What happened to Morgan?" I ask.

"She never married. She waited for Steffan."

"I understand he promised to come back for her. He used to talk a lot about her."

"Do you think he'll ever come back?"

"I don't know. He never married, you know."

"I know you'll want to see Willym. You'll probably have to keep a watch at the pub if you hope to see him though!" she says, laughing.

Chapter 45

The early morning mist hanging over the churchyard only adds to the solitude of the place. I immediately feel an emotion—a feeling I cannot express. On the hillside behind the old chapel many of the granite stones worn by time are now covered with moss and lichen. Some are hidden by tall grass and weeds, and I wonder if I will even be able to find it.

"*Le y mae?* Where is it?" I repeat aloud.

As I make my way through the weeds and toppled stones, I become aware that I am not alone. Turning, I see an aging, gray-haired gentleman making his way toward me.

"Would you be looking for kin?" he asks as he draws near.

"Yes, my brother is buried here. I would like to find his resting place."

After I explain to the old gentleman who I am, he offers to help me find the small stone that marks Brynn's grave. I stop to read inscriptions on several stones and wonder if my father and mother would have known them.

"Here it is!" he calls out.

I kneel on one knee and brush aside the tall weeds from the stone—the weeds that want to choke the marker as if to wipe out that it really existed. But the words are there. "Brynn, son of Tomos and Gwendolyn Jones, 1775, age thirteen years."

I stare at the inscription. Tears are stinging my eyes. I run my fingers over the stone. I remember Brynn. The way he used to tease me. How he wanted to be a man before his time. *But* then hadn't I wanted to do that very same thing. Was it something we had to do?

If only we could have brought my father home to rest alongside of Brynn. He should be here. Over the years I've tried not to think about where my father might be buried, but I've been haunted by the thoughts. Had he been given a proper burial? Where is he? The tears roll down my face. I make no attempt to stop them. There is no one to see me.

"Are you all right, son?"

I had forgotten the old gentleman. I wipe my face with my sleeve and get up. I offer my hand to the old man.

"I did not ask your name, and you have been so kind," I say.

"Rhys is the name. Glad you found the family you sought," he says as he turns and walks down the hill. I watch until he is out of sight. Then I make my way to the chapel.

The old latch yields easily. The heavy door creaks when I push it open. I stand there, allowing my eyes to get accustomed to the dim light. Light filters through the dusty panes of glass, casting an eerie glow in the old structure.

I look up at the barnlike rafters and then at the boxed wooden pews. I remember that my family always sat near the front. I open the little door to the pew, ignoring the dust on the seat, and sit down. I glance up at the pulpit where the preacher used to stand and the seats where the choir sat. As I sit there, I am sure I hear music. *Does the music ever leave one?* I close my eyes, and the sound of the harps fills my head. How long I sit there I don't know, but I know that if I am to make it to Flynt and back today, I need to be on my way.

I turn and look back at the abandoned chapel. The rubble-stone exterior and steep slate roof have withstood the weathering of time. I look to the hill beyond.

"Good-bye, Brynn," I say aloud.

Ruins in the Mist

The footpaths that my brothers earlier walked are now moss-covered in places, softening my steps. I remember how my father used to tell me how these paths were roads built by the Romans centuries before. I know now how very long ago that really was. This network of roads has served as our travel links over the years, and here I am now, still walking those same paths.

As I near the once prosperous town, I notice that dozens of homes are empty, their cracked windows and sagging roofs a testimony to a time that once was. There is no one to hear the birdsong that I hear in the forest canopy above me. There is no one to see the water that is cascading down from a nearby rock outcropping.

In the distance set on the side of the rocky cliff, the ancient castle ruins rise against the clear sky. The walls that once protected the town now lay in crumbling ruins. There is not much left of the castle. The remains of an archway and the porter's lodge are still visible as are three circular towers, but little else is there. There are no sounds to echo over the silent hills—no sounds of galloping horses as there would have been centuries before. My father had told me that Flynt Castle was built during the conquest of our nation. He tried to explain to me how very long five hundred years would be. When it was built by Edward the First, it was considered unique among castles. Built of sandstone on the rocks, it joined the town by a massive drawbridge across wide ditches.

How different today. The mine where Willym and Owen worked is now flooded, and pieces of the weathered colored stone lie scattered on the ground. Bits and pieces of iron and rusted junk litter the area.

Breathing hard, I steadily move up the path. After the steep climb I sit on what is left of a crumbling wall. The view, even amid the desolation, is breathtaking as I look out to the sea. Even now as I look at these massive ruins, I imagine the battles fought hundreds of years ago. The giant fortresses that once protected my people from invading armies now lay in ruins. The thick walls have crumbled in places. The openings that once were shuttered are now bare. No longer do armor-clad knights on horseback exchange blows. No longer is heard the sounds of swords and lances hitting shields and chainmail. The shouts of battle have been quieted by time.

No longer am I seeing all of this through the eyes of a child. The mystery and magical wonderment is gone. What I am seeing now is the fierce strength of our people who had for centuries fought to defend their small nation. Through the years invading armies had tested our people, but even in defeat they had been victorious. They may have taken away our land, our language, and our music, but they will never take away our spirit.

I walked away from that ancient town a different man. I know now that these are *my* people, that this is *my* homeland. No other country can be like this. Every hill and valley is sacred to me. This is my land. This will always be my home no matter where else I live. It was my father's land—the land of my own birth—and it would always be mine.

Chapter 46

For the second time in as many weeks I am pushing open the door to *the Shepherd's Inn*. This time I am hoping to find Willym there. Since *the Swan* is now closed, Gladys says this is where I will most likely find him.

I sit at a table and look around. The innkeeper offers a *cwrw*, but I push it aside. I have never had any desire for it. I remember my father never touched it, and my mother called it "the devil's brew."

"Has Willym been in these past few days?" I ask.

"Willym from down Powys?" the innkeeper asks.

"Yes, have you seen him?"

He looks in the direction of a table where several men are laughing and smoking together. "That would be Willym yonder," he says, pointing to the group engrossed in conversation.

I walk toward the table that is shrouded in a smoky haze. Before I even speak, I know I am looking at my brother. It is as if I am seeing my father after all these years.

"Willym?" I ask quietly.

He puts down the mug and looks up.

"I'm Willym," he says. "Do I know you?" he asks hesitantly.

"I'm Tomos," I say. "Your brother."

Now he's on his feet, and strong hands grip my arms.

"Is it really you? Good heavens, Tomos! What are you doing here?"

"I had to come," I say as he squeezes me tightly.
"When did you get here?"
"Last week. Gladys said you were coming up."
"But it's been so long. I thought you—"
"I know you thought I was never coming back."
"Come sit!" My brother makes room for me to join the others and introduces me.
"So this is the brother we've heard you talk of."
"Many a welcome. Aye, many a welcome!"

It seems strange sitting here with these strangers. Even my brother is a stranger. I was only a child the last time I saw him, and he was already nineteen. He no doubt remembers more about me than I do about him.

"Let's head back, and we'll talk," he says as he takes one last gulp from the mug and quickly bids the others good night. "Lechyd da!"

Each in turn lifts his mug as we get up to leave. "Lechyd da!"
"Lechyd da!"

※

"Tell me all that has happened." My brother says before we are even outside. "What have you been doing?"

On the long walk back we talk about what each of us has been doing and the changes the lengthy separation has brought. We each know that this would be a moment not likely to be repeated.

"I'm so glad you decided to come home," he says as we near Gladys's cottage. "Can you stay awhile?"

"Have to return later next week. I want to get up to Conwy in a day or so if the weather holds."

"Have you seen Owen yet?"

"No, they all hope to get up in a few days."

"Davydd and Evan will not know you either. That's going to be some reunion!"

Ruins in the Mist

"What about you? Can you stay?"

"No. Got to get back to the job."

"Isn't it about time to be giving up the pits, Willym?"

"What else would I do? It's all I've ever known."

Two days later my three other brothers make the trip up from Powys. I wouldn't have recognized any of them had I not known who they were. We talk long into the night, trying to make up for the many years we have missed. There are tears and laughter … and more tears when it is time for them to leave the next day. This truly has been a time I will not soon forget.

※

The time is nearing for my return to Nova Scotia. There is one last place I want to go—something special I need to see. Steffan talked about it, and my father promised that we would see it together. I cannot leave without seeing it, but it is too far to travel on foot. I will have to find someone who is going that way. When I inquire in the village, luck is on my side. Jenkins, the fish peddler, is leaving for Anglesey in two days. I make arrangements to go with him.

I still have time to go up to Conwy before then. When I tell Gladys of my plan for the next day, she is concerned. "It's far, Tomos. Are you sure you're up to it?"

"I'll leave early. Take my time."

"You might even get a ride along the way if you stay on the main roadway."

"I'll probably keep to the pathway. It will be shorter."

I leave early, walking stick in hand. It is a harrowing climb, and after I stop often to rest, I decide to take my sister's advice and take the main roadway instead. By midmorning I hear a cart approaching behind me. I stand and wait, and within minutes a cart hauled by two mules comes into sight.

"Good day" he says as he brings the cart to a halt.

I answer him in the same Welsh greeting.

"On your way to Conwy?" he asks.

"That I am," I say as I quickly climb to the seat beside the young farmer.

The miles are covered much more quickly than by walking, and by noon we've reached the town. I thank him for the ride, and it's apparent that I don't have to ask anyone for directions to the castle—the reason for my visit today.

One of Edward's greatest fortresses rises out of the hills, well preserved, massive, and awe-inspiring. I stand back and look at the giant structure. I am in awe, knowing that at one time the castle and entire town would have been enclosed within its walls. The eight great towers and connecting walls had been built on the cliff, anchoring it to the rock.

As I walk across the bridge that still guards the main approach to the castle, I look up at the massive structure towering above me. Inside I find a stairway that leads to the top of a curtain wall. I walk along the wall, guarding my steps against the fallen stones. A stairway leads to one of the towers. From the top of the tower I get a view of the great hall below with its huge fireplaces and towering walls. Then I turn around and look out over the countryside. Flocks of sheep are grazing on the nearby hills. Beyond the expanse of green fields and trees I am able to see the coastline and harbor. The spectacular view alone has made this trip to the town worthwhile.

I could have stayed there for much longer, but I finally turn and cautiously make my way back down to the inner court. I find a place on the stone floor that is free from crumbling stone. I take out the bag of cheese and bread, lean back against the cold stone wall, and close my eyes. I not only thank God for my food but for the chance to see all of this. It all reminds me of who my people really were, who I am. I finish my food and take one last quick look around and decide it is time for me to be going.

Outside the walls I look back at the ramparts when I reach

the path and then begin my trek back to Denbigh. After two hours of walking, I turn to see a gig with horse and rider coming in the distance. I wait, hoping that I might get another ride. The driver stops and asks if I would like a ride.

"Going to Denbigh?" he asks.

"That I am."

"Going on to Bala myself after a stop in Ruthin tonight for lodging."

"Thank you for the ride. I was getting weary."

"Been walking long?"

"Since I left the castle ruins early this afternoon."

"First time you've seen it?" he asks.

"I was probably here with my father years ago, but I was too young to remember it."

"Quite the sight, isn't it?"

We talk a lot. He has lots of questions when he finds out I am visiting Wales after so many years. Before long we have crossed the wooden bridge and are going down the lane toward Gladys's home. When the gig stops in the lane, my sister rushes out to see who is arriving. She is surprised to see me back before dark.

"Took your advice. Got a ride each time."

The following morning I am waiting on the steps of Jones, the grocer, when the fish peddler rides up with his cart pulled by two mules. I throw my walking stick on the cart with the wooden barrels and climb on the seat beside Jenkins.

"Where does your day take you?" he asks.

"I should like to see Caernarfon Castle."

"Have you seen it before?"

"No, I left here before my father and I had a chance to see it."

"Been away long?" he asks.

"Too long. Nigh on thirty-seven years," I say.

"That's a long time. You would see some changes. So you want to see the castle?"

"When I was a young boy, my brother told me of seeing it often when he traveled to the island."

"So your brother lives on Anglesey?" he asks.

"No, years ago he worked in the slate quarry there."

It is a long ride, which leaves us with plenty of time to talk before we reach the strait. Time passes quickly, and by early afternoon I see that Jenkins is trying to get the mules to come to a stop once more. They are a contrary-minded pair. Even from some distance away I can see the impressive structure. I look up from the roadway as the cart comes to a halt.

Rising out of the mist, the gray fortress stands silhouetted against the sky. I look in awe at the giant structure towering above us.

"It is so big!" I exclaim. "I never would have imagined it being so large."

"That it is. A whole town was destroyed in order to make room for it!" he tells me.

"The size of some of these fortresses! I was up to Conwy yesterday."

"This one was intended to be the capitol of the new domain at the time. The Prince of Wales was to reside here."

"I'm looking forward to seeing more of it."

"I must be getting on. Got to get to the island and back before the day is done."

"I think I'd like to stay here until your return," I tell him.

"Wait by the path, and I should be by this way in about two hours."

Jenkins continues on his way, and I slowly make my way up the embankment to take a closer look at the castle. It is easy to see that the town had once been part of the defense. It was totally surrounded by moats. Two twin towers guarded the gate, and in total I count nine towers. I walk over to a tower that is intact and decide to climb the winding stone steps to the top.

At each turn on the curved stairway I almost expected to meet the ghostly figure of a lady hurrying from the tower with her cloak flowing behind her. I reach the top, and through a narrow slit of a window I look out across the ruins below. From my vantage point I can see for miles in every direction. A mountain range in the distance juts into the mist and seems to disappear. I stand for some time, taking in the island and the vastness of the sea beyond. I cautiously make my way back down the steep, curving stairs and find myself in the great hall. It appears that construction of the massive castle has taken place at different times. Some of it appears to be very early—possibly from Roman times—and the rest might be from a much later time. In one place the roof is partially gone, exposing the great expanse to the weather. I lean against the cold stone wall and look up at the towering space above me. The remains of the huge fireplace sit amid mounds of rubble that have accumulated over the years. Now what remains of the massive stone walls belongs to another time—a time when soldiers moved undetected through the tunnels and dark stairways and made their way along the curtain wall.

My imagination runs rampant now. I hear sounds that would have been evident many years ago as I walk around the massive fortress. I hear musicians playing in the great hall and imagine that someone might be in the chapel in the left tower. Time stands still. In fact, I lose track of time. I must get back down to the path and wait for my ride. I pick my way through the tangle of bushes and thick vines. I look back when I reach the path below. I take one last look at the great gray fortress overlooking Menai Strait. If only my father could have been here with me this one last time— He had wanted to bring me here. Now I know why. I sit near the roadway to await my ride.

Jenkins arrives a little later than expected. I quickly hop up to the seat. The mules are prodded into moving forward again, their loud braying keeping us from carrying on a conversation for some minutes.

"The seas were a bit rough in the strait today," Jenkins says when the braying stops.

"How do you get across?"

"The barge. Ferries me at low tide."

"So still no bridge?"

"There's talk of one. One to be built farther up the strait," he says. "So how was your afternoon?" he asks.

"I'm glad I came today. I've always wanted to see it."

"Quite a sight!"

"It's bigger than any I've seen."

"The biggest in these parts, it was," he says, looking back at the beautiful structure that is fading into the mist behind us.

"It appears to have been built at different times," I say.

"Yes, it was built in 1283 on the site of an earlier Norman castle. A moat and bailey."

"I wonder who lived in it before then," I say.

"The Welsh prince Llwelyn the Great and his son."

"From the time I was a child, I remember my father talking about the great prince."

"Every good Welshman knows about the prince," he says, laughing.

"How long did they live there?"

"They lived there off and on for about seventy years."

"The prince was killed as I recall."

"Killed by King Edward the First in 1282, and after that, England rebuilt the castle. Took them fifty years to complete it, and now it's in ruins again."

"I wonder if it will ever be restored."

"Oh, I don't rightly know. The first English prince of Wales was born there a couple of years after it was rebuilt."

"That would have been quite a while ago."

"It's been over a 150 years now since the last fighting. Hard to say what will happen."

Ruins in the Mist

The castle at Caernarfon is forgotten as we continue to bump along the rough roadway.

As we near our destination hours later, our talk shifts to the changes that have occurred in our own shire. He tells me of the ones who have left as we drive by the many deserted cottages—all a testimony to what has happened over the years.

Chapter 47

Now there is one last thing I have to do before leaving Gladys and her family. I want to take one last walk over the hills and have my last look at the mountains.

I climb the footpath that is now softened with moss from lack of use, and before long I reach the top of the winding pathway. I find a clearing in the trees and look back toward the valley. Off in the distance the gray remains of the fortress overlooking Denbigh appear to guard the town, the very town where I was born. The meadows below are lush and green. The mountains in the distance glow in the late-morning sunshine.

I stretch out on the warm ground and gaze up through the branches of a tall oak tree. I close my eyes and find myself wishing I could stay here. I feel the nearness of my father. I hear his voice in the whisper of the winds through the trees. He loved this land. He was right. This is a special place.

Was this country of ours as beautiful as this when I was a boy? Was it this beautiful when my Celtic ancestors first reached its shores? Was it these ancient mountains that drew them here?

In the quietness of the morning I can almost hear my father's voice. "The wind blows strong over these mountains, and if you listen real closely, you can still hear the choirs coming over the hills." He told me that so often. He believed that if you listened really closely, you could hear the music—the old Welsh songs. Here I feel his presence. It is as if voices are speaking out of the silence of this place.

Between the shadows on the grass, sunlight dances, and I think I hear you, Pa. I think I hear you call. Listen. The tall trees whisper. I hear your voice. I know you are here.

These have been days I will not soon forget. This has been my healing. This, my homeland, with all its memories is who I really am.

There is no need to stay any longer. I have found what I had been searching for. My father is here. He will always be here. Now I am leaving the spirits behind. There are paths on these mountains I will never walk again, but the familiar voices that I've heard today will never go away. The ancient fortresses will continue to crumble, for the weather will take its toll on the remaining walls. Only one thing is likely to stay the same. The valleys will turn green every spring, and the wild daffodils will bloom on the hills. And amidst the bracken, the prickly stems of the fragrant sweetbriar will continue to grow.

Tomorrow I will begin the long journey back to my wife and children. It will be time to say good-bye once again to my sister, time to once again leave my homeland. Will I ever return? Not likely.

The next morning Llandon stops the cart in front of the cottage before we make our way to the coast. I take one last look at the sagging roof and at the tangle of weeds that once had been the garden that my mother so lovingly tended. "This was home," I say quietly as I look at the abandoned cottage.

"This is where we've been a family. But that's been so long ago," my sister says quietly, looking away as if she could not bear the thought of what had been.

"Now our family is separated by many miles."

"Even across the sea," she says sadly.

"These memories will be with me forever."

"I wish you didn't have to go," Gladys says as she dabs at her eyes.

"It's time to return. Mary and the children are waiting."

Hour after hour as the cart rattles along the rough road, we talk of our time together these past few weeks.

"Tell Elen and Megan I shall anxiously await the post for news!" Gladys says.

"I'll let them know you are doing well."

"Do you think you'll return again someday, Tomos?"

"I would like to think I could, but ... I don't know. I'm not young anymore."

"Forty-five is not old!" Llandon says, laughing.

"Perhaps there's still time to bring my own children here one day," I say.

"I hope you do. If only it were not so far," my sister says.

"There's Barmouth just ahead. Won't be long now," Llandon interrupts.

"There should be rooms at *the Sloop Inn*. There are very few ships in the harbor tonight."

"So will you and Gladys take lodging there for the night as well?"

"Yes, the day is spent. We will stay the night and return early tomorrow."

There is no mistaking the old port of Barmouth. The paths and alleys form steps and terraces on the steep slopes behind the streets. Llandon was right. The port is not nearly as busy as it was the last time I was here. We find lodging for the night, and the innkeeper assures me that by early the next day more vessels should be in port. That is good news for me since I still have to find passage back to Halifax.

The next morning when Llandon reins the horses to a stop in front of the inn, I know it is time to say good-bye. I hug my sister tightly and then help her to the seat and hold unto her hand, not wanting to let her go. I fight back tears. I watch until they are out of sight, and then I go back inside. By now quite a few seamen have gathered for their morning meal. I see that there is an empty chair at one of the tables, so I join the four sailors who are there.

"Looks as if the fog will lift. Should be a good day," one sailor says.

"Where does the day take you?" I ask casually.

"Headed down to Fishguard and then across to St. John's eventually," he answers.

"Really?"

"And then on to Halifax," another adds.

"Any chance I might—"

"Are you looking for Atlantic passage?" a sailor asks when he sees my excitement.

I cannot believe my good fortune when I am told they can take me along. Shortly afterward, the ship sails down the coast, and within days we have left the port at Fishguard and are heading out into the North Atlantic.

The last rays of sunset filter through the rigging as I stand gripping the railing, straining to get my last glimpse of home. I am unable to take my eyes away from the retreating shoreline. Sailors are hustling about and shouting commands as they prepare to unfurl and hoist the sails in preparation for the crossing. I listen as the waves lap against the hull, still unable to tear myself away, even though the shoreline is now nothing more than a blur in the distance.

Now clouds are creeping across the darkening sky. The sails are slapping in the wind, and the air is damp. I think it's time to go below.

"First trip?"

I turn to see the burly seaman who had come up behind me in the semidarkness.

"No. Once before," I reply.

"No concerns with the war over there and all?"

"Not really. Seems safe enough out here at sea."

"Guess you're right!" he says. "The shipping lanes seem to be safe enough."

We talk for a few minutes, and then he suggests it would be best to go below.

The seas are favorable for sailing that first week, and rather than stay below, I often spend time on deck with the crew. Weeks later we arrive at the port in St. John's. The British naval base there has been the first to hear the news. There around the docks the sailors hear of the recent battle in the ongoing war.

"They burned York a week ago!"

"How did they get their forces to Upper Canada? I thought the coast was guarded," I say.

"Sailed a fleet across Lake Ontario," the sailor answers. "From Fort Meigs, I guess."

"After a bloody battle they burned the town," another says.

Weeks later I find myself once again in the town that held only sad memories for me. I was anxious now to get home and lost no time in finding a ship going to Canso. Luckily for me the captain was eventually going on to Chedabucto.

The first day out of Halifax a windstorm comes up as we are sailing along the coast, blowing the ship off course. But by the next morning the storm has passed, and the vessel is again making progress. A brisk breeze is now catching the sails, and by nightfall the sky is bright with stars. As the vessel dips and rolls, I stand on the deck and think about all that has happened these past weeks.

I think of the memories—so recently brought to life—that will in time fade and even disappear. But for now I remember the boy, the hills of a beloved country, the winds whispering. The storms of my life have become my memories.

I find myself praying as I stand there. God's presence has been near.

I finally leave the star-filled night and go below.

Two days later, I am awakened by the sounds coming from the deck above, and before I can make my way there, a seaman announces that we were nearing Chedabucto Bay. I pick up my satchel and make my way on deck.

Even in the morning mist I can see the shoreline and the dim outline of the wharves and the masts of the vessels at anchor. As the vessel draws nearer to the wharf, I am thinking how glad I will be to see my family again after so long. I wonder how Mary has made out, and if John has been able to help get the garden plot ready. I am getting home just in time for planting. I see that the snow is gone. The ground should be thawing.

I need not to have worried. As I near our home, I see that John is tilling the garden plot and that two of the girls are helping him. Mary rushes out to meet me when she sees me coming up the lane.

"Your father's home!" she yells to the rest of the family.

Chapter 48

Over a year has passed since that time. A lot has happened. Our oldest daughter, Anna, has married, and Mary and I are blessed with another son. The daily chores keep me busy, and I often remember the unforgettable journey I took—the journey that took me to my homeland.

Often at the end of the day I walk to the stream near our home when I want to be alone. One day shortly after I return home, I am standing on the bridge, listening to the sound of the rippling water making its way over the stones, lost in my thoughts when I hear footsteps on the pebbled path.

"Da! I found you!"

I turn to face the small figure running in my direction.

"Fishing, Da?" he asks when he reaches the bridge.

"Just thinking, Tommy."

"John said you went to Grandfather's home."

"That I did."

"Is it far? You were away so long?"

"Aye, it's far. Very far."

"Did the ship take you there?" he asks excitedly.

"For most of the way. Then I had to walk for many days."

"Will you take me there someday?" he asks.

"Perhaps one day when you're older."

How could I promise my six-year-old son something that I knew was not likely to happen? I had no reason to return.

"Is it a special place, Grandfather's home?"

"Aye, a very special place. I'll tell you about it later."

I reach out and take his hand, and together we walk toward home.

Epilogue

One year later–

Mary stands motionless, tears streaming down her face as she watches earth being shoveled unto the box. She holds her young son's hand as the rest of her family stand nearby, clinging to one another.

In Anna's arms a young boy whimpers. Steffan supports his aging mother as he helps her up the hill to where the others are standing.

Mary wills herself to concentrate on what the preacher is saying. "To everything there is a season ... a time to be born ... a time to die—" The preacher keeps talking, but she doesn't hear it. "A time to weep ... a time to mourn—" The rest of his words fade away.

She remembers the day so well. Has it really been only five days ago.

"Mother, come quick!" John shouted that day as he rushed from the pasture where he had been helping his father clear trees.

"What's wrong?"

"It's Father!" He's hurt!" he said, barely able to catch his breath.

She rushed to the pasture with John and Elizabeth. A large

tree had fallen, pinning Tomos to the ground. The children ran for help, but it was too late.

The preacher's words bring her back to the present. He is reading now. "In the shadow of thy wings will I make my refuge. If I take the wings of the morning, and dwell in the uttermost parts of the sea, even there shall thy hand lead me ... and thy right hand shall hold me."

He goes on, and now he is talking about her husband's life. "If it is true that one's life worth is told by the dash between the two dates on your headstone, then the life of this man was a full one." He pauses. Then he goes on, "Let's remember this brave man who suffered much hardship. As his forefathers before him, he leaves a legacy to his family here today."

He pauses, and then he says, "May he always hear the music of the mountains—the music of his homeland."

Mary falls to her knees before the fresh mound of earth that now covers her beloved Tomos and weeps. Steffan stands nearby as his mother lays the bunch of daffodils on her youngest son's grave. Then in a feeble but sweet voice, the Welsh words float over the hillside as she sings, "When for a while we part, this thought will soothe our pain; That we shall still be joined in heart, and one day meet again."

All is silent, except for the soft sobbing.

Mary stands there with her family around her as the others slowly make their way down the hillside. Then she takes her son's hand, all the while dabbing her eyes with the other, and together the family follows the others.

"Mommy?"

"Yes, Tommy?"

"What about Da?"

"Your daddy's in heaven."

Author Note

This story was inspired by actual historical events and real people.

Apart from the historical facts and actual events and places, most incidents related are fictional, although some of the characters actually lived where they are portrayed.

About the Author

The author, being a Loyalist descendant herself, became interested in the history of the American Revolution some years ago, and that led to the writing of her first book *Wilderness Home*, the story of the founding of Country Harbour by Loyalists.

Her love of history is evident in her writing.

After years of living in various parts of Canada and the United States, she returned to Country Harbour, her hometown. There she writes, paints, and enjoys her gardening.

CPSIA information can be obtained at www.ICGtesting.com
Printed in the USA
LVOW12s0201080814

397878LV00002B/13/P